PRAISE FOR
A CATHEDRAL OF MYTH AND BONE

"[A] Brothers Grimm tale for the contemporary reader"

—*School Library Journal*, starred review

"Strong and satisfying."

—*Publishers Weekly*

"Sidewalk saints and scholarly sorceresses populate Kat Howard's collection of new stories for old ceremonies. The ferocious bonds of girls and women are the focus of these myths for the modern age, drawn from two thousand years of lore, ritual, and witness. In them, Howard has created enchanted narratives of hard-won survival."

—Maria Dahvana Headley, author of *The Mere Wife*

"Kat Howard's short stories are by turns revelatory, transformative, and magical—and often all three at once. Howard writes a modern mythos where her heroines and heroes (no matter how familiar the setting seems, Howard's characters are never mere protagonists) confront curses, magic, love, madness, and the supernatural. They emerge stronger, as does the reader. I dare you to read these stories and not look at your life differently afterward.

With *A Cathedral of Myth and Bone*, Kat Howard cinches her place as a new generation's vividly different answer to Zelazny."

—Fran Wilde, award-winning, Hugo and Nebula-nominated
author of The Bone Universe series
and *The Jewel and Her Lapidary*

"There is magic in this book. You just have to crack it open."

—*Spectrum Culture*

PRAISE FOR *ROSES AND ROT*

"Kat Howard is a remarkable young writer, and she's written a powerful first novel, as strong as Emma Bull's *War For The Oaks*. This is a book about family, about the price we're willing to pay for art, and the strange music and haunting glades of faerie."

—Neil Gaiman, #1 *New York Times* bestselling author of
American Gods and *Trigger Warnings*

"Captivating, fiercely smart (about sisters, artists), utterly transporting. I read it so consumingly, it was more akin to swallowing."

—Megan Abbott, bestselling author of
You Will Know Me and *The Fever*

"Howard weaves a dark and enticing tale of sisterly bonds, fairy promises, and the price of artistic success in this lushly written debut fantasy set in the present-day U.S. This story will resonate with readers long after the last page."

—*Publishers Weekly*, starred review

"The realm of fairy tales meets the harsh world of the Fae in this starkly enticing debut. With undercurrents of darkness in the midst of the beauty of the arts, this is a Brothers Grimm tale for the contemporary reader."

—*Library Journal*, starred review

"What are you willing to do for your art? What would you sacrifice? Kat Howard's *Roses and Rot* takes you to the dark and older fairy tales, where things are not as they seem and 'be careful what you wish for' is the refrain. It is a story of two talented sisters, a writer and a dancer, who attend an artists' retreat. It seems like the perfect place to create, yet as with all perfect places, something is not quite right. Kat Howard seems to possess a magic of her own, of making characters come alive and scenery so vivid, you forget it exists only on the page. *Roses and Rot* is both beautiful and dark, lovely and haunting."

—Anton Bogomazov, Politics and Prose Bookstore

PRAISE FOR
AN UNKINDNESS OF MAGICIANS

"Strong characters and a captivating revenge plot make this a fun, absorbing read for those who like their magic, and their magicians, dark and twisty."

—*Kirkus Reviews*

"*An Unkindness of Magicians* will please fantasy fans, but mainstream readers looking for mystery, mayhem, and a strong female protagonist will fall in love with it as well."

—*Shelf Awareness*

"The characters and the Unseen World flourish in her gorgeous prose."

—*Publishers Weekly*

"Howard's vengeance-fueled urban fantasy is stylish, macabre, and spellbinding."

—*Booklist*

"This is an amazing book filled with magic, consequences, and what happens when you fight rather than turning away. This is Omelas, for magic. This is the price that must be paid. This is the story the others forgot to tell."

—Fran Wilde, award-winning author of *Updraft* and *Horizon*

Also by Kat Howard

Roses and Rot

An Unkindness of Magicians

A CATHEDRAL OF

OF

MYTH

AND

BONE

STORIES BY

KAT HOWARD

SAGA PRESS

LONDON SYDNEY NEW YORK TORONTO NEW DELHI

SAGA PRESS

AN IMPRINT OF SIMON & SCHUSTER, INC.

1230 AVENUE OF THE AMERICAS, NEW YORK, NEW YORK 10020

Compilation copyright © 2018 by Kathleen Howard

"Once, Future" and "Saints' Tide" copyright © 2018 by Kathleen Howard

The following stories were reprinted with permission: "A Life in Fictions"—*Stories: All New Tales*. William Morrow, 2010 • "The Saint of the Sidewalks"—*Clarkesworld*, August 2014 • "Maiden, Hunter, Beast"—*Lightspeed*, January 2016 • "Translatio Corporis"—*Uncanny*, March/April 2015 • "Dreaming Like a Ghost"—*Nightmare*, February 2014 • "Murdered Sleep"—*Apex Magazine*, August 2012 • "The Speaking Bone"—*Apex Magazine*, March 2011 • "Those Are Pearls"—*Guillotine Series* #10, 2015 • "All of Our Past Places"—*Unlikely Story*, 2014 • "Painted Birds and Shivered Bones"—*Subterranean*, Spring 2013 • "Returned"—*Nightmare*, January 2015 • "The Calendar of Saints"—*Beneath Ceaseless Skies*, October 2011 • "The Green Knight's Wife"—*Uncanny*, Nov./Dec. 2016 • "Breaking the Frame"—*Lightspeed*, August 2012

Cover photograph copyright © 2018 by Amy Haslehurst

This Saga Press trade paperback edition October 2019

SAGA PRESS and colophon are trademarks of Simon & Schuster, Inc.

For information about special discounts for bulk purchases, please contact Simon & Schuster Special Sales at 1-866-506-1949 or business@simonandschuster.com.

The Simon & Schuster Speakers Bureau can bring authors to your live event. For more information or to book an event, contact the Simon & Schuster Speakers Bureau at 1-866-248-3049 or visit our website at www.simonspeakers.com.

Interior design by Vikki Sheatsley

The text for this book was set in New Caledonia LT.

Manufactured in the United States of America

1 3 5 7 9 10 8 6 4 2

The Library of Congress has cataloged the hardcover edition as follows:

Names: Howard, Kat, author.

Title: A cathedral of myth and bone : stories / Kat Howard.

Description: First edition. | New York : Saga Press, [2018] | Description based on print version record and CIP data provided by publisher; resource not viewed.

Identifiers: LCCN 2018000666 | ISBN 9781481492157 (hardcover : alk. paper) | ISBN 9781481492164 (paperback) | ISBN 9781481492171 (ebook)

Classification: LCC PS3608.O9246 A6 2018 | DDC 813/.6—dc23

LC record available at https://lccn.loc.gov/2018000666

ISBN 978-1-4814-9215-7

ISBN 978-1-4814-9216-4 (pbk)

ISBN 978-1-4814-9217-1 (ebook)

To Becky, who asked for a story

CONTENTS

INTRODUCTION

Writing, for me, is an act of faith. When I sit down to write, I have to believe in what I am writing. Any hesitation, any loss of faith, and the story breaks down, falls apart. I have words scribbled on pages—maybe even beautiful words—but without belief, they're not a story. And the faith doesn't end there. I have to believe that the story will find an audience. That somewhere out in the world, there is a reader who will also believe in that story, and in that act of belief is where the miracle occurs: the story becomes real.

I grew up steeped in story. Not just fairy tales and myths, but hagiography as well. The richness and strangeness of these stories, their glorious impossibility, their connection to the numinous, made them the first stories I'd found that I wanted to believe in. At recess I was as likely to pretend to be Joan of Arc fighting the English as I was Artemis shooting her bow. But as I grew older and started writing, I realized that for all their power, the old stories—the myths and the fairy tales and the lives of the saints—told a very narrow sort of story, one that closed off more doors than it opened. Here was one way to be, they said. Here was the set of rules that led to the happy ending; be careful lest you break them. It was a narrow view of stories that held such potential. When I wrote my versions of these stories, I wanted to look at them with new eyes, break them out of the frames they had been displayed in, tell their truth slant.

And this, too, is an act of faith: the belief that there is life and truth in the old stories, that I can find that truth and make it recognizable even as I turn it inside out. If I didn't believe in these stories, if the way they were told didn't matter to me, there would be no reason for me to spend time in them—to listen for the silenced voices, to look for the gaps in the narratives. To believe that there are important stories in the silence and the gaps, even if those weren't the stories that were originally told.

I am drawn to short fiction because it distills the beauty and the darkness that are possible in fiction, and particularly in the fantastic. It allows stories to be more intense, more dreamlike, for me as a writer to hang a skin of myth on the skeleton of the strange. This collection, which includes previously published work as well as original material, showcases my quest to re-envision those old stories that first made me love fiction and the fantastic. To give an ancient Irish king new life in New York City, to see the burden of sainthood when prayers can be sent by email, to tell and retell the story of King Arthur on a modern college campus. To show that the power in the old stories can be extended, carried on, made fresh, and opened up for a new audience.

And of course not every story here is a retelling of something older. Some of these stories engage more directly with questions of faith: of how belief—or its lack—can be the thing that pushes you outside of the story that you are comfortable in, and into a story that's altogether stranger.

Turn the page. I have miracles to offer you.

A Life in Fictions

He wrote me into a story again.

I told him to stop doing that, after we broke up. In fact, it was one of the reasons that we broke up. I mean, being a muse is all well and good, until you actually become one.

The first time it happened, I was flattered. And it wasn't like my normal life was so great that I was going to miss it, you know? So getting pulled into that world—a world he had written just for me, where I was the everything, the unattainable, the ideal—it was pretty powerful.

When he finished the story, and I came back to the real world, the first thing I did was screw him until my thighs ached. It was our first time together. He said it was the best sex of his life.

When I asked him if someone had ever fallen into a story that he had written before, he said not that he knew of. Oh, sure, he had based characters on people he knew, stolen little bits of their lives. A gesture, a phrase, a particular color of eye or way of walking. The petty thievery all writers commit.

I asked what he had done differently this time.

"I was falling in love with you, I guess. You were all I could think of. So when I wrote Marah, there you were in my head. Always."

I hadn't fallen into the story right away, and I didn't know what happened in the parts where Marah didn't appear. Reading the finished draft was this weird mix of déjà vu and mystery.

Apparently inspired by my real-world sexual abandon, the next thing he wrote me into was an erotic novella. Ali was a great deal more flexible than I was, both physically and in her gender preferences.

I really enjoyed that story, but one night I tried something in bed that Ali thought was fun but that he thought was beyond kinky. After that, the only sex scenes he wrote me into involved oral sex.

Men can be so predictable, even when they are literary geniuses.

Maybe especially then.

The next time he wrote me into something, I lost my job. It was a novel, what he was working on then, and when he was writing Nora, I would just disappear from my life as soon as he picked up his pen. For days, or even weeks, at a time, when the writing was going well.

He said he didn't know what happened to me during those times. He would go to my apartment, check on things, water my plants. When he remembered. When he wasn't so deep in the writing that nothing outside registered.

I was always in his head during those times, he said, at the edges of his thoughts. As if that should reassure me.

It happened faster. He would begin to write, and I would be in the story, and I would stay there until he was finished.

The more I lived in his writing, the less I lived in the real world, and the less I remembered what it was like to live in the real world, as a real person, as me.

When the writing was going well, I would be surrounded by the comfortable, warm feeling that someone else knew what was going on, was making all the decisions, was the safety net under the high wire. Everything was gauzy, soft focus, fuzzed at the periphery.

I could have an adventure without worrying about the consequences. After all, I was always at the edges of his thoughts.

Until the day I wasn't. Everything froze, and I was in a cold white room, full of statues of the people I had been talking to.

I walked from person to person, attempting to start

conversations, but nothing happened. Walked around the room again, looking for a way out, but there was nothing. Solid white walls, floor, ceiling. It was a large room, but I could feel the pressure of the walls against my skin.

I walked to the center of the room and sat, cross-legged, on the floor. Waiting.

Have you ever had your mind go blank? That space between one thought and the next when your brain is just white noise, when there is not one thought in your head—do you remember that feeling?

Imagine that absence extending forever. There's no way of escaping it, because you don't know—not don't remember, don't know—what you were thinking about before your brain blanked out, and so you don't know what to do to get it started again. There's just nothing. Silence. White.

And there's no time. No way of telling how long you sit in that vast, claustrophobic white room, becoming increasingly less.

I never was able to figure out how long I waited there. But suddenly I was in a room I had never seen before, back in the real world, and he was there.

There were wrinkles at the corners of his eyes, and grey threading through his hair. Writer's block, he explained to me. He had tried to write through it, work on other projects, but nothing helped. Finally, that morning, he had abandoned the novel as unworkable.

I asked if he had tried to bring me back, while he was stuck.

He hadn't really thought of it.

That was when I broke up with him.

He had, I discovered, become quite successful while I was away. A critical darling, praised especially for the complexity, the reality, of his female characters.

Speaking of Marah in an interview, he described her as his one lost love. The interviewer found it romantic.

I found the interviewer tiresome. Being lost was not romantic at all.

Parts of me stayed lost, or got covered over by all those other women I had been for him. Sure, they were me, but they were his view of me, exaggerated, slightly shifted, truth told slant.

I would turn up a song on the radio, then remember that it was Ali who liked punk. I abandoned my favorite bakery for two weeks when I convinced myself that I had Fiona's gluten allergy.

For three months, I thought my name was Marah.

During all of this, there were intervals of normalcy. But I still felt the tugs as he borrowed little pieces of me for his fictions. I would lose my favorite perfume, or the memory of the first time I had my heart broken. Tiny bits of myself that would slough away, painlessly. Sometimes they would return when he wrote, "The End." More often, they did not.

I reminded him that he had promised not to write about me anymore. He assured me he hadn't meant to. It was just bits, here and there. He'd be more careful. And really, I ought to be flattered.

But then a week of my life disappeared. I loved that short story, and Imogen was an amazing character, the kind of woman that I wished I was. That wasn't the point.

The point was he had stolen me from myself again. I was just gone, and I didn't know where I went. And there were more things about myself that I had forgotten. Was green really my favorite color?

I flicked on the computer, started typing madly. Everything I could remember about myself. But when I looked over the file, there were gaps that I knew I had once remembered, and duplications of events.

Panting, I stripped off my clothing and stared at myself, hoping that my body was more real than my mind. But was that scar on my knee from falling off my bike when I was twelve, or from a too-sharp rock at the beach when I was seventeen? Was that really how I waved hello? Would I cry at a time like this?

Anyone would, I supposed.

I tried to rewrite myself. I scoured boxes of faded flower petals and crumpled ticket stubs, paged obsessively through old yearbooks. Called friend after friend to play "Do you remember . . . ?"

When I remembered enough to ask. To know who my friends were.

It didn't work. Whatever gift he had or curse that I was under that let him pull me into his stories, it was a magic too arcane for me to duplicate.

And still, the gaps in my life increased. New changes happened. I woke one morning to find my hair was white. Not like an old woman's, but the platinum white of a rock star or some elven queen.

I didn't dye it back.

There was a collection published of his short fiction. He appeared on "Best of" lists and was short-listed for important literary prizes.

I forgot if I took milk in my coffee.

He called, asked to see me. Told me he still loved me, was haunted by memories of my skin, my voice, my scent. I missed, I thought, those things too. So I told him yes.

It took him a moment to recognize me, he said, when I walked across the bar to meet him. Something was different. I told him I didn't know what that might be.

He ordered for both of us. I let him. I was sure he knew what I liked.

There was a story, he explained. He thought maybe the best thing he would ever write. He could feel the electricity of it crackle across his skin, feel the words that he would write pound and echo in his brain.

He had an outline that I could look at, see what I thought. He slid a slim folder across the table.

I wondered aloud why, this time, he would ask permission. This one was longer. An epic. He wasn't sure how long it would take him to write it. And after what had happened the last time, when I had . . . Well. He wanted to ask.

I appreciated the gesture.

I drummed my fingers across the top of the folder but did not open it.

A waiter discreetly set a martini to the right of my plate. Funny. I had thought that it was Madeleine who drank martinis. But I sipped, and closed my eyes in pleasure at the sharpness of the alcohol.

I said yes.

To one more story, this masterpiece that I could see burning in his eyes. But I had a condition.

Anything, he said. Whatever I needed.

I wanted him to leave me in the story when he was finished.

He told me he had wondered if I might ask for that. I was surprised he hadn't known. He nodded agreement, and that was settled.

We talked idly through dinner. Occasionally his eyes would unfocus, and I could see the lines of plot being woven together behind them.

I wondered what he would name me this time, almost

asked, then realized it didn't matter. Then realized I wasn't even sure what my own name was anymore. Grace, maybe? I thought that sounded right. Grace.

He started scribbling on the cover of the folder while we were waiting for the check. I watched him write.

"Rafe fell in love with her voice first, tumbled into it when she introduced herself as . . ."

The Saint of the Sidewalks

J oan wrote her prayer with a half-used tube of Chanel Vamp that she had found discarded at the Thirty-Fourth Street subway stop. It glided across the cardboard—the flip side of a Stoli box, torn and bent—and left her words in a glossy slick the color of dried blood: "I need a miracle."

You were supposed to be specific when asking the Saint of the Sidewalks for an intervention, but everything in her life was such a fucking disaster, Joan didn't know where to start. So, she asked for a miracle, nonspecific variety.

She set her cardboard on the sidewalk, prayer-side up. Then lit the required cigarette—stolen out of the pack of some guy who had been hitting on her at a bar—with the almost-empty lighter she had fished out of the trash. You couldn't use anything new, anything you had previously owned, in your prayer. That was the way the devotion worked:

found objects. Discards. Detritus made holy by the power of the saint.

Joan took a drag off the cigarette, then coughed. She hadn't smoked since her senior year of high school, and she'd mostly forgotten how. Thankfully, she didn't actually have to smoke the whole thing. Cigarette burning, she walked three times around her prayer, then dropped the butt to the sidewalk and ground it out beneath her shoe.

Then she waited to see if her prayer would be answered.

Other people waited too, scattered along the sidewalk where the saint's first miracle had occurred, with their altars of refuse and found objects, prayers graffitied on walls or spelled out with the noodles from last night's lo mein.

The rising sunlight arrowed between the buildings and began to make its progress down sidewalks lined with prayers. This was how it worked: if the sun covered your prayer, illuminating it, the saint had heard you. There was no guarantee of an answer, but at least you would know you had been heard. For some people, that was enough.

If your prayer caught fire, if holy smoke curled up from its surface as the sun shone down on it, that was a sure sign you had been blessed. Heard and answered, and your intention would be granted. A miracle. If she just had a miracle, things would be better.

Joan didn't need to watch to follow the progression of the sun. Cries of disappointment and frustration were common. Gasps of joy and gratitude much rarer.

Everyone had theories about how the saint chose to grant prayers. Some said it was whether she liked the altar or the things you used to make your prayer. Others said she could feel the need in your heart and mend your broken life that way. Joan hoped it was the latter, since it wasn't like her hasty scrawl and filthy cardboard were that impressive. Certainly not compared with what was next to her—a salvaged player piano, painted with neon daisies, tinkling through a double-time version of "Music Box Dancer." Though really, Joan hoped the saint had better taste than to pick that one.

She tapped the toes of her left foot on the sidewalk as she waited, just below the cigarette. Maybe it was bad form to be impatient about a prayer, but Joan didn't care. She just wanted to know. Plus, she really had to pee.

The sun crept closer, the light crawling over her ancient Docs. It licked up her legs, over her chest, illuminated her hair, a brief halo.

Then paused, on the sidewalk again, inches from her prayer. Joan bit her lip hard. *Come on, come on, come on,* she chanted inside her head. *Please.*

A drop of rain. Then another and another. The sky greyed, then grew storm-dark. Then opened, rain sheeting down. The worst of all possible signs.

Soaked to the skin, Joan ran into a coffee shop. She shouted her order as she passed the counter so she could use the FOR PAYING CUSTOMERS ONLY toilet. After she washed her hands, she rubbed the smeared mascara—waterproof, her ass—from beneath her eyes.

Well then. No miracle. She would figure out something else.

The voices woke Joan the next morning. A crowd of people outside her apartment, congregating on the sidewalk, on the steps. She angled her head to better see out her sliver of window.

There were the beginnings of altars, but these were made to honor some sort of saint she had never seen before—coffee cups and lipstick cases, worn Docs and tights with holes. The hair on the back of her neck stood up.

Joan checked her Book of Hours, but there were no saints scheduled to appear on her street today. It wasn't a feast day either.

She shrugged into a thrift-store kimono, worn at the hem and wrists but its embroidered peonies still bright, and went down to see what the fuss was about, hoping she was wrong.

Cries of "Our Lady of the Ashes!" and "Our Lady of the Lightning Strike!" greeted her as she opened the door.

The people outside had smeared ashes on their faces, were waving scorched pieces of cardboard like holy relics. Most had painted their lips with dark lipstick. The front line of them fell to their knees before her.

"Oh, fuck no," Joan said, and fled back into her apartment.

Joan hadn't been online to do more than check her email in over a week. Nine days ago, she had discovered that her (now ex) boyfriend was cheating with her (now former) best friend, which would have been bad enough on its own, but Joan had still been drunk and angry enough the day after to punch the asshole who liked to grab her ass when they were in the elevator together. Except. Said elevator was at work, and said asshole was her (now former) boss. Joan had gotten fired.

On reflection, it had not been her finest twenty-four hours.

In the wake of all of that, she hadn't wanted to scroll through social media feeds full of pity and snark, or pictures of the happy new couple—because, of course, the best friend and the boyfriend were in love—so she hadn't looked at anything.

She did now.

She had run fast enough ahead of the storm that she hadn't seen it happen, but lightning had struck the cardboard on which she had written her prayer. Had scorched it, but had not consumed it. Even stranger—although the cardboard had been prayer-side up, her words had been seared onto the sidewalk, still in the same shade of elegant goth Chanel lipstick she had scrawled them in.

Nothing else had been touched.

People were already calling it a miracle. Apparently, every major department store in the city had sold out of Vamp, it was back-ordered online, and tubes were going for upward of $100 on eBay.

Joan closed her laptop. "This is too weird," she said. She looked out her window again. There were even more people out front. She shrugged into a hoodie and pulled the hood tightly over her hair. Then she slunk out of the back of the building, holding her breath against the stench, and very carefully not looking at the spatters and smears as she passed the dumpster.

Things were even crazier on the street where she had made her offering yesterday. Her *rejected* offering. Because whatever this was that was happening, it was not how the Saint of the Sidewalks worked. No one had ever heard of her making a new saint before.

Ash-smeared people wearing bloodred lipstick waved scorched pieces of cardboard. Some were calling out, "Saint Joan of the Lightning! Strike us!"

Great. Not only did they know where she lived, but they knew her name. Joan pulled her hood tighter over her head and walked as fast as she could back to her building.

That was how saints were made. Some piece of strangeness happened, and it hooked itself in the heart of someone who saw it and called it a miracle. Once they decided that's what it was, people tried to reenact the miracle's circumstances. They ritualized its pieces. They named the person at the center of it, gave them an epithet, something memorable.

The Saint of the Sidewalks had been a homeless woman, with a pile full of belongings, broken and worn. Perhaps relics from her previous life, perhaps more recent scavengings. She sat on it like it was her throne.

One day, it caught fire. Spontaneous combustion, said the witnesses. Too hot and fast to save her.

Except. No body was found. Surely a miracle, in and of itself. But then the stories started, saying that everything the fire touched had been made whole, restored. And so she became the Saint of the Sidewalks, her altars made of broken things, refuse her relics, and prayers sent to her in fire and smoke.

Joan did not want to be a saint.

The crowd at the front of her building had grown even larger, and there were peonies, baby pink and fuchsia and striated with color, woven through the handrails on the front steps. Those gave her pause for a moment, then she realized—the pattern on her kimono. Scary, that that was all it took.

The press of people was terrifying, the number of them, the fervency. She could feel the want, the terror and desperation, rising from them in waves. It made her dizzy, seasick, and again Joan slunk in through the back entrance, trying to remain unnoticed.

Joan thought she heard someone yell her name, but she pulled hard against the door, not letting go until she felt the lock engage, and then ran up the steps to her apartment.

She had forty-one new emails and thirty-six direct messages on Twitter, and there were 407 new pictures that she was tagged in on Instagram. She herself was in only thirteen of them. The rest were of her building, the lightning-struck sidewalk where her prayer was.

Almost all the messages and tags were requests for prayers, for interventions, for help.

Joan didn't even make it through ten of them before she wanted to punch something—the world, maybe—and a few more after that and she was crying. Hot, angry tears, that these people were so desperate as to see her as their best option.

She wasn't. She didn't even know how to fix her own life, much less theirs. The lightning had struck her prayer, not her—she had no superpowers. She was just a woman with a cheating ex, no job, and no coffee in her apartment.

Joan ordered in groceries and promised an obscene tip if the delivery person would meet her at the back. Nine text messages from her ex came in while she waited, all variations on how he was "So sry, bb." Not sorry enough to type entire words, apparently.

Plus, he was selling the cardigan she had left at his place on Craigslist, calling it a holy relic. He was also not sorry enough to just give it back to her when she asked him for it, the dick.

Getting the groceries was a fiasco. The crowd of people had found the back of her building, and by the time she got back inside, three of her eggs were smashed, someone had stolen her grapes, and she had gotten smeared with ashes, her arms covered in people's handprints. She wondered if yelling "Get the fuck away from me, you fucking freaks!" would make people see her as any less of a saint.

She wondered if they'd see her as normal if they saw her hiding in her bathroom, wiping away tears, or if they'd just hold out vials to collect them in.

For some people, the saints were like candles bought at bodegas: a series of interchangeable names etched on glass, to be forgotten when the too-vivid wax burned down. They were the equivalent of love spells found on the internet, tarot cards bought to be party tricks.

If Joan was honest, that's what they had always been for her. Even the intention that had gotten her into this mess—"I need a miracle"—had been desperation, not piety. In the darkest part of her heart, she hadn't really expected anything to happen, even if the sun had immolated her request. She had hoped something would happen, sure, but the gesture had been more of a way to feel like at least she had done something, than out of any fervent belief.

It was after midnight now, and raining, and there were still people clustered around the doors to her building. She had been braced all day for management to complain, but the message that pinged her inbox wasn't a noise warning, but an offer of a month's free rent. The publicity her presence generated had been a real boon. Oh, and he'd be happy to get her oven fixed too. (It spontaneously turned off after twenty minutes, no matter what temperature it was set to. Joan had put in the maintenance request three months ago.) He just had a quick prayer he wanted to send her way. Joan looked away from it. It seemed too intimate, to read what someone was praying for.

There was a GIF of a lightning strike at the bottom of the email.

Joan typed "Yes"—meaning the rent and the working oven—and copy-pasted the GIF because she didn't know what else to do with it. She felt sick to her stomach. She wasn't a saint, she wasn't, but this had to be better than just ignoring the guy, right? She hit send.

Blue-white lightning cracked outside her window.

There was a crash. A scream. Then cheering.

"Saint Joan of the Lightning!" they cried.

She did not get up. She did not look.

Joan sat at her computer, staring at the "message sent" icon, hands covering her mouth. I need a miracle, she thought.

This time, the voices that woke Joan weren't from the chaos outside. They were in her head. People begging, beseeching: "Strike me with your holy fire, Lady." "I cover myself in ashes until I am worthy of your light." Other things she understood less—languages she didn't speak, incoherent weeping. She sat up in bed and clung to her blankets.

This was insane. She was no saint. She couldn't answer prayers. Didn't want the responsibility. Certainly didn't want other people's fucking voices inside her head.

She opened up her laptop and started to type.

Turns out, once people decide you're a saint, they're reluctant to let you stop being one. They retrofit your actions to their desired narrative. So even though Joan wrote an explanation to her followers—ugh, that word—that she was just like they were, denied all ability to help people, to work miracles, they took her words as a sign of humility, of caring, of becoming modesty. The devotion to her only increased. She couldn't walk anywhere without prayers reverberating in her head.

The constant press of people sent her into trembling panic attacks, and so she lied, said that any unwanted physical contact would shock people, a result of the lightning that still passed through her.

She'd picked the ability because she wished she'd had it around her grabby ex-boss. But the story spread, and people gave her space. Almost enough that she could breathe.

Joan was never sure, after, how it had happened. If the man had acted deliberately or not. But there was a hand on her upper arm, and then there was a spark and snap, and then there was a man, flung backward, heaped up against a wall.

Joan stood, frozen to the spot. The man scrambled to his feet, then prostrated himself before her on the sidewalk. Already, the branching tattoo of the lightning strike was visible on his skin. He apologized and begged her forgiveness.

She gave it to him, of course. That was what saints did.

"It gets worse, the more they believe in you, not better." The woman sat on a stoop, bright fuchsia sequined Converse scattering sunlight from beneath the hem of an unbelted cream trench coat. "All the supernatural bullshit, I mean."

"How do you know that I—" Joan started.

"You look haunted. Hollow. Like people have been biting off pieces of your insides.

"Plus, you're all over the internet. Our Lady of the Lightning Strike."

There was a clink as a piece of a shattered flowerpot

replaced itself, making the terra-cotta whole again. A sensation like flame passed over Joan's skin.

Down the block, a flat bicycle tire refilled itself, and the bent wheel of a homeless man's shopping cart straightened.

Refuse made whole. Tiny, spontaneous miracles of proximity, accompanied by the heat of flames that did not consume what they touched. Joan felt pretty sure she knew who she was sitting next to.

"Right. Of course. What do you mean, 'it gets worse'?" Joan plucked at a torn cuticle, worrying the skin until it bled, then winced at the pain.

"The more they believe, the more you become a part of those beliefs. Or did you think hearing voices and being electric were just talents you picked up?"

Joan shook her head. "Does it stop?"

"Maybe. If you're lucky." There was longing in the woman's voice.

"I only wanted a miracle," Joan said.

The woman stood up, her shoes blinding in the sun. "And what makes you think you didn't get it?"

For the first time in her life, Joan desperately wanted to pray. To pray fervently, devotedly. To light candles before an altar, to obscure the sand of a mandala with her feet.

And she couldn't. Every time she opened her Book of Hours, every time a text alert popped up on her phone to notify her of a holy day, she thought of someone else, trapped by the weight of people's desires. Someone who, like her, could not sleep without being woken by voices raised in prayer, who could not leave their apartment without becoming the unwilling head of an impromptu pilgrimage.

She couldn't pray, not when doing so might trap someone else.

So she left. Joan wasn't sure if you could abdicate sainthood, but she would try. She hoped that if she could just get far enough away from the ecstasy of belief, find somewhere that people didn't know her face or care where she lived, she could go back to being normal.

She dyed her hair in her sink. She left in darkness. She used the last of her tube of Vamp lipstick to scrawl "Do not Look for me. I will not be Seen" on her mirror, and she left the door to her apartment wide open.

She did pack her peony-covered robe. She really liked it. And then she ran.

Far, far away from where things had begun, Joan watched as the devotees of Saint Joan of the Lightning staged a service in her honor.

They wore masks now that completely obscured their eyes, so that they could not accidentally see her. It had been that, more than the distance, that had helped—she could grocery shop in peace, most days, and usually the people who recognized her only thought she looked familiar. They didn't quite know why. And if she had peony plants in her yard, well, so did most people. She stood out less, having them.

She watched on her laptop screen as people slicked dark lipstick over their mouths, then wrote their prayers on pieces of cardboard and pressed them to the sidewalk. She thought she saw a pair of fuchsia sequined Converse walk through the crowd, and she smiled.

Joan felt the hair rise on her arms, felt static electricity crackle across her skin. She would hear the voices—she had learned to listen without going mad, to separate out the pleas—and when she heard people asking for their own miracles, she touched her screen and struck their prayers with lightning, burning them to ash, letting hope rise up like holy smoke.

She was very careful to choose only the most specific prayers. She knew very well that without direction, miracles were never what you expected them to be. She observed those who called out in her honor, and touched her finger to the computer screen. In a crackle of lightning, at a distance, a prayer was answered.

Maiden, Hunter, Beast

S he had never intended to be a nineteen-year-old virgin. She wasn't opposed to the idea of sex, didn't think the simple act of having sex with someone had to be a big deal, and sure, she went to Mass and knew what the priests taught, but she figured God was actually a lot less concerned about that sort of thing than they were. She just hadn't ever wanted to badly enough.

Which, since there was an actual fucking unicorn walking down the alley outside her apartment, seemed in retrospect like a really good decision.

Not that she really thought unicorns cared about virginity either. It was pretty clear from the art and the mythology surrounding them—the hunt for the unicorn ending with its horn in a lady-maiden's lap—that the whole "unicorns only like virgins" thing was just another way the patriarchy policed women's sexuality. If unicorns cared so much about virginity, where were the pictures of unicorns with their heads in the laps of dude-maidens? That was what she wanted to know.

That wasn't exactly the point right now, though. What with the unicorn being here. Which was amazing. And maybe it would still be here even if she'd screwed her entire high school football team and then had an orgy with the cheerleading squad as a palate cleanser. But whatever the reason or the rules, a unicorn was here, and she could see it.

She climbed through her window and clattered down the fire escape. Then stopped at the bottom, pinned by its gaze.

The unicorn raised its head and saw the maiden. It held her gaze as it swayed on its feet. Tired, so tired. It had been running forever, it seemed. Running to find itself here. This great forest of steel surrounding it, its feet aching from asphalt and concrete. Endless.

It stepped toward her. This was almost finished. It could rest. An end was all it wanted, and she was an end made flesh.

Then.

A crash. A clatter. Shouting. The maiden ran up the side of her building and disappeared.

The unicorn ran too.

The hunter stood in the mouth of the alley. The unicorn had been here—she knew the signs. The shimmer that clung to the ground, visible under ultraviolet light. The tiny white feathers that looked like down from a pillow but that chimed like glass when they hit the ground. The scent of summer and roses and frankincense that lingered to mingle with the other, less pleasant scents of a city alley.

She picked up three of the feathers and put them in the ancient leather bag that she wore slung across her chest.

It bothered her, though. The location. It was an itch between her shoulder blades. She could believe that a unicorn would make its way here, to this city. It was a place made of myth as well as of concrete and steel, and myth called to myth, even when both were tangible. But this alley was a piece of nothing. Unremarkable. Why come here?

The unicorn was gone. It had run when her roommate had yelled that the takeout was here, goddammit, and she had better come pay for it now, which was bad enough, she thought, but the fact that it had been replaced in the alley by a platinum-haired older woman with a spear slung across her back—an honest-to-God spear, not some cosplay fake—was worse. She knew what the woman was. A hunter.

Which was some kind of fucked-up shit. What kind of person saw a unicorn and thought, Yeah, you know what I'm going to do? I'm going to hunt it down and kill it. People were assholes.

Maybe she could find the unicorn first. It had looked right at her. Like it saw something in her. She had felt the look all the way into her bones. That had to mean something.

She grabbed her jacket, and some apples off the counter—because Jesus, who knew what unicorns actually ate, but apples seemed like a possibility—and left.

She stopped. Went back into her apartment and took the leathery pomegranate out of the basket too. She had seen a unicorn tapestry with pomegranates in it once. It might help.

Legs trembling with weariness, the unicorn stepped onto the patch of grass, which reeked of animal urine, of the tracks of thousands of feet, of stale earth, and of worse things besides. The unicorn thought of forests that smelled of cool water, of pine resin, of the dark comfort of leaf mold.

It could not say how long it had been since it was in such a forest. A lifetime. Two. Or three.

The unicorn could go no farther than where it was. Not right now. It barely had the strength to stand.

It could feel the heart of the maiden. It could hear the pursuit of the hunter. This, this too-long life, it would end one way, or it would end the other. But it would end, and soon.

For now, the unicorn would stand on this grass, this filthy, disgusting grass, and it would dream of remembered forests, and it would rest.

Tracking a unicorn wasn't a difficult thing, not if you were a hunter. The signs—roses growing up from cracks in the sidewalks, store windows turning to stained glass, streetside trees coming into fruit all out of season—were obvious, once you knew them.

Finding the unicorn was never the hard part. Certainly some hunters used maidens as lures, but that could cause complications, and the hunter wanted none of those. She preferred to rely on herself.

Even without the signs, without any of them, she could have tracked the unicorn. She often had, in the past. When it was younger. When it was more cunning. She had learned to rely on her intuition, on her sense of the unicorn, on the weight of the hunt, which hung, like her spear, across her back. And while she had not yet caught it, she had always found it.

There were only so many places it could go.

She had no idea where the unicorn could have gone. It wasn't like she could listen for the clip-clop of hooves over the noise of the city. And you would think that you would hear shouts, you would hear people yelling about a unicorn walking down the street—that shit should have been blowing up Twitter, Instagrammed everywhere—but no. Nothing.

Maybe it really was true that only a virgin could see a unicorn.

Not that that helped right now, because clearly the hunter could see the unicorn too, and that was the bigger problem. Because not only could the hunter see the unicorn, the hunter was also better at finding it than she was.

Her feet ached from running all over the city, and her jeans chafed, and she hadn't seen it again, and it would be easier to go home and not care.

But the unicorn had come to her alley. Had looked straight into her eyes. She had seen something in that look—age and time and the world's one remaining miracle, maybe. Or maybe just something alone and hunted and tired, in need of one kind thing, and with no one to give it. Either way, she had to care.

Think. Where in the city would a unicorn go? She knew what she would want if she were lost and wandering. Food. Water. Shelter. Unicorns probably wanted those things too. Where would it find those things in the city?

The park. She turned and ran toward it.

The unicorn wanted nothing more than to sleep. To stop. To curl its aching limbs into a cool shadow, to lay itself down on a hill of sweet grass. But it could not rest, not while it was hunted. That was the way this worked—once the hunt began, it ended only in death. The unicorn left the corroded grass, the oil-tainted water, and continued on.

It could smell the hunter's sweat, could feel her footsteps, even though she walked smoothly, even though her movements were deliberate.

That was the way of things, that the hunted beast would know of its pursuit. It had been a game before. The unicorn had exalted in its own cleverness, had laid false paths, had given counterfeit signs of its presence. Had stood in the hidden places, and watched, and delighted in the hunter's confusion.

Had remembered when it was a hunter, before it had been changed, and had used all that past knowledge to lengthen this chase.

In those early days, when this body was still new, the unicorn had felt like it could run forever.

But now it was tired, and it wished to stop. It wished for an end to things, and it very nearly didn't care how that end came about.

Very nearly. There was a hunter, yes. But there was a maiden, too, and above the strange steel forest, a bell rang, a familiar calling, and so there was something else as well.

The hunter felt the change when it happened. The air shifted. There was an undercurrent to it that hadn't been there before. It licked along the hunter's skin like electricity, and she did not like it.

Hunts were not about unpredictability. There was a quarry, and there were signs, and the quarry was tracked, and then there was the kill.

She knew what would happen, had been there before,

had been the maiden that had lured the beast. When that hunt had ended, she had pulled the spear from the corpse and claimed her new role. That was the way of things. Simple. Straightforward.

This was not.

Fuck her aching feet. She ran. She could feel time getting small, slipping away from beneath her boots as they pounded on the sidewalk. She had passed two parks already and hadn't seen the unicorn anywhere. She had called out to the people she passed, asking for help. It had gone about as well as she expected. Some asshole had grabbed his crotch and told her, "I got something better than a unicorn for you, sexy." Most people just stared.

She stopped. There had to be a better way to do this. She closed her eyes, trying to think, to feel. To remember the weight of the unicorn's eyes, looking at her as if it knew her.

If she were hunted, if she were pursued, where would she go? Where in this city was there a place of safety, of sanctuary?

Sanctuary.

The unicorn walked, as it had walked forever. But not away. Toward. Back along a path that had already been walked, back closer to a fate, instead of away from it.

The bell rang again.

The bell was the sound of sanctuary. A holy ringing, calling the faithful to a place of safety. This was something the unicorn knew, something it understood. There would be water there, holy and cool, and hands that might take the knots from its mane and the burrs from its flanks.

It could stop there. It could even sleep, and not violate the rules of the hunt. There was no time on hallowed ground.

Sanctuary.

The cathedral bells rang through the hunter. She felt them in her bones. They were a warning. There was no hunt without a quarry, and there was no hunter without a hunt. She needed to find the unicorn now, before it could cross onto hallowed ground.

She looked to the sky, to the spires and towers clawing at the horizon. She tossed the three glass feathers the unicorn had shed into the air to check the wind.

They shattered before hitting the ground, each chiming the same note as the cathedral bells.

Sanctuary. The hunter spat the word, and she ran.

She saw the unicorn fall on the cathedral steps, and she ran, her blistered feet in her too-small boots nothing to her now. Up close, she could see that it was old. Ancient maybe. Rheumy eyes and thinning hair. Hooves that were cracked.

Still a miracle, born into flesh and bone. She didn't see the hunter, but she wasn't sure that mattered now.

She stroked her hand down its trembling flank, over ribs too close to the skin. Her skin gleamed like stardust where she touched it. "You poor thing," she said. "Rest now. I'll stay with you."

Its nostrils were rimmed with red, and she moved so that the fallen unicorn could rest with its head in her lap. She offered the apple, now bruised, from her pocket, and then tore the pomegranate seeds from their leathery skin. It ate one, two, three. Not even a winter's worth. It was, she thought, eating them for her, not for itself.

She did not notice she was weeping, even as her tears fell like shadows onto the unicorn's moonlight-colored skin.

The unicorn closed its eyes.

The hunter stopped at the bottom of the cathedral stairs, just outside the bounds of what had been sanctified. She unslung her spear from her back.

"You. Will. Not." The maiden's voice was sharp as fate.

"I am a hunter. This is what I do." But the spear felt heavy in her hand, strange in a way it never had before. She was unsure of her words, of her very name.

"No. This hunt is finished."

The cathedral bell rang.

• • •

She kept her hands on the unicorn as the hunter walked toward them. She didn't know what else to do, so she hunched over its fallen body, shielding it with her own, bracing for the hunter's spear.

She felt the unicorn stop breathing.

In that moment, she felt as if the spear had pierced her heart, felt a world end.

She did not want to be the maiden, if this pain was what that meant. She would be something else.

Beneath her, the unicorn disappeared, the sound of its leaving a thousand shatterings of glass.

The hunter's spear fell apart in her hand, scattering to nothing, to uselessness. She stumbled to her knees, unbelieving. Lost.

The hunter was nothing without her quarry. There was no hunt without a beast.

She got up from where the unicorn had fallen and walked to where the older woman crouched among the pieces of her shattered spear. She spoke one word.

"Run."

The woman who had once been the hunter stood awkwardly. She waited for the thing that must happen—for her feet to form into hooves and her skin to harden into hide. For her body to turn strange and monstrous, moonlight-colored and spiral-horned, for the change to give her the advantage of the hunt.

Nothing. Her own heart thudded, frantic in her chest. Her aching legs—two, only two!—shook beneath her.

Again, that terrible, merciless voice: "Run."

She did.

Once, Future

— 1 —

The scent of apples is everywhere. Cloying and too sweet. The thick white of their blossoms, the sharp crispness of the fruit, the heady cider of the overripe bodies fallen to the ground. The rot where they lie. It should be impossible for each version of the fruit to exist at once, all together, but really, everything about this should be impossible.

Like. For example. On a bier, as if we were in some sort of fairy tale and she were waiting to be kissed awake, Sabra. She's not dead. Not quite. She won't die, not if things play out the way everything else in this stuck-pattern has. She can't. Once and future, that's the deal. She will stay, not quite alive, not quite dead, on this island of impossible apples, this almost Avalon, and I will . . .

I will . . .

Time is ticking down. I have done everything I can to put this moment off. To look away from this action, this thing that waits at the end. Because the story might survive if I'm wrong—almost certainly will—but some of us won't. I drop down into the grass, closer to the scent of dying apples, and stab my hands through my hair. The white dog sitting at Sabra's side noses her once again and whines softly when she doesn't move. I stretch my hand to pet him, not sure which of us I'm comforting.

I am terrified that I'm wrong about what I have to do. I'm also terrified that I'm right. And there's no one here I can ask.

This is the part of the map that has monsters on it. We are beyond the end of the story.

Maybe I should start at the beginning.

"Once upon a time" is the traditional start to a story, but I don't want to open with a lie. The problem with this story is, it was never only once. It was, and has been, over and over. So: the beginning. Well. Our beginning.

Our once upon a time was a sunny September afternoon in Professor Viviane Link's Severn University seminar, The Arthurian Legend in Time. The syllabus promised a semester-long engagement with all the variety of ways the story of Arthur and Camelot and its fall got told and retold, across time and medium. It was supposed to be one of those classes you take to give yourself a break. Not an easy grade necessarily, but a fun one. The kind of class that always has a waiting list, because everyone who took it before you loved it and you've heard stories about how great it is since you first got to campus.

It was the third week of the semester, and on tap that day was a discussion of T. H. White's *The Once and Future King* and two adaptations of it—the Disney version of *The Sword in the Stone*, and the Lerner and Loewe musical *Camelot*—and how they all connected in the mythology around the Kennedy administration in the early 1960s. Fantasy being rewound around the narrative of reality and vice versa. Circles of events and circles of influences and repeating patterns that drew them together. The symbolism and iconography layered in the same way one would tell the life of a saint—that everything that happened had been destined from the beginning, that all the signs were always there to be seen.

"I just think it's interesting," Sabra said, "the way it's so easy for the same story to be retold and reshaped. Like there's a pattern somewhere, and it pulls at the pieces until we recognize them."

Sabra Michaels. So strange to be taking classes with her. In undergrad, we both had been Gamma Alphas at our tiny liberal arts college in Virginia. I'd liked her, but we hadn't been particularly close—she had pledged when I was a junior, so while our paths had crossed, there hadn't been that much overlap. I hadn't even known she was doing grad school, much less here at Severn, but I'd been delighted to see her walk through the doors. Her girlfriend, Niv, was doing her graduate work here too—I'd had dinner with them last week.

"Of course there's a pattern," Nora said from the opposite side of the table. "We're looking at retellings of the same story. Written by writers making their characters jump up and down like puppets. If we didn't recognize what was going on, the retelling would be a failure."

"Obviously, I get that it's fiction, that writers are writing, and things aren't just happening, but it's easy to make things fit. The story works as well in a medieval Celtic setting as it does in 1960s America. I think that's worth thinking about." Sabra was animated, flushed.

"I think you're seeing connections because brains like patterns," Nora said. "But that's all there is. The Arthurian legend isn't magic, and it doesn't have self-replicating DNA."

Professor Link sat back and let the discussion range. Her teaching style was basically that since we were graduate students, we were capable of learning from one another, and she would stay out of our way while we did, unless it looked like actual blood might be shed, or that the class might go silent. I wasn't sure which she would have thought was worse.

During a lull, she spoke up. "Anyone else? Liam, Morgan, you've both been quiet."

Liam shook his head. "All I had to say was that I really liked the wizards' duel in the cartoon. I wish that had been in one of the other stories—I was kind of surprised that it wasn't."

"I think it's both," I said as Professor Link turned her gaze to me. "Of course the writer is manipulating things, making sure the underlying pattern of the story is recognizable. But I also think this particular story has a pattern that likes to fit. It is almost like self-replicating DNA. The story makes it easy for the writer. That's why there are so many retellings."

"So you're saying that if you just took a bunch of people sitting around today and named them Arthur and Gwen and Lance and Mordred, they'd wind up repeating the fall of Camelot?" Nora asked, scorn in every syllable.

"That's not what—"

"I think we should find out," said Professor Link.

The seminar room fell silent. Dust motes spun in a slant of light that slashed across the long oval table that we sat around for class.

"I propose an alternate project. If you want to participate, let me know by the end of this week. I will randomly assign the participants to names from the story—big players and small. Once you get your name, keep a journal for the rest of the semester where you record anything that happens that makes you feel like it might possibly be related to the Arthurian legend or any of the variants of it that we've studied here. Tell me if you think the pattern is trying to replicate."

"That's it?" Liam asked. "Just a journal. No walking around campus pretending to be Merlin, or teaching my section of freshman comp while I'm cosplaying Lancelot?"

"Or Guinevere," Professor Link said. "Random means random. But no. Aside from keeping the journal, what you do—or don't do—once you've been assigned your name is up to you. If there is a pattern, it will assert itself regardless. And if there isn't, well, a bunch of blank notebooks will be a nice change from the usual end-of-semester requests for extensions on seminar papers."

"So we can still get an A even if nothing happens?" Liam asked.

"If you legitimately observe nothing—no changes in yourself, in your fellow students, anything of that sort—then that's all you need to write down. Just be honest—and yes, I'll know if you're not."

"What if everyone chooses a name?" I asked. "Will you still hold class, if the final is only determined by our journals?"

"You'd still need to do the reading, to familiarize yourself with the various versions of the story, since you will, after all, be looking for similarities. But I'd probably drop the attendance requirement. Still, I suspect there will be those who prefer a more traditional classroom experience, so don't get your hopes up."

"I'm in," Sabra said.

"So am I," said Nora.

There was a flurry of voices and hands. Professor Link held up hers. "Before things dissolve into chaos, let's do this by email. That way, I can also make sure I have enough names for everyone before I start handing them out."

"Do we tell anyone who we are?" I asked.

"Once you've committed to participating, everything else is up to you. You choose your level of involvement. Get your name, tell no one, do nothing, or spend the entire semester in costume, acting the story out. As long as you turn in the journal at the end of it, you will have fulfilled your obligations, and will be able to earn an A in the course."

Monday of the following week, I got a card in my campus mailbox. Heavy cream paper, like an invitation. I slid my finger under the flap and winced as the edge sliced my skin. Blood from the paper cut smeared the card inside, but I could still read it.

Even without knowing who anyone else was, I wondered how honest Professor Link was being when she'd said things would be totally random. What I saw made me suspect they weren't, not completely. There in the scrawl of purple ink was the one name in the story that matched mine: Morgan le Fay.

Once

A BELL TOLLS, AND AS ITS ECHO FADES, I AWAKEN. Around me are black-feathered birds, taking wing. When they are all airborne, when the sky itself looks to be black and feathered, the last blanket lifts from the magic.

My magic.

It sleeps, in between things, with my brother.

I sit up, slowly stretching my unused muscle and sinew into a semblance of function, and look around. He is not here. Not yet. Even with as many times as the story has started, I have seen him only twice since that first time I sent him to sleep on the Isle of the Apples, long and long ago. Both times, I have only seen him sleeping.

He has not woken since he fell.

My brother. Arthur. King once and future, the Pendragon. The stories will tell you that he sleeps now so that he may awaken in his country's hour of greatest need, arising so as to save it.

The stories lie.

He sleeps because I made a mistake. Because I loved him, and I did not want him to die. Because I bound him too well into a story he was supposed to leave, and bound myself, too.

Bound us, and one other. The one who would have a different story told. She is why I am awake, now, again.

Magic fizzes like acid in my blood as it uncurls from its sleeping, cramping my muscles, and sending aches through my joints. The pain of reawakening gets worse each time, and I wonder if she knows that. I wonder if she hurts too when the story starts again.

The ravens wing away, and the air here, this here, this now, smells like apples. In the distance, I hear waves breaking on a shore. It is as it always is: once upon the next time. Perhaps this time an ending.

In the darkness, an apple falls.

— 2 —

If there is a pattern, it will assert itself regardless.

If I'm going to be honest, if I am going to be the one who tells this story, who goes back to my fake journal entries and rewrites them into the truth about how a seminar project led us here—

(Sabra's still breathing. I can feel her pulse. But she won't wake up. I think I know what will end this, what will break the strange once-future we're caught in, but I'm afraid. Afraid that under all the weirdness of the past few months, I'm just a grad student from Idaho, not some out-of-time, kairos-ridden version of a sorceress, afraid that this is the place where the pattern that got stronger all semester finally refuses to recognize itself and falls apart, afraid that if I'm wrong, not only does Arthur wind up dead, but Sabra does too.)

—I should be honest.

Part of the reason I was in Professor Link's seminar was my name. I liked Morgan le Fay. I always had. She was the reason that I'd read the King Arthur stories in the first place. I liked that she was a sorceress, or maybe a fairy. The Queen of Air and Darkness. I liked that she was a woman with power. I wasn't there for Arthur, who came across as being sort of dim in a lot of the stories and too good to be real in others; or the knights of the Round Table, who were way too invested in smiting; or Excalibur, which, at the end of the day, was only a weapon. I was in that class because of the woman who took her dying brother to the isle of Avalon and made sure that he was future, not just once.

I was in that class because of Morgan, and she was why I sent in the email and asked for a name. Not because I wanted an easy final or truly believed that the pattern of a story I was pretty sure was mostly fiction was going to re-create itself in our seminar, but because hers was the name I wanted to get.

Because I wanted to pretend, just for a moment, that I could be a sorceress. That I could be a woman with power.

Cabal raises his head from my legs and whines.

I am a woman with power.

I know what I have to do.

Liam, of course, did show up to our next seminar meeting in his best attempt at a suit of armor. It looked like it had started out as football or hockey pads, which he then spray-painted silver, but he seemed so pleased with himself as he clanked around the room calling people "foul varlets" that it was impossible to do anything but go along with his delight at being Lancelot.

Well, almost impossible.

"You get that Lancelot was an asshole, right?" Nora asked.

"Come on. He was the greatest knight in history. He won all the jousts and rescued all the ladies. No one could beat him." Liam struck a pose reminiscent of the Wart's fencing lessons, off-balance and akimbo. "En garde!"

"The greatest knight in history. Who committed treason. Fucked his best friend's wife. Then ran off and left her to almost get burned to death because he couldn't cope with what a giant douche he was." Nora ticked her points off on her fingers.

"Ever heard of courtly love? Lancelot was just doing what his culture told him to when he flirted with Guinevere. Besides, it wasn't his fault that Arthur couldn't keep his wife happy."

"It was, however, Lancelot's fault he couldn't keep his lance in his pants." Nora rolled her eyes and shoved her chair away from Liam's, opening up a gap at the far curve of the table.

Professor Link didn't comment, just began the discussion on Guy Gavriel Kay's Fionavar trilogy, "a series that has a more charitable conception of Lancelot, and the triangle, than the one that's been articulated here."

Our class hadn't been meeting for very long, and as far as I could tell, Nora was one of those people who enjoyed being contrary. Still, I wrote the conversation down, later,

in my journal. Like any good academic, I dutifully specu-
lated whether Nora really hated Lancelot, or if she had been
assigned the name of someone who hated Lancelot in the
stories. Agravain, maybe.

Guessing people's alternate identities became a sort of mental game. I knew who I was. I knew who Liam was. Nirali,
who was working on her MFA in dance, was Gawain, so
maybe things were more random than I thought, because
there was nothing about her that called to mind the bulky,
quick-tempered Gawain of the stories.

"Though if anyone thinks I am jousting, or smiting, or
doing any other random knight things, they are mistaken,"
she said. "All I am doing is keeping a journal."

"Well, the knights in Monty Python dance," Liam pointed
out. "You could do a very knightly sort of soft-shoe."

"You put your suit of armor back on and show up at the
studio, we'll do a kick line. Otherwise, no."

Liam grinned. "I just might. Wearing it was pretty damn
fun."

Nirali shook her head, laughing.

Even though I knew we didn't have to guess who the
other people in the seminar were, it itched at me that I didn't
know who had been assigned Arthur, Guinevere, Mordred.
The big names, the ones that anchored the story. Sabra and
Nora had both announced that they were in, but maybe they

had changed their minds. They acted the same way in class as they had for our first few meetings, so there were no clues there.

Plus, I knew that some of the people in the seminar hadn't wanted to participate in this little experiment. The whole idea was too weird, they said. They were only sticking around because it was too late in the semester to drop the class. I was pretty sure I knew who they were, though, a knot of five, nearly one third of the seminar, who grouped together along one curve of the table, fiercely taking notes as if grounding themselves in the world of academe would keep them safe from being infected by whatever wild bits of story might be floating about the room.

So I wasn't sure exactly how many people I was guessing about. Maybe we had a Merlin and a Lady of the Lake and a Galahad. Maybe we had none of those people. I wouldn't put it past Professor Link to dig deep into Malory, or wherever else she was getting the names from, and bring out some lesser-known players, like Sir Marrok, the werewolf knight.

No, I wouldn't put it past her, but random assignment or not, Arthur, I thought, was a guarantee. He was the one constant in all the patterns, all the stories. There was no Camelot, not without Arthur.

Once

MY ISLAND IS STILL FORMING ITSELF OUT OF PAST time and old magic. Even the apple trees, most days, are barely more than scent and memory.

I make myself walk the island's bounds, such as they are, every morning. Relearning how to walk, how to breathe, how to taste the air. To be reminded, once again, of the ways of living in flesh.

It is limiting.

Neither the island nor I am yet strong enough to bear my leaving it, and so I send out my ravens.

They bring me news, carried on wing and wind, and they are the eyes through which I see. It begins as I have come to expect it to—Arthur's story, *my* story, is barely more than a fairy tale to them. It is names on a page, marvels and monsters, not people who bled and died.

It is a strange thing, the first time you realize you have become a fiction.

But some of them want to believe the story is more than that, the girl who takes my brother's role in particular. There is a clarity to her desire that makes me think she could have sat the Siege Perilous and survived, had she been in that telling.

I can use that desire.

The spell moves sluggishly through my hands—I am less awake than the magic that woke me—but my fingers unstiffen and remember their patterns.

It helps that the story remembers how it begins.

With a sword, and a stone.

— 3 —

Two days later, I came home from a seminar on medieval poetry to see Sabra sitting on my front step. "Have you found anything weird lately?" She hesitated between the words, as if she hoped that, given enough time, they might change in her mouth.

"What sort of weird?" I slid my bag from my shoulder and sat next to her.

"Well, there was a sword in my front doorstep this morning."

"An actual sword."

"Sharp and everything." She held up a Band-Aid-wrapped finger. "It looks like it should be in a museum."

"Who are you? I mean, for Professor Link's class."

"Arthur." She grinned. "Let's hear it for random assignments, right? Niv's full name is Gwenivere, and she thinks it's hysterical. Plus, I always wanted to be Arthur when I was a kid, and was so pissed when my brothers made me be Guinevere and get rescued all the time just because I was a girl."

A sword as a gift for Arthur made at least some kind of sense. "Does anyone else from class know? Giving you a sword seems like something Liam might do—he's pretty into this whole thing."

She shook her head. "You're the first person from class I've told. Besides, I don't think it was a prank. The sword was literally *in* the stone doorstep." She pulled out her phone, showed me the picture. The sword was sunk down, almost to the forte of the blade, flush with the surrounding stone, as if it had grown there.

Not just a sword for Arthur. A sword in a stone.

"I know," she said in response to the wonder on my face. "I know."

"How did you get it out?"

"I just . . . pulled." She shrugged. "It didn't seem like a big deal—no light from heaven, no chorus of voices telling me I was the rightwise king, or whatever—but then I was standing there, holding a sword that I had pulled out of a stone as easily as cutting butter, and I really needed to sit down.

"So, like I said, have you found anything weird lately?"

I shook my head. "But I'm Morgan. I don't think I get any sort of symbolic weird shit."

"Maybe you'll get magic." She wiggled her fingers like jazz hands. "That would be cool."

"It would, actually. If I get a letter from an owl, I'll let you know."

Sabra was laughing as she left.

I wasn't.

I was beyond laughter. I felt electrified, like the wind had stood all my hair on end, as if I were perched on the threshold of a hidden door.

Something was beginning.

Professor Link's office was in one of the oldest buildings at Severn. The kind of building that location scouts searching for "picturesque seat of higher learning" would drool over. Ivy-covered walls of faded red brick, diamond-paneled windows that sparkled in the sunlight, and a tower. Professor Link's office was at its top. After walking up three stories of winding steps, I knocked on the doorframe.

She looked up from her papers. "Morgan. Come in."

I sat in the worn wooden chair in front of her desk. "I was just wondering—with this whole we get names from the Arthurian legend, let's see if the story happens thing—are you participating?"

She set her pen down and leaned back in her chair. Behind her, the window was open wide enough to let in the sound of the wind on the lake. "Participating?"

"Doing something more than just assigning names. Like, leaving presents or something related to who we're assigned to be." The breeze made her office chilly, and I pulled my cardigan closer around me.

She smiled, shook her head. "I put the cards in the

envelopes without looking at them. So while I know which names are in play, I don't know who has been assigned to each one, except for people like Liam, who have made that public. And much as I might like it to, I'm afraid the departmental budget doesn't stretch to giving gifts to students."

"That makes sense," I said. Which, of course, it did.

"Why do you ask?"

The entire room changed around the question. The wind from the lake grew frigid and picked up enough that I could see white on the waves. An ache throbbed in my temples. The hair rose on the back of my neck, and the only thing I wanted more than to get out of that room was to tell Professor Link everything I knew about the mysterious sword, and Sabra. The desire to speak was so strong my stomach ached.

"Oh, just something Liam said. Maybe about his knight costume? I guess I misheard." I leaned down, biting my lips around the words that were trying to crawl from my throat, and picked up my bag. "I'm sorry, but I have a terrible migraine coming on."

I stood and covered my mouth with my hand. "I get nausea with them. I should go."

"By all means. Feel better soon."

I did, as soon as I left her office, and better still by the time I had—at a near run—gotten to the bottom of the twisting staircase. I slowed then, catching my breath and allowing my racing heart to get closer to normal. My head no longer ached, and I didn't want to vomit other people's secrets.

Maybe Professor Link was telling the truth when she said that she didn't know what names we'd been assigned. But I didn't believe she was disinterested in what would happen next.

That was when I started writing fake entries in my journal. I wanted to keep the truth of the story, of *our* story, hidden. As if by not speaking it, I could keep it—keep *us*—safe.

At the time, I thought that would be enough.

Once

THE AIR SHAKES, AND THE WAVES SMASH THEM-selves against my island. The reek of the lake is everywhere. She cannot set foot here—she is as bound in these things as I am—but she does not let me forget that she is close.

I do not know what name she is using this time. She sheds them as a snake sheds skins. But I do not need a name to know that what I feel is her—the anger of the lake, the scent of the water.

She is here, and she has been thwarted.

In her tantrum, something else: a door, cracked open. Magic brought into play. She has used hers against one of the players, and so I can use—or share—mine in a way that is more direct than simply making sure that someone finds a sword. I gather what I need.

A mirror, in which I can see myself and this story's reflection, the one who shares my name and shares it twice.

A cord to knot and bind us both together.

Glass, that I may see her clearly, and feathers to carry the magic on their wings.

Blood, because it is life.

And finally, a light to bring life, flame against the darkness.

I take all these things in my hands, hold them tight together, and I speak her name, my name, our name, and release the spell to the sky.

— 4 —

There was no owl with a letter waiting when I got home. I didn't expect one either—leaving aside the more obvious issues, that was the wrong story. But I wondered if magic—real, true magic—was possible.

I knew how that sounded, but I was Morgan. If someone in this story, or this pattern, or whatever we were calling it, was supposed to be magic, it was me.

So I decided I would try something small, something simple. I cast about for ideas but kept tripping over mental images of stage magicians flourishing wands and pulling rabbits from hats by saying "abracadabra." The Morgan of this story was not a stage magician.

Then I remembered: the end of *The Once and Future King*. Arthur, who knows full well that he will fall in battle, asks his page to remember his story. To tell it as a light in the darkness. A candle. I would try to light a candle, and when it didn't work, I would laugh at myself and move on.

I poured a glass of wine and found a fat pillar of beeswax, set it on the kitchen table, far away from everything else. Just in case.

I drew a breath and let it out. Held the image of flame in my head.

"Light."

Nothing. Not even the scent of smoke.

"Let there be light!" Focus, plus dramatic hand gesture, and I was so glad that I didn't have a roommate. No one should see you trying very seriously to be a wizard when you are completely certain that you're not one.

One. One more time. I'd try once more before I gave myself up as ridiculous. Maybe with better magic words. Something Morgan might have said—words full of ritual and power.

I placed my feet flat on the floor, looked straight at the wick, and said, *"Fiat lux."*

And there was.

Without looking away from the flickering candle, I reached out for the glass of wine. I drank all of it.

I stayed up all night lighting the candle. At first because it seemed impossible, and then because it didn't. Over and over again until it was almost nothing—a breath, a thought—to set it burning. Just past dawn, I stumbled into bed, exhausted. I dreamt of candles. Flickers and glows of light against the darkness.

I slept poorly, and only for about two hours. The first thing I did when I woke up, sand-eyed and muzzy-headed, was to turn to the candle next to me on the nightstand and command it to light.

It did.

My grin stretched huge across my face. Magic was real, and I could do it.

You forget the end of the story when you're living in it. I mean, it's right there in the name: *Le Morte d'Arthur. The Death of Arthur.* Death. There are no versions of the original legend where he gets out alive, unless you count that whole once-and-future bit, where he's taken offstage to sleep on the island of Avalon. The story of Arthur is always a tragedy. The only question is what the rest of the body count looks like.

Intellectually, I knew that. Everyone in Professor Link's seminar did. We spent hours talking about it every week, the way each version of the story either stopped just before the end or walked headlong into disaster and grief.

But it didn't occur to me that we were in for the same thing. Not at the beginning, anyway. Not when Sabra pulled a sword from stone, not when magic became like breathing for me, not until later. Not until too late.

Maybe that's the nature of tragedy. That you don't notice. Or you see the signs gathering around you, and still you think: not us.

Or maybe I was the only one who didn't see. Because Morgan is always there, at the end, when that black-covered barge comes to Avalon. In every version, she survives.

If I was going to be able to do magic, I wanted to be able to do more than just light candles. Don't get me wrong: lighting a candle with just words was cool, but it wasn't exactly useful, especially considering that I lived in a world with easily accessible electricity.

My previous experience with anything remotely connected to magic and witchcraft had been limited to the high school rite of passage stuff—Ouija boards that predicted death in grisly ways; slumber party games of "Light as a feather, stiff as a board" that worked just well enough to make us believe we were powerful; small curses and big wishes, both of which were cast around events that likely would have played out as they did even without our efforts. I had liked playing at magic and was secretly sad that I didn't have any real evidence that any of it had worked. I still read my horoscope in the backs of fashion magazines so I could take advantage of my guaranteed lucky days, and I had an app on my phone to tell me when Mercury was in retrograde.

Some days I sort of believed in some of it.

Unfortunately, the offerings of the Severn University library were a lot closer to the history of the Ouija board and how to do sleight of hand, and nothing like how to do actual magic. Not that I thought I was going to find an old spell book stuffed on a forgotten shelf somewhere, but I figured that something in the medieval section might be helpful. Alchemy was once an actual science, after all, and the history of magic was an academic discipline. But no. I spent a frustrating hour searching the stacks, and another making interlibrary loan requests so I could pretend I'd accomplished something, before deciding anything else was futile and gathering my stuff.

Tired, I slumped against the wall of the ancient, creaking elevator, rolled my eyes when it stopped after one floor. The library elevator was notoriously cranky, sometimes deciding to stop on every floor, regardless of what buttons had been pushed, and often coming to a halt on the third floor and refusing to move in either direction for hours. This stop, at least, had been needed—a clutch of undergrad women crowded on, mid-conversation.

"I heard he knocked out the guy with one punch!"

"And then kept him there until the police came."

"He walked her back to the house and stayed outside all night, not even sleeping, so she could feel safe."

"I'm sorry," I interrupted their conversation. "Mei, right? You were in the Shakespeare class I TA'd last fall, I think?"

"Oh, hi, Morgan! I didn't notice you when we got on." She smiled and shifted her bag to her other arm.

"What happened?" I asked. "Who are you talking about?"

"One of our sorority sisters got followed home from a party—this douche-bag guy wouldn't leave her alone, you know how it is. And when she tried to walk away, he grabbed her by the hair and yanked her to the ground. Like he would have . . . ugh, I can't even say it. It was almost horrible."

"But she's okay?"

"Yes! Totally fine. This grad student—Liam O'Brien, he taught my freshman comp section—he came out of nowhere and rescued her. Knocked the guy out, stayed with her till the police came, called out their bullshit when they asked if she had been drinking or had 'accidentally' invited the guy home with her. The whole bit."

"Like a knight in shining armor," I said quietly.

"Exactly," she said. "Like, I thought he was nice before, but this is like superhero stuff. Plus, he's hot."

"We've got a class together. I'll be sure to tell him you said so."

She laughed. The elevator stopped with a thud on the ground floor, and Mei and her sorority sisters waved goodbye and walked into the grey drizzle of the evening.

I didn't know Liam well, not at all outside of our seminar. So rescuing a woman from an attempted assault and helping her deal with the aftermath could have been completely in character for him—some people truly are that decent.

Still. He was Lancelot, and Arthur's knights had all been required to take a vow to come to the aid of any woman who required it. Helping someone once was an isolated incident, not a pattern, and I didn't want there to be enough women attacked for there to be a pattern. But. Still.

The bells in Severn's clock tower rang out as I hurried across campus. Rain was sheeting down, and the wind turned my umbrella inside out and useless. I didn't see the woman until I ran into her.

We both went tumbling to the ground in a collected heap of limbs and books. "I'm so sorry," I said as I pulled myself up and held out my hand to her. "Are you all right?"

She looked windblown, tossed. Dark hair in soaked ropes, shadowed hollows under eyes that were tawny and sharp, like a bird of prey's. "Yes, yes," she said. "It's this cursed rain—I didn't see you. Oh, all your books!"

My tote had gone flying, spilling my books across the path and into the grass. "Shit. The library is going to kill me."

"Let me help you." She gathered a stack and dropped them into my bag.

I settled my bag back over my shoulder, readjusted to the weight of it. "Is the clock still ringing?" Minutes had passed, but I would have sworn I still heard the deep, sounding chimes tolling the hour.

"Are you sure you're all right?" she asked me, her hands on my shoulders.

"Just dizzy, I think. Thanks." Soaked and mud-smeared, I decided to skip my evening class and limped back home.

I was shivering by the time I got back, aching from my fall, and in a mood as foul as the weather. All I wanted was a steaming-hot bath, a glass of wine, and a pizza. Possibly eaten while in the bath.

I kicked the door shut behind me and let my bag drop.

A book I didn't recognize fell out. Heavy, and bound in old, worn leather, pages warped with age. A lock held it closed but snicked open when I touched it.

Words I didn't recognize swam dizzily across the pages, then halted and resolved themselves into English. Instructions for magic, all neatly organized. It was, I thought, a grimoire. My head throbbed, but I couldn't stop reading. Each page was full of spells, their ingredients in recipe lists, followed by incantations. A variety of ways of making magic, all written out. Inside the front cover: "*Ex libris Morganae.*"

Morgan's book.

Morgan's.

My hands shook as I turned the pages, then closed the cover.

Reasonably sure that this constituted finding something weird, I thought of calling Sabra but set the phone back down. Before I shared this, I wanted to know what I could do.

Thoughts of bath and pizza pushed aside, I lit my candles, opened the book back up, and read.

I didn't leave my apartment for a week. I cut all my classes, even the ones I was supposed to be teaching, and Professor Link's seminar. At the end of those seven days, I was exhausted, held together by coffee and will, but I could do much more than simply call flame to a candle.

There were birds drawn in the margins of the manu-
script: perching, mantled, in flight. They flew me through
the pages, guided my way through the spells.

The first thing I learned was their calling. Not just the
sounds, the way of changing the shape of my voice in my
throat to fit, but the way to send that call to their ears, to be
able to bring a response. Next I learned their speech, how to
shape my ears to their voices.

Even now, a flock of ravens was a set of smudged shadows muttering amongst themselves in my trees. A comfortable, reassuring cohort in the pale-silver light of dawn.

The pages of the grimoire moved like feathers beneath
my hands and brought me to the next spell, and I learned to
fly like a bird. To shrink myself down into wings and talons,
to have a heartbeat that raced and eyes that saw forever compared to my human ones. I flew everywhere, all over campus, through the orchard and to the shores of the lake where
every morning Sabra went to try to outrun herself.

Back in my own body, I felt light-headed and strange,
as if I were living outside my skin, as if the air were a lightning storm I walked through. I could feel time, stretching
and branching in all directions, until seconds met and coiled
themselves round as clocks, and I could feel the worms
crawling beneath the ground, and the wind on the water, and
the quiet drowsing of the trees as fall came upon them.

Magic came faster and faster to me after that. It was as

if I were a glass, and magic the sand that poured in to fill me.
I learned words for binding things, for knitting skin together
once torn, for closing a mouth that would speak an untruth.

I could pour ink on a map and find a person as they
walked, and I could shield my own self from seeking eyes.
(Thinking of Professor Link, I cast that one every day as soon
as I woke up.)

There were others, too, that I didn't try. Spells to stop
time. Spells to bend another's will to mine. Spells to cause
obsession.

A spell to prevent death in battle.

No, that's not what I'm supposed to use.

Trust me.

That was the spell that started all this.

Sitting through that week's seminar was like bracing for an
explosion. Magic surged beneath my skin, looking for a way
out. Static in my blood. I couldn't concentrate, could barely
sit. My discomfort was so obvious that Sabra, sitting next to
me, typed "R U OK?" into her notes and angled her laptop
toward me. I nodded, lying.

"Well, we've gone longer than I meant to, but this is a
good stopping point. Rather than taking a break and starting
a new topic for half an hour, why don't we just go home early
today?"

I was packed up and out of my seat before Professor Link had finished talking, knocking my chair over in my hurry to get outside. I kept going until I got to a small clump of trees. Stopped and leaned against one, letting the soft, cold rain wash over my face until my heartbeat felt like mine, and not like a bird's in my chest.

"Morgan?" Liam's voice.

I opened my eyes.

"I thought this might help." He held out a to-go cup.

"Normally, I'd say yes, but I don't think coffee's a good idea right now."

"It's tea," he said, turning the cup so I could see the string from the tea bag. "And lots of sugar."

"Thank you." I sipped at it, the warm sweetness easing whatever it was that had been trying to shake me apart from the inside.

Liam leaned against a tree of his own.

"You don't need to stand out here in the rain with me. I'll be fine."

"You're still shaking, and you're currently the palest live human I've ever seen. A little rain won't hurt me."

"You really know how to flirt with a girl, Liam."

"I'll do better later." He grinned.

The rain fell harder and was cold enough that I was shaking from the temperature, rather than an excess of magic. "I should go home."

"Do you mind if I walk with you? I mean, I'm sure you're fine, but it would reassure me."

"A 'verray, parfit gentil knyght,'" I said.

He laughed. "My mom gets low blood sugar. Hot sweet tea helps steady her. More chemistry than chivalry."

I thanked him when we got to my apartment.

"You're sure you're going to be okay?" he asked.

"I really am much better," I said.

The rain silvered around him like armor as he walked away.

I did feel better, but I wanted to know why I had felt so strange in the first place. I paged through the grimoire, wondering if I had missed some warning against combining certain spells or using an excess of magic.

Nothing. Maybe it was just my body adjusting. But it had been unpleasant, and I wanted to avoid something like that happening again.

I closed the grimoire, rested my fingers on top of it. They tingled, like I'd grasped a nettle in my hand.

There was, perhaps, someone I could ask.

I got out a map. A campus map, the scale small enough to see the paths and buildings. There was no guarantee, but our class was here, we were here, and she—whoever she was— had come here to give me the book.

I said the words of the scrying spell, poured ink in a thin

stream over the map, and watched as it beaded up in the middle of Lake Severn.

Which, unless she was out rowing with the crew team, meant I had done the spell wrong. There were no islands in the lake.

I cleared my thoughts of everything but the woman who had given me the book. Held her image so bright in my mind I could see her raven eyes. I spoke the spell again, and this time . . .

Once

THE AIR OPENS BEFORE ME LIKE A MIRROR, BRIGHT as lightning, and a face that is not mine looks up from a book that is. I do not usually see my shadows, my story-selves, at times when I haven't gone looking for them. And never before has one come looking for me.

But here she is.

I reach out and bind my magic to hers.

— 5 —

This time, I could see her. See her, and the island she stood on, with impossible apple trees, in bloom and in fruit all at once. It was fog-draped, but I could hear the susurrus of waves against the shore. A jolt, electric. My flesh lumped up, and all my hair stood on end. She seemed real enough to touch.

"Can you hear me?" I asked.

Her head cocked, birdlike. "I can."

This was amazing. Impossible. Beyond. "I have so many questions."

She held up a hand. "In three days. When the clock chimes. The ravens will bring you."

Her voice pulled farther and farther away with each word, a tide going out. With the end of the sentence, the link between us was broken.

I leaned back in my chair, an ache throbbing behind my eyes.

Three days.

The discussions in Professor Link's seminar grew more contentious as the semester went on. It was as if by sharing the names of the characters, we felt like we were also particularly connected to them, that their actions somehow reflected back to us, and so we had to defend them, because otherwise we were the ones who were being smeared.

I'm not saying it made sense.

"Here's the thing I want to know," Nora said. "What was actually so great about Camelot? It gets talked about like it was some sort of second Eden, this perfect paradise of happiness and good government, but none of the stories talk about Arthur's tax policies. Or his judicial system, at least not till it's time to burn Guinevere at the stake for treason, and I don't really want to hold that up as a model of greatness.

"So why do we care that Camelot fell? What's the tragedy?"

"Aside from all the death?" Nirali said.

"Whatever. I'm talking about the actual tragedy here, not how to categorize Shakespeare's plays. Why don't we just wash our hands of Camelot like we do of every other failed monarchy? Why do we give a fuck that it's gone?"

"Well, Camelot was about ideals, wasn't it?" Sabra said. "The idea that everyone sits equally at the table, no one lower or higher. That no one's above the law, even the queen."

"Except the king," Nora said.

"What? No, Arthur sat at the Round Table too, just like everyone else."

"You mean, just like every other knight. There weren't any women sitting there, not even Guinevere. And even if we ignore the sexism, it wasn't a parliament. The Round Table wasn't a congress or his advisory board. Arthur made the law. He may have sat with them, but he wasn't equal." Nora tipped back in her chair, then dropped it to the ground with a thud. "Which, honestly, makes the whole Guinevere thing worse. He could have saved her, commuted the sentence, shipped her off to a convent, whatever. Instead he's all fake-noble. 'The law ties my hands. Sadly, I must burn the unfaithful whore.' He's no better than Henry the Eighth—I mean, if Guinevere's dead, Arthur can marry again and fix his lack of a legitimate heir problem. The whole thing is bullshit wrapped up in the name of being a nice guy."

"The reason we mourn isn't about Arthur, it's about Camelot. Camelot was about the idea that you look for miracles," I said. "That Christmas didn't start until a wonder had walked into the hall, that when the kingdom faltered, instead of going to war, they went on a holy quest."

"So religion fixes everything? Not likely," Nora said.

"Not religion. Myth. The numinous. Magic. The idea that there was something more, something better, and that the solution to the problem was to find that," I said. "They went looking for something bigger than they were."

"Plus, they tried to be good," Liam said. "The quests and stuff, they weren't about going out and stealing land and conquering, they were about helping people. Protecting the oppressed."

"Yeah, because a system with royalty at its heart is always about protecting the oppressed. You just keep believing that, golden boy," Nora said. She reached over and patted him on the head as if he were a puppy.

"I think it's about time for a break, everyone," Professor Link broke in. "Get up, stretch, get some air. We'll meet back here in fifteen."

"Nora's a bitch about things most of the time, but I think she's kind of right," Sabra said. She shouldered the recalcitrant vending machine, which then coughed up two packets of peanut butter cups. "Want one?"

"Thanks," I said. "I'm starving."

She unwrapped the candy and delicately bit the top layer of chocolate off. "I mean, Camelot is supposed to be this good place, with everyone equal at the Round Table, no might makes right, all that, but if it was just Arthur sitting around like everyone's dad, telling people to be their best selves but not really doing anything to make that happen, why do we care so much?"

"I don't know," I said. "I get Nora's point—things weren't perfect. The knights were supposed to defend the ladies, but 'ladies' meant social status as well as gender, so the serfs were still fair game. And what happened to Guinevere was shitty. But when was the last time you heard anyone in power say, 'Be good, dream bigger, look for wonder'? Maybe the fact that Arthur did doesn't count for everything, but it does count for something."

"Yeah. I just feel like I should be doing more."

"I?" I repeated the pronoun, waiting to see if Sabra noticed what she had said. The rush of ravens' wings filled my ears. "I?"

Sabra held the door for me. "You look like you're a million miles away. Are you coming back in?"

"Yeah, thanks."

When we reconvened, Nora's chair was empty.

Here are some of the things that happened at Severn that semester: The library received a $5 million donation, to better develop its special collections, with the specific directive of acquiring works from populations traditionally under-represented in academic libraries.

The Molecular Biology Department was selected to be part of a multidisciplinary research push, with the objective of finding a cure for all forms of breast cancer in ten years. The department head, Dr. Kalinda Mansouri, would coordinate the research team across all participating institutions.

A record number of grants were won by faculty across the university, in all disciplines.

The Panhellenic Council established a "Yes Means Yes"

campaign, designed to end sexual assault and harassment at social events. By all accounts, it was taken seriously, and actual assault numbers—not just the reports—went down.

The events were background noise at the time. The good kind, to be sure—much better than announcements of yet another football player assaulting a woman, or of cuts in funding, departments unable to fulfill course offerings due to lack of faculty and hiring freezes. I remember, vaguely, getting the email announcements for all the good things that happened over the course of those fifteen weeks. Seeing the posters. Being happy. But they were nothing that made me stop, made me realize that something was going on. That things were trying to be better, that we were living in an idyll.

The morning of the third day came. I spent it half-distracted: listening for a chiming clock, watching for a flock of ravens, and explaining Anglo-Saxon alliterative verse to a classroom full of undergrads.

The carillon in the center of campus chimed as class was ending, but it was nothing more than its customary song, background to campus bustle, and not accompanied by corvids.

I stopped for coffee. When I stepped out of the small café, I nearly dropped my latte. The ravens—hundreds of them, a black cloud draping the trees—had indeed found me.

Clock chimes rang through the air, and I glanced at my

phone: 10:17. Not the normal marking of the hour. "Okay then," I said to the ravens. "Here I am."

They flew. The flock so enormous its passing dimmed the sun. People held up phones, recording. The birds flew toward the lake. I followed them, and the dark-haired woman waited there, standing in a low boat, tangled in the reeds of the shore.

"Why did you give me that book?" I asked.

"Because in every story, Morgan is a sorceress," she said. "And to be Morgan, you need magic."

"How do you know what name I have? Did Professor Link ask you to do this?"

"Oh, no. Oh, hardly that at all." Her mouth twisted. "But you needed the book," she repeated. "The magic is important—necessary—for the proper ending. Giving my book to you directly was the best way to ensure you would have it."

"How did you know it would work—that I would be able to read it, that . . . Wait. *Your* book?" My voice broke over the words, over the terrible reality of speaking them aloud.

Ex libris Morganae.

My head felt as if some enormous crack had opened up inside it, a chasm similar to what had just fallen away beneath my feet. The entire world was a great, ringing bell.

She—Morgan—laughed. So loud the waiting birds all took to the air, a storm wind and hurricane rustle of wings.

Then, still standing in the boat, she grabbed my hands. "This will be faster."

Something ran through me, electric, setting my hair on end, snapping my eyes back in my head. Apples. The scent of apples, so thick I could barely breathe.

With her hands on mine, her magic coursing through me, I saw everything.

A bright-haired boy laughing as he pulled a black-haired girl up behind him on a horse. Fencing with her, practice swords in hand, fierce grins on both faces.

A skip then. Electricity in my head, and time passing.

That little boy grown to adulthood, the bright hair turned ruddy. A king now. The sister grown too, and into something else altogether. The Queen of Air and Darkness. The woman who held my hands.

Arthur and Mordred and the blood-soaked fields of Camlann and Liam somehow there too, with blood on his hands and sorrow on his face. My hands, too, were sticky-wet.

A great, round table, cracked in two, snakes slithering in the gap, and the oval conference table in our seminar room knocked askew, chairs overturned and scattered.

A low black barge, and an island of glass, and air that smelled like apples. On the shore, this woman. Morgan.

On the shore, me.

One thing and the next and the next, faces I didn't know, and stories I did, and then our faces too: Sabra and Liam and

Nora, her face turned away from all of us. Professor Link, high in her tower. Nirali, weeping.

A body on a bier with a sword in her hands.

I yanked my hands away, stumbling back. My breath rattled hard in my throat and my eyes burned with grit.

Morgan watched me. She looked reduced, drawn. "I am," she said, "almost out of time. So are you, if you are going to stop the story, change it before the ending becomes inevitable."

"What are you talking about?" I asked.

"Arthur's fall will rewrite itself again and again, one time after the next. It will always end the same way, unless it's stopped. You are in the story now. You can change it. He sleeps. Wake him."

"Oh, is that all?" The question came out halfway between laughter and a sob.

"Yes," she said. "That is all. I will give you what aid I can, but you will not be unopposed." She gasped, bent forward, clutching at her side, her face even paler than before.

"What's wrong?" I put my arm around her, tried to hold her steady. Apples, I thought. She smelled like apples. But something else. The smell of algae, rot, rose from the lake, choking me. The surface of the water grew rough, the waves chopped by wind.

"Too long away." The words dragged from her throat. "I need to go back, before she sees."

"Where do you need to go? I'll help you." Her weight heavy against me.

"You can't. Not yet. Change the story, Morgan." A shove, hard, and I stumbled away from her, fell. In an explosion of ravens, she was gone.

Once

TOO LONG FROM MY ISLAND, AND TOO LONG ON the lake that is not mine, and too much magic used. My bones ache from the effort and my breath shakes. But at least she knows, my story shadow, her role in this. At least she knows what is necessary.

The boat shakes its way onto the island's rough beach, and I stumble from it. Pick my way on trembling legs through the trees. There is a proper orchard here now, the Isle of the Apples. Small bits in the story working their way through time, waiting for an ending.

Better, it would be better if I could help the ones in this telling of the story, set the gears and move the pieces. But I moved too much, once, or some thought I did, and now I am bound. Now I wait and I watch and I may do so little, even in my own life.

The story knows the way of its telling.

The ravens land in the apple trees, dark stars in the white sky. I curl against a trunk and fall asleep.

— 6 —

I had no idea what to do.

Change the story.

Look, we all know how the story goes, right? Once upon a time, when miracles still occurred. The kingdom is in chaos after Uther Pendragon dies, presumably without a legitimate heir. And then, somehow, just when everything is on the edge of falling apart forever, Arthur is found. Maybe he pulls a sword from a stone. Maybe the Lady of the Lake raises her samite-clad arm from the water and hands him his destiny. Either way, he gets an incontrovertible and appropriately phallic symbol that proves his paternity, and hence his right to rule.

For a while, things seem to go well. In fact, they go better than well. Wonders occur on a regular basis. Miraculous objects are sought for and found. There is a Round Table and knights who take their seats at it, and they do good and have adventures. There is no war, no threat of invasion. Peace throughout the land, and a specific, wonderful kind of peace—so well-governed is England under Arthur that a maiden carrying a bag of gold can walk unescorted from one end of the kingdom to the other, her maidenhead and her gold both intact at the end of her journey.

Truly, it is a golden age.

But then, something goes wrong. Maybe it's Mordred. Maybe it's Guinevere and Lancelot. Maybe, in the way of all epic tragedies, it's Arthur's own hubris. But whatever it is, there is a worm at the heart of the apple, and Camelot destroys itself from the inside. At the end, Arthur is struck down on the field of battle—maybe Mordred means to kill him, maybe not, but the knife still lands.

The stories tell us Arthur's not dead, not really. That he's *rexque futurus*. That in our hour of greatest need, he will return. At least, that's how the story goes.

Don't let it be forgotten.

I stumbled through the door to my apartment, the visions heavy in my brain, throbbing like a cluster of hangovers.

So. That was what we were, Morgan and I, bound.

Except. No. I was still myself, solely myself, no matter that I shared a name with her.

There was a shadow-voice that spoke another truth: that I certainly was myself, as much as she was hers, but that together we were a third, other Morgan. That this was no longer a story of once and future, but one that would weave us both in its ending.

That night, I fell into exhausted sleep and dreamt of

a sleeping king. The king from my visions, child to man. Arthur. The Pendragon. He rested on a bier of glass, so that it seemed as if he floated above the ground that was meant to embrace him. He lay with his hands across his chest, as if they had once held a sword, a still-breathing effigy.

His bier stood on an island, and it was an island of bones. I knew, in that terrible, certain way you know things in dreams, that the bones were the remains of everyone who had ever gotten caught up in this story, the ones who had never made it back out. My own skeleton pushed closer to the skin, on its way to join them.

The sleeping king opened his eyes and saw me, even through the dream.

"The story ends where I do."

I woke late in the day, untangled myself from the ropes of my sheets. Then climbed from bed and tried the scrying spell. Ink poured first on a world map, because there had to be some logic to the process, even though part of my brain was reminding me that I was using magic to look for a sleeping king I had seen in a dream, and the other part was telling me to just skip to the Severn campus map, because if Arthur was anywhere, he had to be here.

I used the spell again and again, map after map, each smaller and more specific than the last. It was, of course, the campus map the spell halted at.

Except the ink, after collecting itself on that same spot in the center of the lake where the previous spell had told me I would find Morgan, sank into the map and disappeared.

I lifted the piece of paper from the table. Nothing. No ink. No stain.

Which, great. Because there was still no island—of bone or otherwise—on Lake Severn. Maybe there once was, and it sank, but Arthur hadn't been underwater in my dream.

Then, a welling up of ink. Not on the table, but in the air in front of me. Letters written in a hand I knew: "He sleeps out of time. Find him in the ringing of the bells."

The words fell, into a heap of blue-black feathers.

Bells rang, and I started from my seat, but it was only the alarm on my phone. Class. I had to go teach.

I brushed feathers from my hair, washed spilled ink and the shadows of dreams from my hands, and stepped back into the world.

Nora had missed the past three meetings of Professor Link's seminar. I figured she'd gotten fed up and dropped. But as I called goodbye to Sabra and Nirali and pulled my scarf closer against the late-fall chill, she stepped out from against the wall.

"So, you're still going? Has she made any changes to the course requirements?"

"You mean, are you suddenly going to have to write a paper instead of keeping a journal?"

She shrugged. "Something like that."

"Nope, nothing. You're fine to keep avoiding us. Though, if you're concerned, why don't you just drop the class? Or—and I know this may sound crazy—show up sometime and find out for yourself?"

"Too late in the semester to drop, and besides, I need the credits. But, God, if I had to listen to that twee moralizing for one more class, I was going to throw something. I mean, who does Sabra think she is?" She rolled her eyes so hard that even in the dying light of the evening I could see it.

"Arthur, actually," I said.

"Huh. Well, that was a good match of random name with person."

That was not the sentiment I expected. "What do you mean?"

"Well, I've never thought of Arthur as being particularly smart. Sabra seems to get by mostly on being nice too."

I would have agreed with her, had we just been talking about Arthur, but her words jarred, directed at Sabra. "I assume you're someone smarter."

"I didn't even read my card."

I didn't believe her. "Seriously? You're doing this, and you don't even know who you are?"

"I know exactly who I am: Nora."

I understood. I did. But she was so vehement about it. "You know what I mean."

"Does it matter what name I got for this class? I mean, either it does, and my role will be so obvious and clear I won't be able to hide who I am no matter what I do and we're all going to re-create the rise and fall of Camelot around a seminar table, or it doesn't, and you all can just continue along in your little role-playing game and leave me the hell out of it. Either way, I'm done."

"So then why stop coming to class if you think the names don't matter? You seemed really into all of this at the beginning, so ready to prove Sabra wrong."

"Because I know how the story ends. Arthur dies. In every version. And he may be once and future, sure, but I'm pretty sure Sabra isn't. No matter what name I'm assigned, I'm not up for seeing that part of the story play out, and I'm sure as hell not up for having a role in causing it."

I felt my stomach drop.

"Not so fun now, is it?"

"Professor Link wouldn't let that happen." The words sounded weak, feeble, even as I said them. Morgan from Camelot was here, and I could do magic, and if there really was a fate that needed Sabra as Arthur dead, I seriously doubted there was anything a literature professor could do to stop it.

Nora's contempt for my response was visible in every line of her body. "If you believe that the story makes its own pattern, that doesn't matter."

. . .

"Change the story," Morgan had said. The problem was, I wasn't sure how. I couldn't see enough of our version of the story yet to know what parts we were living, much less to know what parts needed to be different. Sure, Sabra had a sword, but it wasn't like she was convening knights and riding off to harry the giant Ysbaddaden. Though, really, I would have preferred that to grading midterms. There was no in-seminar love triangle that she and Liam were two points of, and I'd heard no rumors of a Questing Beast leading people on a chase through Severn's campus.

We had the names and some similarities, but we weren't reliving past events. Even knowing what it was supposed to be, I could barely see the story, considered as a whole. Without seeing the whole, I didn't know what needed to be changed.

I told Sabra about my magic. She was surprisingly calm about it. "Can you do that thing like Merlin in the movie where you sing a song and shrink all your stuff to be super tiny so it all fits in your backpack?"

I blinked. "I don't know."

"I hate packing. It stresses me out. Niv almost broke up with me when we moved here for grad school because I was such a horrible person when we were packing our old place. So that would seriously have been the first thing I tried."

"Well, if I figure it out, I'll pack your apartment for you next time."

"Excellent." She grinned. "So what was your first spell?"

"Hang on. I'll show you." I tore a piece of paper from my notebook, wadded it into a ball, and dropped it on the sidewalk. *"Fiat lux."* The paper caught, flared, and burned itself out.

"'Let there be light'?" she said.

"Or 'life.' 'Illumination.' It doesn't work if I use English, so thank God for being a medievalist and having to learn all these weird languages to get my degree."

"They should put that on the grad school advertising. 'Get your PhD in medieval lit. If you can't get a tenure-track job, you can always be a wizard,'" Sabra said.

I snorted a laugh. "Sad thing is, there are people here who would see wizardry as a poor second choice."

"Right? So what else can you do?"

"I can talk to ravens. Do binding spells. Find people using ink and maps. Basic healing. Transformation."

"Right. Basic healing and transformations. The usual, then," Sabra deadpanned. "Normal wizard stuff."

"Yeah. Magic 101." I grinned, and we both laughed.

But I didn't tell her anything else. Didn't say, "Oh, hey, remember how you die at the end? Got any plans to avoid that?" Or that I'd been scouring the grimoire and memorizing healing spells that went far beyond basic ever since Nora reminded me about that death.

94

Because when it came to that, the death at the end of the story, Arthur's death, and one I would not let Sabra share, every choice I saw before me was wrong. There was the choice to do nothing, which only worked if I was certain that nothing would come from the little cards with our new names written on them in purple ink. Far too much had happened for that to be an option I believed in anymore. I couldn't say for sure that we were fully bound on some careening, irrevocable path to tragedy, but I also couldn't say for certain that we weren't.

Option two: Tell Sabra. Tell her everything I knew. Show her the grimoire and drag that other, impossible, Morgan before her and . . .

And then what?

Morgan didn't kill Arthur. Neither did Lancelot or Gawain. Mordred did. It was his hand that held the blade in every version of the story—the tragedy of the father slain by the curse of an unwanted son. If we didn't have a Mordred, Sabra was safe.

Unless.

Unless Nora was Mordred, and by taking herself out of the story, she had already changed it, and by telling Sabra that I thought the story might want her to die, I would be putting that possibility back in there.

Besides. Even with everything, magic and swords and everything else, we knew we weren't the people in that story. We *knew*. None of us would kill Sabra.

Everything would be fine.

* * *

Sabra's pulse flutters beneath my hand like the spasms of a dying bird. The wind off the lake is harsher now and smells of algae and rot. The scent, mixed with the perfume of the apples, is nauseating.

Time is stretched and strained here, and I have held it in place as long as I can. I feel night coming on, darkness crouching, waiting. The bells aren't ringing. I wonder if they will.

There is something I must do.

Excalibur lies next to the bier, fallen. I reach down, and I pick it up.

After a while, we stopped bringing up our characters in classroom discussion unless we had to. It was too weird, to talk about Lancelot's struggle against his desire for Guinevere causing him to run wodwo, and have Liam sitting across the table. We focused instead on the characters whose behaviors we could pick apart without it seeming like we were passive-aggressively snarking at one another.

"Here's the thing I don't get," Liam said. "Merlin's this great and powerful wizard. Plus, he lives backward. He doesn't just see the future, he's already lived it. So why doesn't he ever step in and stop Arthur? Or, like, magic Mordred to somewhere else? At the very least, tell him that his snake of a son is going to breach the peace, and make sure Arthur doesn't get killed."

"It's the free will problem. Merlin can warn Arthur about the consequences of his actions—in some of the stories he does—but Arthur still makes his own choices," I said.

"Yeah, but getting stabbed by Mordred wasn't a choice."

"Merlin was gone by then," Nirali said. "Locked in the tree by Nimue. Who either didn't bother stealing Merlin's foreknowledge when she sexed him out of the rest of his power, or didn't bother telling Arthur what she knew."

"Earned," Professor Link said.

"I'm sorry?" Nirali asked.

"Nimue earned her power. Not sexed it out of Merlin." Professor Link's voice was the coldest I'd ever heard it.

"What version of the story was that in?" Nirali asked, fingers poised over her keyboard.

"The true one."

Nirali opened her mouth, then closed it again at the expression on Professor Link's face.

"Earned, stole, whatever," Liam said. "The fact is, someone knew that Arthur was going to die, and did nothing to stop it. Didn't even bother to tell him. That's not right."

"If it were me," Sabra said deliberately, "if I were the one who was supposed to die, or whatever, I wouldn't want to know."

"Why not?" Liam asked.

It was a question I wanted an answer to as well.

"If it was fate, truly meant to be, unavoidable fate,

knowing wouldn't stop it. And if Merlin or whoever really can see the future, if he can see the future because he already lived it, then it happens. My death. The only thing that my knowing would mean is that I would live those last days dreading what would happen, making myself insane trying to avoid the inevitable, rather than doing normal things.

"If it was my fate, I wouldn't want to know."

I still wasn't comfortable with the idea of silence, but that seemed the end of it. Enough to know that Sabra didn't want the direct reminder of the end of the story. A clear sign that she'd thought about it and didn't want to have the discussion.

So I held my tongue.

Once

THESE CHILDREN.

They talk about fate as if they understand what it means, as if it is simply a thing that happens—someone falls in love, as fast as a heartbeat, and of course it is fate. Someone achieves glory, status, a name written in the stars, and what else could have caused that blaze of greatness but fate? Someone dies cruelly young, and that, too, they comfort themselves, is fate.

They do not understand that fate is the thing that happens no matter what. That its signs are written everywhere, and cannot be evaded or escaped. That it is both map and prison.

They cannot know that it binds like shackles and sinks into your skin, as you watch again and again, as you cast cards and look for signs writ on the water and in the flight of birds. As you bloody your hands with sacrifices, hoping that it will change its iron grasp, and still there is not enough to satiate its hunger.

My brother was fated to die, and I did everything I could to save him. I broke three lives and a story in the attempt.

I will not pretend remorse: I would do every single piece of it again.

— 7 —

It was the sort of day that fall is made for. The air just cool enough to make your wool jacket comfortable, the leaves bright flames against the grey of the sky. The wind rippled the mirrored surface of Lake Severn, and the path was crowded with joggers out for a run.

Liam ran by, then stopped and circled around. "Morgan! How are you?"

"Good." I smiled.

Leaves crunched beneath our feet as we traced the curve of the lake. Then we turned a bend in the path and stood in a grove, and all the trees were full of ravens.

They spoke to me.

Change the story. Find the king. Soon. Now.

Over and over, the words intermingling into a cacophony. I stood in the whirl of their feathers and voices. They landed on my arms and on my shoulders, the weight of their attention far greater than the bird weight of bones and feathers. I changed my voice to match theirs and asked: "How do I change the story? Do you know where he is? How much time?"

They didn't answer, only continued to call out their questions. Then, as one, flew away.

Liam pulled in on himself. "What the fuck was that?"

"I'm Morgan," I said, as if the name itself was an explanation.

"You spoke to them. Like you were a raven. What are you?" His voice, just on the edge of horror.

"Morgan is a sorceress. You know the story."

Silence stretched between us and was broken by the crash of wind on the water.

"No. That doesn't happen. This does not happen." He didn't run from me.

Not quite.

My phone rang before the sun was even up. I reached to hit the ignore button, but it was Sabra's number on the caller ID.

"What is it?" I asked, my voice froggy with sleep.

"There's a . . . It's . . . Look, can you just get down to the crew launch, please? It's important. It'll make sense when you get here."

"Okay."

I pulled on the nearest clothes, ran to the lake, and hesitated for a beat when I saw Sabra standing on the end of the launch. She had her sword in her hand, which wasn't helping with the promise that this would make sense.

I ran out onto the deck. "What is it?"

"There." She jerked her chin toward the center of the lake, where a whirlpool spun. Water spat and splashed around it, and the surface shimmered like an oil slick.

"Okay, that's weird, but I'm not sure if your sword is going to help."

"Just watch."

The whirling stopped, changed direction, and then. "Sabra. That is a fucking sea monster."

Scaled and reptilian, fanged and clawed. Shades of green in fish-scale shimmer. It roiled and bent, in and out of the water. Opened its mouth and howled and howled, and in the roaring, such pain that I almost went to my knees before it.

"She's hurt," Sabra said. "Really hurt. I don't want to have to kill her, but if I swim out there right now, she'll drown me, and if I leave her alone, she'll attack whoever goes into the lake next, and I'm pretty sure there's crew practice today. So I called you."

I turned from the impossibility in the lake. "Sabra, how do you know all of this?"

"You can't understand her?"

"No." But I thought of the magic that had let me be a bird, of the way I had learned to shift my hearing and my sight, to take myself out of my world and step into theirs. I whispered the words under my breath.

The air shook around me and I could see the lake the way the creature saw it—some strange new place she had been pulled into, away from home and safe haven. Could understand her words. *Not a sea monster,* she said. *An afanc.*

Her voice was the sound of the last gasp of the drowned before the water took them, the crack of wrecked ships as they groaned and splintered, the hurricane's howl. She was begging for release from chains.

"Chains?" I asked Sabra.

"Look again," she said.

I hadn't noticed them at first. Too overwhelmed by the immensity of the strangeness, at the sight of something out of myth swimming in the same lake where the crew team practiced, where we burned a boat at Homecoming while drunken undergrads shout-sang the Alma Mater. But there. Like creases in her skin, deep lines of muddy greyness, edged in rust.

Chains. An ancient, heavy horror, there so long that they had become near part of her.

"Oh, you poor thing," I said.

"I did that to her." Sabra's voice a hollow glass.

"Sabra? Are you okay?" That same pronoun slip I'd heard before, and it raised the flesh on my arms. Time stuttered beneath my feet.

"Arthur. Arthur did. I know that. Not me. But it feels like I did. Morgan, I can see my hands holding the chains." Pain in Sabra's voice then. Pain to almost match that of the impossible creature, shrieking in Lake Severn, who had been chained for a small eternity.

"I need you to help me get them off."

"Okay. But I need to go back to my apartment. I don't know the magic for something like this." I wasn't sure if I had seen a spell in Morgan's book that would help—even the unbinding spells I had read had been for metaphorical chains, not physical ones. But at least if I had the book, I would have something that might tell me what to do.

"You don't need to. Just ask her to come here, and tell her I'm going to help."

I wasn't sure that was a good idea, but it was better than Sabra swimming out to meet the afanc like something out of *Beowulf*, and definitely better than leaving the afanc alone and hurt and liable to eat the crew team in a rage.

"Hello!" I called. The magic that changed my language to hers shredded my throat, and I tasted copper, penny-bright. "We'd like to help you." I coughed, spat blood on the dock.

The churning of the lake slowed, and the afanc's head rose above the waters. "You are small and weak. How would you do that?"

"We can take off your chains."

"Do you swear? Swear true, your lies a poison in your mouth?" Her eyes, deep and ancient, fixed on us.

"Yes," Sabra said before I had a chance to ask. "Tell her yes."

I did, praying that Sabra knew what she was doing.

"The last time I trusted, moons and tides ago, I was bound. Cast out. Made into this. Why should I come near?"

"We can help—" I began.

"Tell her I offer myself as surety," Sabra said.

"What? Sabra, no. I get that you have good intentions, but I am right on the edge of out of my depth here, and all you have is somebody's SCA sword."

"You know it's more than that, Morgan. Tell her."

I thought for a moment of lying. But Sabra could— somehow—understand the afanc's language; she just couldn't speak it. I drew in a deep breath. Fuck it. If Sabra was all in, so was I. "We offer ourselves as surety."

"Prove it." Bitter, bitter, the afanc's words.

Before I could say anything, Sabra drew her palm against her blade and held her hand out over the water so that the blood dropped in. I sucked in a breath and then, less poeti- cally, coughed and spat again, this time letting my blood fall into the water. "We swear by blood."

The lake stopped spinning.

The afanc sank down beneath its surface, and I could track her progress toward us by the ripples on the water. "I hope you know what you're doing."

"I do." With a splash, Sabra stepped off the edge of the dock.

The monster rose up next to her, wrapping herself around Sabra. The afanc reeked of blood and rot, her sickness caused by those ancient chains. Sabra raised the sword, and in that moment, it didn't look like a prop, like a too-thin piece of metal. It looked like a weapon, like power. Like it held death.

"Your promise!" the afanc shrieked, and sank her claws into Sabra's other arm.

"Let her go!" I screamed.

"Morgan, I've got this," Sabra said.

I wasn't sure at all that she did. I jumped in the lake with her, sinking up to my chest in the cold, wishing I had some better grip on magic, that I knew a spell that would let me do something more effective than just yelling at the afanc in the event she decided that we were brunch.

"I will break open the cages of your ribs and swallow your beating hearts." The afanc's voice like drowning.

"Morgan, will you please ask her to hold still." Sabra, calm and measured, as if the monster were a recalcitrant toddler.

"Please," I said. "Hold still. She can't help you if you're moving."

The afanc's claws slid deeper into Sabra's arm. "You lie so you can bind me further."

"No," I said. "We don't."

Then, in the soft silt of the lake, a thud. Another. The monster stopped her struggle. "How?" she asked, her voice softer.

I didn't need Sabra to tell me. "The sword." I could feel the charges of magic as it sliced through the ancient iron of the shackles. "Brought out of time to right a wrong."

It went much faster after that. The afanc let go of Sabra's

arm and moved to give her better access to the chains. I had memorized a small healing spell from the grimoire, and I cast that, over and over, to help soothe the old wounds.

When it was finished, when Sabra and I had climbed, soaked and exhausted, back onto the dock, the afanc bowed her head. "Thank you," she said, and sank below the calm waters of the lake.

"I can try to cast something," I said. "Something mild. Just enough of a binding to keep the crew team safe with her here."

"No." Sabra shook her head. "We just unbound her. I won't have her in chains again. Even magical ones. We will leave her free, and they will be fine."

The carillon rang out, the sound of its bells carrying over the water.

Even though we learn time and again that they are as mortal as we are, even though we know they will all eventually be dust, there is still a small part of us that thinks that somehow the rules are different for our heroes. I knew that she could bleed—I spoke the words that knit up the wounds the afanc's claws had made in her shoulder. But if you had asked me that morning, as I walked home, soaked in lake water, I would have told you that Sabra would live forever. That she would always be just as she was—standing on the shore, sword in her hand.

. . .

We waited, all of us, around the table as the clock ticked past the time our seminar should have started. Fidgeting, checking phones in case there was a last-minute email announcing the cancellation. Nirali looked up Professor Link's office phone and called. "No answer."

"Right," Liam said. "I'm out of here. I'm not wasting one of the last warm days of the semester waiting for an instructor who isn't going to show."

None of the rest of us were inclined to wait around either, especially on what was a glorious, golden day, the air rich with the leaf-crackle scent of fall. We gathered laptops and notebooks and headed for the door, quickly, so that if Professor Link were to dash in late, we would already be free.

Instead of being gone, Liam was waiting outside. "Does he belong to anyone?"

There was a white dog standing next to him. Muddy-pawed and bedraggled, a wolfhound with mats in his coat, and ribs too visible beneath his skin. He walked right up to Sabra, then sat, patient, at her feet.

She bent down to scratch his ear, and he leaned into her. "Fine. Niv has been talking about getting a dog anyway. You can come and live with me, okay?"

His tail thumped once.

A gust of wind blew through, sending shivers across my skin even in the sunlight. Raising a memory that wasn't mine, of a white dog that I had loved, blood red on his flank, and the king who wept for his loss. Dead already when they brought him to me, from the wounds sustained when he threw himself between Arthur and a boar's angry tusks, and none of my magic could bring life back into that great heart. Another click as the pattern tightened. The clock tower chimed.

I watched as they walked off together, Sabra shortening her stride to make it easier for the dog—who I was sure would be named Cabal by the end of the day—to keep up with her.

I met Liam's eyes, but he dropped his gaze from mine, readjusted his bag over his shoulder, and walked away.

Professor Link sent around an email that evening, apologizing for missing the class, and for not getting word to us sooner. Something unexpected had occurred. We should move our discussion of Tolkien's *The Fall of Arthur* to the next meeting, and she would adjust the syllabus as necessary.

I wouldn't have thought about it for longer than it took to make a note in my planner and press delete on my email, but for the next message that came up. The campus newspaper, and on the front page a photograph of the building where Professor Link's office was. The outlines of the trees were fuzzed and obscured by what sat in their branches: ravens. Possibly hundreds.

There had, it seemed, been an incident that afternoon,

right around the time when our seminar should have been meeting.

One of the collective nouns for a group of ravens is an "unkindness," and that was certainly what they had been. They had surrounded the building and harried anyone trying to get in or out—dive-bombing people, pulling at hair and bags. Some of the ravens had even managed to get into the building and had wreaked havoc in the offices. It had been enough of a mess that campus safety blocked the building off, not letting anyone in or out.

"I will give you what help I can," Morgan had said. Morgan, whose spell book was full of drawings of ravens. Morgan, who had loved Cabal too.

I wondered what would have happened to that poor white wolfhound had we not left class early, had someone else found him. What he would save Sabra from this time.

I cast the spell looking for Arthur again when I got home. And again, the ink collected in the center of Lake Severn, where no island was, and disappeared.

Once

"HAVE YOU SIMPLY DECIDED THAT THE RULES don't matter anymore?" I asked. "Once the roles are filled, we do not bring outsiders into the story."

"The lake is mine, and the afanc dwells within it," she said. She was calling herself Viviane this time. Viviane Link. It was as good a name as any. "I broke no rules. She awoke, and I reminded her of her chains.

"Not that any harm came of it, in the end, so put away your righteousness, Morgan. I did no more than you are right now." Viviane gestured at the window, where my ravens covered the trees.

"Have you ever thought," I asked, "that we could end this ourselves?"

She laughed. "I am sure I have thought that exactly as often as you have, Morgan. But that does leave the question of which of us chooses the ending. So tell me now that you will ensure Arthur dies and passes out of history and story as he should have, tell me now that the proper story will be told, and yes. I will help you end this."

He was my brother. I could, at the end of all of this, let go of his life. He deserved sleep, the true sleep of death. But

I would not let go of his story. Whether he should have had it or not, it had been told, and he deserved to keep it.

"Indeed," she said, nodding at my silence. "Besides, I am sure you have tried to end this on your own as many times as I have."

I said nothing. There was no need to give her a truth she held already.

Viviane smiled. "But we don't get to. Not anymore. Not beyond that once. We are, as we always were, characters in his story. Observers in our own."

As much as I loved my brother, that, too, was a truth. "Are you not tired?"

"Morgan. I have been tired for at least a thousand years. But that's hardly the point now, is it?"

— 8 —

Most of the strangeness that occurred that semester disappeared from campus memory almost as soon as it happened. It was—for all that it became to those of us who lived through our parts in the story—a relatively self-contained phenomenon. Ours was not a Camelot that ended in a state funeral.

But there is one thing you can see even now if you go to Severn's campus. The paw print of a dog, in concrete, next to a half-sunken sculpture of a giant boar made from razor blades.

Sabra had invited me to the sculpture garden to help walk her new dog—and she had named him Cabal, though she insisted the name had been Niv's idea. "She said that if the story was going to give us a dog, we should respect the story."

Children ran past us, in and out of a series of tiny, rainbow-colored doors, unconnected to anything, even to walls, the last one barely hobbit-size. A mobile that looked like a disarticulated dragon spun from one of the trees.

Cabal froze in front of Sabra, hackles raised, teeth bared. He howled, and the sound raised the hair on my own neck. Then I felt it. Something waking.

I flung my arm in front of Sabra as well. "Wait."

Then.

A groaning. Harsh. Metal rending, deep and shrieking all at once.

Screams. The children.

We ran toward it, until we saw what it was, and then we stopped running.

The centerpiece of the sculpture garden was a wild boar, made entirely out of razor blades, edged and deadly. The rending we had heard was that same sculpture tearing itself from the ground. The metal screamed as the boar lowered its great head, swung it back and forth, as if the blank spaces where eyes should have been could somehow see.

"Morgan. The kids."

"You get them," I said. "I'll deal with that."

She ran, Cabal with her, and he herded the children as if they were sheep.

I anchored my feet in the earth and stared straight at the boar, focusing only on that, and not on the chaos unfolding around me. I prayed that focus would ensure that none of my magic would go astray, and started casting.

Spells to make things decay, hoping that the metal would rust.

To weaken bones, that its joints and hinges might break.

To disorient, to distract, to make clumsy.

Nothing I did had any effect.

"Morgan, we've got all the kids. Just blast the fucker."

Liam's voice. I turned toward it, and in that moment, the boar ran toward Sabra.

A white blur in the air, a howl to pull the dead from their rest, and I would not let the story have what it wanted. Instead of the boar, I aimed my magic at the ground, softening it to a pit that grabbed at the sculpture's churning legs.

It tossed its head as it sank, and red stained Cabal's white fur. But he stood, and Sabra stood too, picking herself up from the ground where that best of dogs had knocked her out of harm's way.

I spoke the second spell, my words rumbling from my throat like granite, and solidified the ground that held the boar. The metal shrieked in protest, but the sculpture did not shift from where I held it.

Unmoving, vigilant, I stood until Cabal nosed my hand, stepped one foot onto the hardening ground. I knelt down beside him, ran my hands over his body, and checked for other injuries.

"He's okay," Sabra said. "He's fine."

He was. The scratch was minor. My voice shook only a little as I spoke the words that healed him. "Good dog," I said when I had finished.

"The kids?" I asked.

"All fine too. Most of them thought it was some sort of game, especially after Liam came in out of nowhere and helped."

I looked at him.

"I heard a voice," he said. "It sounded almost like yours, Morgan. Saying you needed help, that my king was in danger. Telling me to come here. I tried to ignore it, but it got louder. So." He shrugged.

"Thank you," I said.

"I'm going to take Cabal home so Niv and I can make a fuss over him, and give him a big steak. Morgan, call me later." Sabra walked away, Cabal leaning against her.

"I'm surprised you came," I said. "Knowing how you feel about magic."

"I'm sorry I couldn't cope at the lake. With the birds and everything," he said. "It was not my best moment. It seemed so crazy, what I had seen, what you were telling me, and instead of remembering that you were underneath all the magic, all I could think was that it was too much, too strange."

"And now?" I asked.

He looked at me. "It's still weird, Morgan. I'm not going to lie—this is not what I thought I was signing up for. But if I can help, I should."

Professor Link gave no explanation for her previous absence the next time our class met. I hadn't really expected her to— she seemed to want to keep pretending that she was nothing more than a professor, that the names were only an academic exercise.

It was the week before a major paper was due, and there was a small contingent that hadn't opted in to the Arthurian names project, so she was fielding their questions and concerns. I let my mind drift over ravens and Arthur and an island of bones. Then there was the question of how to wake him, and whether, dream or not, that was necessary. Things might be easier if he never opened his eyes.

"Ah, shit!" Liam yelled.

I looked up just in time to see a flood of latte headed for my laptop. Without thought, I held up my hand. *"Desisto!"*

The coffee paused, puddled, halted as if there were a wall in front of it, pooling up against my invisible barrier.

The table was a flurry of people, yanking their own laptops and notebooks up and away, pulling wads of tissues from pockets and backpacks to mop up the mess, generally not paying attention to anyone who might have used magic to keep her laptop dry.

Professor Link's gaze never left mine.

At the end of class, she stepped in front of me before I could walk through the door. "I'd like it if you could come with me to my office, Morgan. I think there are some things we should discuss."

I thought about refusing. Acting like I didn't know what she was talking about. But there were things I wanted to discuss too. "Of course," I said.

I walked with her in silence, on the red brick path,

through grass in the process of browning before the winter. Flame-colored leaves hugged the tree branches, and the wind chased wisps of clouds across a sky turning sunset lavender.

As cool as it was, the window in her office was still cracked open, to let in the sound of the lake. I kept my jacket on, my bag in hand, and perched on the very edge of her visitor's chair.

"She's taught you, then."

"I'm sorry," I said. "I'm not sure who or what you're talking about." I was pretty sure I knew both, but I wanted Professor Link to be the one to say it.

"Morgan, of course. And magic. Let's not waste time pretending either of us is stupid. Has she been giving you lessons?"

"Nothing like that. We've only ever spoken a couple of times." My knuckles were white around the strap of my bag, the sharpness of my nails digging into my palm a reminder to take care.

"She'll have told you her version of events by now, an attempt to play on your sympathy. She'll want you on her side of the story."

I didn't say that she hadn't, that she had simply given me a book of magic, a series of visions, and an order. "Why don't you tell me what really happened, then? Give me a chance to make my own decisions."

Professor Link tapped her fingers against her lips, considering. "The first thing that you need to know is that Arthur was always supposed to die. Die completely, none of this once-and-future business."

I didn't so much as blink.

"There were fates," she continued. "Auguries and omens, and no matter which ones were cast, no matter who read the signs, Arthur died in all of them. Young, and not particularly heroically. It was Guinevere who was supposed to bring the peace while acting as regent for Mordred. Arthur should have passed quietly out of history, been a footnote at most. Had things simply been left alone, it would have been a true golden age.

"Merlin couldn't bear it. All his plans, all his manipulation of Uther's line, to be lost because of an infected battlefield scratch. Something so petty, and all his power couldn't defeat it.

"So he lied. He went to Morgan, who was far greater at magic than he was, and cast the one spell that was his great strength."

"Illusion," I said, remembering the story of how Merlin disguised Uther, made him appear exactly as Igraine's husband, and brought about Arthur's conception through deceit.

"I'm glad to see you've been doing the reading," Professor Link said. "Merlin told Morgan there had been a new omen in the stars, and asked her to recast Arthur's fate. As she did, he cast his magic, and for all her power, it broke Morgan's heart every time she foretold her brother's death. So it was easy for Merlin to make Morgan see what he wanted: that she could save Arthur. That there was one magic strong enough."

"Excalibur's scabbard," I said.

"Precisely. She wove it with her own hands, wove her magic into it. Whoever wore it would be protected from any wound received in battle. And it worked. Arthur lived for decades longer than he should have. It was one of the greatest sorcerous achievements of any age.

"But Camelot itself, everything around Arthur, turned sour as a result. Guinevere grew bitter over Arthur's neglect, and the knights grew quarrelsome, pushing against one another in hopes of petty advancement. Fate tried to rewrite itself, to undo Arthur, to put back into play what should have been. All of it Merlin's fault."

"Not Morgan's?" I asked.

"She did the magic, yes. But she was as used by Merlin as Igraine was. He took her love and twisted it for his own ends. I didn't blame her for it, but that didn't mean I could let it stand."

"You?" I asked.

The wind came in stronger, carrying the scent of the lake. "Come now, Morgan. You know the story well enough. Think about the names."

"Viviane," I said. She had a different name in almost every story—Viviane, Elaine, Nimue, and variants of each.

"Your name is Viviane. The Lady of the Lake. You did those things." My mind bent itself around the recalculated story line, and I almost missed her next words.

"It was easy enough to put Merlin into the tree. Easier still to whisper to Mordred of his mistreatment at Arthur's hands, of the need to take hold of his own destiny. And magic is a tricky thing—a spell designed to keep you safe in battle will not turn away a knife slid into an embrace of peace." She pushed back from her desk, the chair creaking as she turned toward the window, the lake.

"What I did should have worked. It should have been enough to set things back in order. But Morgan's spell had woven itself into Arthur's fate, making itself the new omen Merlin had lied to her about seeing, and things changed.

"Arthur didn't die. Not on the field at Camlann, not when Excalibur was cast into the water, not when Arthur himself was set adrift on the lake. He should have floated out past time and memory, should have disappeared, but instead, this.

"He lingers, and the story lingers with him, and I am dragged through time with him and his interfering sister until someone gets the story right." Her face, a study in long-held rage.

"What does that mean?" I asked. "To get the story right."

"And here I thought you were paying attention. The story doesn't end unless he does."

"Great. So you want him dead and Morgan wants him alive and—"

"No. His death is a side effect. I want his story gone, and Morgan wants his story to live forever. Too late to make the story be what it should have been, but at least he'll be out of it."

"Whatever," I said. The distinction was unimportant to me. "Not my fight. What I want is Sabra. Alive. At the end."

"Whatever." She shrugged. "Not my fight."

I got up. "It will be."

"Nirali, you did your undergrad here too, right?" Sabra asked as she shoved her chair against the table.

"Yeah. It's a good dance program that doesn't think it's weird to cast a brown girl as Odette, so there was no reason to leave. Why?"

"Is there any sort of campus legend about a giant?"

Nirali narrowed her eyes. "You mean like an actual fee-fi-fo-fum giant, don't you?"

Sabra nodded. "I overheard some of my students talking about seeing some giant-type thing in the woods, but I want to make sure this isn't them just taking the piss out of me."

"I've heard about that too. Just this past week or so," Liam said. "They were describing this huge guy who sounded almost like one of those walking tree things from Lord of the Rings."

"An Ent?" Nirali asked.

"Talks really slow, carries the hobbits around?"

Nirali nodded.

"Then sure," Liam said. "An Ent. Is that what you've been hearing about too, Sabra?"

"Sounds like it. So, probably not just students playing a joke, then?"

"What else would it be?" Nirali asked.

"The Green Knight," I said. "I don't know if I've ever read a version where he looked like an Ent, but huge, like a giant, all in green, even his hair and skin, and carrying a tree for an axe? Definitely sounds like him."

"Why would something like that be wandering around campus, though?" She seemed genuinely puzzled, and I reminded myself that not all of us chose to dress up in armor, or were given gifts of swords and magic.

"Because he's in this story, or at least the Gawain part, and the story's not giving you a choice, Nirali."

"That's not funny," she said. "I told you guys I wasn't doing anything other than keeping a journal."

"I'm not sure that matters anymore," I said. "Although, I can't remember—didn't Gawain volunteer to answer the Green Knight's challenge? So maybe you don't have to do anything."

"Not maybe. There is no maybe about it. I don't care what the story wants. I am not part of this."

She shoved her laptop into her bag and left. I thought of Nora, who'd also wanted out of the story before it forced her into something she didn't want, and hoped that Nirali was right.

She walked in a few minutes late, but Nirali did come to the next seminar meeting. Liam hooked his foot around her chair leg, sliding it out, and smiled. She smiled back as she sat down, and it seemed everything was forgiven and back to normal.

Wham.

Wham.

WHAM.

After the third shuddering knock on the door, it flew open, coming to rest half off its hinges.

For a moment, we all sat, shocked. The Green Knight. Tall enough to have to bend his head—a head out of which grew oak leaves and ivy as hair and beard—as he strode through the door. Wildness filled the air around him. "Someone has called for a wonder!" His voice the rubble of rocks, the creaking of sap in branches.

Liam stood up, angled himself in front of Nirali. "I—"

"Liam. No. I've got this," she said.

"Are you sure?"

Nirali nodded. "Thanks, though."

She walked around the table, to where the Green Knight

(and I could see why students had called him a giant—Nirali wasn't short, and the top of her head barely reached the middle of his chest) stood. "No one has called you here."

"You are wrong." He slammed his axe onto the floor, and holly branches burst from it.

I flicked my glance at Professor Link but couldn't read anything in her face.

"I'm not. But even if we had," Nirali continued, "our time is not your time. Things have changed since the first time you were called to this court. Had a wonder been required, your presence alone would suffice."

"How can that be?" His voice the rustle of wind in branches.

"Look outside," Nirali said. "Think of what you have seen and not seen on your journey here. There are no more great forests, no standing stones to serve as clocks. We do not ride in pursuit of wishes granted by the white hart. You are a thing unique, sole and unexpected. Like nothing any of us have seen. Truly, a wonder, and so you have fulfilled your quest."

"Truly?" The boom of his voice quieter now.

"Truly." All around the conference table, faces of awe and agreement. Even—maybe especially—the faces of the students who hadn't agreed to take cards and names. I wondered what this semester must be like for them, if they regretted their decisions to live in the safety of papers and research.

A pause. Then he bowed, deeply to Nirali, and walked three steps backward before standing up again. "Then I take my leave of you."

He thumped off, through the broken door, and down the hall.

Sabra stood and started clapping. The rest of us followed, cheering Nirali.

"You were fucking amazing!" Liam said. "How did you do that?"

"I knew the story," she said. "Just because I don't want to dress up in armor doesn't mean I wasn't curious about who I'd been assigned. Arthur calls for a wonder at Christmas, like usual, and the Green Knight shows up. While there, he offers the challenge, which Gawain accepts. That leads to the whole striking heads off with axes bit, which is what I really wanted to avoid—though, thanks for stepping up."

Liam grinned.

"But all the Green Man had to do to fulfill his role in the story was be a wonder. The rest of everything came from Gawain, really.

"I just figured, if you guys weren't being collective jerks, and if some weird part of the story was going to show up here, I was going to meet it on my terms.

"Besides. I mean, it's not like I was lying. A giant fucking green man just came to our seminar. If that isn't a wonder, I don't know what is."

We left then, to celebrate with Nirali. Drinks and pizza and feeling invincible. Like we, too, were wonders.

It wasn't until I woke, dehydrated and angry-headed in the small hours of the morning, that I remembered one thing: Professor Link had not applauded. She had looked away from Nirali's triumph.

And the Green Knight had said he had been called for.

This time, when I went looking for Arthur, I didn't use the locator spell.

My plethora of interlibrary loans had finally come in. As I had suspected, none of them gave any real hints about magic. But like Nirali, I had wanted to know everything I could about the name I had been assigned. So I'd also ordered thick, scholarly tomes on Morgan, and those coughed up a couple of pieces of relevant information.

Morgan, it seemed, was associated with ravens because one of her original titles was that of necromancer, a magician with power over the dead. Ravens were psychopomps— creatures that carried souls between life and death. Another thing that was said to carry souls was the sound of church bells, which would ring the souls of the dead home on the tide.

Lake Severn didn't have tides, and I knew Arthur wasn't drowned, but if ravens could pass between those two states, maybe they could find a sleeping king who was neither one of those things nor the other. Maybe they were the locator spell I needed.

But when I looked through the birds' eyes, they didn't show me a king sleeping on a glass bier. Instead, I saw Sabra standing on Lake Severn's shore, a white dog next to her.

I ended the spell, blinking until my eyes readjusted to human sight. Then I went down to the lake.

"I've been dreaming of him," Sabra said. "Arthur." Lake Severn's waves lapped at the shore, crisp in the darkness. "Sometimes I see him asleep, on a bier of glass. But usually, I see pieces of his life. I remember what I did.

"Sometimes it's me, on the bier."

Cabal whined, pressed against her side.

"He's out there," she said, looking at the lake.

"Yes."

"We can find him," she said. "But I think it needs both of us."

The boathouse lock broke with a word, and Sabra and I carried one of the crew shells down to the shore.

"Do you need me to wrangle a second set of oars?" I asked.

"I rowed in high school and undergrad," Sabra said. "I've got this." And so I had nothing to distract myself with as we glided over the still lake. The cool night air and the dip of the oars in the water, and the smell of apples as we approached.

"Sabra. There's an island." There hadn't been, before. Not built on bone, but all the same, as she rowed us closer, I felt like we were approaching a graveyard, a dead place.

The boat fetched gently up against the shore, and we climbed out. The air was full of ravens. "I think," I said, "we follow them."

Sabra nodded, and we walked in silence.

The scent of apples was stronger now, and I could see them hanging in the trees, ripe and waiting. White fell through the air, and my first thought was that it was snow, but then I realized: blossoms hung on the trees as well, and it was their petals falling, bright in the moonlight.

From somewhere over the water, bells began to ring, a calling of souls.

Sabra stopped at the edge of a clearing, and in its center on a bier of glass, so that it seemed he floated above the earth, the sleeping King Arthur.

Time froze, and we froze with it.

Having seen Morgan, I could see the resemblance between the siblings. Arthur had the same generous mouth as his sister, the same blade-straight nose. His hands, crossed over his chest where the hilt of Excalibur would have rested, had the same long fingers. But he was red and gold to her dark and pale.

His clothing looked worn, functional rather than royal, and the left side of his shirt was stiff and stained. I wondered if he was sleeping in the same clothes he'd worn at Camlann, at the end.

He wore no crown, and he had no scars. Which seemed strange—he had been, after all, a warrior king. But then I remembered: Morgan's spell. The scabbard.

The spell to protect him from all injury in battle.

The reason I was here.

The reason he was.

Cabal walked to the foot of the bier, laid himself down, and whined as if his heart was broken.

"Morgan," Sabra whispered, "can you wake him?"

"Are you sure he needs to be awake?"

"Yes."

I stepped forward, then halted, my hands curling at my sides. "You're linked. If I fuck this up, you could wind up like he is."

"I could wind up like that anyway," she said. It was the closest I'd heard her come to directly acknowledging the expected end of things.

"Sabra—"

"Morgan, wake him."

But nothing I did worked. As I tried, as I stood for what felt like hours, weaving magic out of air and words, the temperature dropped. The wind picked up, and the smell of the lake mixed sickeningly with that of the apples. Hackles rose on Cabal's back, and he started to growl, low and terrible.

I stopped mid-word. "Sabra, we need to go. Now." I didn't wait for her to agree, just grabbed her arm and ran back to the boat.

"Hang on," I told her.

Instead of sitting, I stood. The buffeting winds tore my words from my mouth as I guided us back over the water.

We hit the shore with a crash that spilled the three of us out.

"We left the oars," Sabra said after we'd hauled the shell back to the boathouse.

"Sorry," I said. "Other things on my mind."

"What was that?" she asked.

"A sign we were on the right track. Sabra, you're sure he needs to be awake?"

"Yes."

"Okay. Then he will be."

She grabbed my wrist. "Soon, Morgan. It needs to be soon."

Once

VIVIANE'S MAGIC FALLS AWAY FROM MY ISLAND AS they leave. I go to the clearing at its center to see what they did to make her so angry. I step through the trees, and my heart stops beating.

My brother. Arthur. Here.

My heartbeat an ache in my breast as it starts again. I stumble to his side and I fall, landing on knees turned to bird bone and unable to support my weight. Arthur. I press my face to his folded hands.

Weeping, because what else can I do? I wasn't even the one to bring him back.

My brother's hands in mine are pliant and unmoving as clay. Scenes of his, our, life play out in the glass of his bier: all the branches, all the fates, all the choices that led us here.

I was supposed to say goodbye to him, long and long and too long ago. But it would have been too soon then, and who agrees to that? I didn't care if he became a legendary king; I just wanted him alive, and my brother. But now that he is as he is, I will not let her unwrite him.

All he has left is his story.

In the darkness of the glass, white moths flutter, like apple petals, like falling stars. And then they, too, fall, and my brother lies sleeping on their stilled wings, white as death.

— 9 —

"And, of course, those of you participating in the journal option must turn in those journals in person during the last class meeting of the semester," Professor Link said.

"The last class meeting? Not during the finals period?" Liam asked.

"Well, it's not precisely a final project, now is it?"

"It has to be in person?" I asked. "We can't just leave it in your mailbox or give it to a friend?"

"In person. During the class meeting," she repeated. "If you're feeling charitable, perhaps you might tell your less-attending fellow students."

She smiled, and I understood. Nora. She meant Nora. Who was the only one of us who didn't attend. Whatever name she had been assigned, Link wanted her here, to put her desired ending in motion.

"Of course," I said. "I'll be sure to pass that along."

I emailed Nora. Five minutes later, her response pinged.

"Thanks for the warning. Don't worry. I'd rather fail."

The next day, I got another email from Nora.

"Link's done this before. We need to talk."

She asked me to meet her at one of the less popular coffee shops on campus that afternoon. Shadow-eyed, she slid into the bench across from me, clutching a mug of the largest possible mocha, extra chocolate drizzled across the top. Not bothering even with "hello," she opened her laptop and slid it across the table. "I started wondering, after you emailed yesterday, and did some research. It's all here."

I read the opening of the article, then looked up in shock. "How did you find this?"

"Like I said, I know how the story goes. So I ran a bunch of searches, using every string of terms I could think of that might pull up any relevant information. I'm getting my master's in information science. This is what I do."

We hadn't been the first group of students. Of course we hadn't—I was an idiot for not realizing it sooner. This was a story that retold itself. A story she wanted retold. Professor Link had a different name then—Elaine Lac—but it was definitely her, directing a class of theater students performing *Camelot*. The article included pictures, and the only thing different about Link, or Lac, or whatever her real name was, was her wardrobe.

There had been, it seemed, a love triangle, and not just the one onstage. The paper spoke in language cautious enough to hide exactly how many points in the love triangle had been involved with each other, but the one thing that was made clear was that on opening night, the actor playing Lancelot had stabbed the actors playing Arthur and Guinevere, and then had slit his own wrists. Arthur and Lancelot had died. At the time of the writing, Eliza Williams, the actress who had played Guinevere, had been in the hospital with significant injuries.

"That's awful, Nora. I mean, really fucking awful. But I don't know how that changes anything for us." I slid her laptop back to her.

"Read this one." She clicked something on her screen, then shoved the laptop back.

Eliza Williams had never recovered. The doctors hadn't been sure why—infection, maybe, from something on the blade. But her wounds had never healed. She was unable to leave her house, unable to have anything like her previous life. The article went on to mention that she had inherited a collection of art—historical objects from the medieval and Renaissance periods, some even earlier. She lived in a house that was like a museum.

"The Fisher King," I said quietly. The guardian of a sacred object, with an unhealing wound, ruler of a dying land. "She's not Guinevere, not anymore. She's the Fisher King."

"I emailed her," Nora said.

"What?" I yanked myself from my thoughts.

"She's still alive, and in the area. She'll talk to us. If we come to her. I want to go today, Morgan. I don't think we have a lot of time."

There were only two more class meetings left in the semester. I didn't think we had a lot of time either. "Okay," I said.

"Great. I'll drive."

"Drive" in this case meant a motorcycle. "Are you kidding me?" I asked.

Nora tossed me a helmet. "Get on."

I muttered a spell for protection as I climbed on behind her.

"Are you praying?" she asked.

"Something like that."

The drive was beautiful, though. Deep into the woods, which were casting off their fall colors and stretching their branches toward the starkness of the November sky. Everything was crisp and sharp.

Nora turned off onto a winding drive, beneath an arcade of trees. She stopped in front of a building that looked like a sixteenth-century abbey, all soaring arches and stained glass. From the distance of the road, it had looked splendid, intimidating. But now, up close, the truth revealed itself.

The trees were dying. Twisted, full of dead limbs, some completely rotten and bare. Not the temporary dormancy of fall and winter, but true death. There were sere patches on the ground. The stones of the building itself were moss-covered and ivy-vined, beginning to crumble in places. The doorbell chimed like a mourning carillon.

A woman in scrubs opened the door. "I'm Molly. I take care of Eliza. She said to bring you right up."

"Just stay close. The house can be a little odd."

Nora and I looked at each other and stepped inside.

It was like walking into an abandoned cathedral—the same sense that a place once vital, even perhaps sacred, had been left alone to time and colonized by the transient.

Molly led us into a large, open room, full of long tables. Seated at them were what had once been guests and had turned into something altogether other. "Don't talk to or touch them," she said. "Just keep walking."

The tables were set for a feast—all crystal and silver and heavy candelabra, lit with unflickering flames. Sleeping Beauty's castle after the spindle pricked her finger. Everything caught in stasis, except for the guests at the feast. Even without Molly's warning, I wouldn't have touched them. Six dead knights sat around the table. Formerly rich clothing hung in tatters from their bones. In front of each of them, a goblet. All but one filled with what I was very certain was blood. That empty goblet stood in front of an empty chair.

"You walk through this every day," Nora said, low and flat.

"Yes."

"What happens when the last one fills?" I asked.

"It doesn't," Molly said.

"Do you actually like working here?" Nora asked.

"You get used to the house," Molly said. "This way."

Stained-glass windows lined a cobweb-strewn hallway, weeping spills of color to the floor where the light came through. Not the expected saints, but kings and queens and knights, some wearing faces I knew. The final panes, an entire flock of ravens.

Crack-snap-shatter behind us as glass fell to the floor.

Molly knocked on the frame of an open door, then gestured us in. The room was like a jewel-box museum. Unicorns raced across tapestries hung on the walls. Two suits of armor stood sentry. Display cases held chalices, chatelaine keys, rings and bracelets in rows. In a bed, made as much as possible not to look like a hospital bed, the woman we had come to see.

She looked exactly as she had in the newspaper picture, taken over fifty years before.

"Holy shit," Nora said as she exhaled.

"Trust me," Eliza said, her voice barely above a whisper, almost more breath than sound, "it has its drawbacks."

The shadow of an antiseptic scent burned at the back of my throat. There were stacks of gauze, scissors, medical tape, next to the bed; a stainless stand to hold an IV bag, pushed just off to the side.

"Like the dead guys down the hall?" Nora asked.

"Among other things." Eliza spoke slowly, pausing for

breath between words. Remnants of the never-quite-healed stabbing.

"Are you stuck with them forever?" I asked.

"Until the story ends."

"Except it's started over," I said.

"It never ended." She coughed then, put a hand to her side, and her hand came up bloody. Red leaked across her shirt. A spasm of blood-flacked coughing, and the stain on her shirt like a pool.

Instead of being calm or smart, calling for Molly, I ran forward, grabbed a stack of towels, and started the words of the binding spell I'd used to heal Sabra.

When I touched Eliza, it felt like lightning exploded inside me.

I woke up on the floor, Molly shining a penlight into my eyes. "Welcome back," she said.

"What." My chest ached as if I had been kicked dead-on by a draft horse.

"Apparently, you did some magical matter-antimatter deal, and the blowback knocked you ass over tit," Nora said. She was standing in the far corner of the room, eyes narrowed. "Which, maybe next time mention the whole being a fucking wizard thing."

"Sure. Okay. Next time.

"Eliza!" I sat up and the room tilted.

"Is fine," Molly said.

"I don't heal. Or die. Until the story ends," Eliza said. "It's her idea of an apology."

"Apology?" I echoed.

"Elaine's. Because I wasn't supposed to get hurt."

"But the ones who died, that was fine. No apology for them, and they're still dead," Nora said.

Pain across Eliza's face, and I remembered that she had loved at least one of the dead men. "Yes. They are. But I can help you make sure no one from your story dies. Molly, the cauldron."

It looked like something from a witch's stash. Small enough to be carried, the outside tarnished and dinged, the lip ringed with smearily iridescent black pearls. The inside, silver and immaculate.

"Great. A goth fantasy movie prop," Nora said. "I'm sure it will help."

"It resurrects the dead," Eliza said.

"Of course it does," Nora said, stepping back again.

"Blood. You need the blood of a willing sacrifice. One life for another."

"How do you have this?" I asked.

"The knights downstairs. They traveled with Arthur, in search of the great treasures of Britain. To Annwn, the land of the dead. This is one of the things they brought back."

"'Except seven, none returned,'" I said, quoting a poem

141

that was likely one thousand years old. "That's why the chair hasn't filled," I said. "It's his."

Eliza nodded.

"And you're just giving this to us," Nora said.

"Your friend is, as you said, a fucking wizard. She'll know what to do."

I didn't, beyond taking it. But I felt the weight of eternity in my hands, the echo of miracles in my bones. It was a possibility, where before there had been none.

"Thank you," I said. I thought I heard a whispered "good luck" as Nora and I followed Molly out of the house, but it could have just been a breath.

"Are you coming back to class?" I asked Nora as I climbed off the motorcycle.

"I don't know. Maybe. I don't think so."

I raised an eyebrow.

"I don't trust Link. Or any of this, really. Because whether or not the names would have done a damn thing on their own, it's clear that something else is going on. Link hasn't aged in over fifty years. That poor woman in that house is immortal, for all the fucking good it does her. I *felt* you do magic today. So it's not just names, and the story is still a tragedy."

"Maybe it's not if you're there," I offered, tucking the cauldron more securely in my bag.

"Morgan, I'm Mordred. So no. My being there helps exactly nothing. This? Today? This was my best guess at something, anything, I could do to make sure that Sabra doesn't die. And now maybe she won't, if that thing really is what Eliza says it is.

"Take the cauldron and save Sabra's life with it, and call me when it's over." Nora started her bike and drove off.

I sit on the ground, cauldron in my lap. It should be heavier.

A noise, half laugh, half sob, breaks from my mouth. If I'm going to get all metaphorical, it could never be heavy enough. Not for what it will hold.

"Are you ready?" I ask.

I spent the last days of the semester trying to wake Arthur. I rowed my hands raw going back to that strange island in the middle of Lake Severn, cast spell after spell over and around his sleeping body, all to no apparent effect. I put myself into the body of a raven and tried to fly after the part of his soul that was somewhere on the border of life and death, of waking and sleep. Before I got to that border, I was cast from the sky like Icarus, to fall, broken and dazzled, in a field of apples.

I had to wait, cold and lonely, on that island, until I was strong enough to call magic to bring myself back to the other side of the lake, and it wasn't until the next day that I could set the break in my arm. I don't think I got it quite right.

I tried to go to the island in a dream and wake Arthur that way. A dream had been the first place I had seen him, after all, when he told me to find him. But all I dreamt were nightmares of past Arthurs, past failures. And, over and over, Sabra dead, my hands red with her blood.

The night before our last class meeting, I dragged myself across campus to Sabra's apartment. Niv opened the door, Cabal wagging his tail behind her.

"I'm sorry it's so late. But I need to talk to Sabra," I said.

"You look like you're about to fall over. Come in, and let me get you something. We've got pizza I can reheat."

"You don't need to go to any trouble," I said.

"You're trying to save my fiancée's life," she said. "I think I can put some pizza on a cookie sheet."

"Wait, you guys are getting married?"

Niv smiled. "She proposed the day after that sculpture came to life. Which is not how I started the story when I called my parents."

"Congratulations. That's wonderful."

"You'll come to the wedding?" She put pizza in the oven, poured me a glass of wine. My face must have shown more than I wanted it to when she handed it to me.

"Don't even," she said, her hand shaking. "Don't even say it. I know. And I know you wouldn't look like you do if you were here with good news. But Sabra and I are getting married, and you are going to be there to dance."

"Okay," I said.

"Glad that's settled." Sabra sat down.

Niv set my plate on the table and kissed Sabra. "I've got papers to grade, so I'll leave you two. Morgan, thank you."

I nodded. Cabal woofed hopefully at my pizza. I passed him a pepperoni, and he settled in at our feet. "Sabra, I can't wake Arthur."

"You didn't look like you were here with good news. But maybe he doesn't wake up until, you know, tomorrow. At the end."

"You should maybe think about not coming to class." I couldn't look at her as I said it.

"I'm going," she said. "Niv said the same thing, but seriously, if something is going to happen, it doesn't care where I am. Trying to fuck around with fate is what got us here. I'll be there, and it will be fine."

"I think you should bring Excalibur, then," I said.

I could see the question flash through her eyes, and was glad when she didn't ask it.

"I will," she said.

I didn't sleep. I lit candles and thought about pieces of stories.

The last day of class was bright and clear, the chill November sky ice-blue as we wandered in, leaving our journals in a pile

145

next to Professor Link's chair. There were no flocks of angry ravens, no Green Knights, no anything to suggest that this room was something other than what it appeared—a room full of graduate students.

Nora wasn't there. I hadn't expected her to be.

Even now, I can't tell you what it really was. I thought I saw a weapon. I know—staggeringly unspecific. But my brain said "knife" and I heard a voice yell "gun" and I jumped from my seat, flinging myself into Sabra, in some desperate attempt to shield her from whatever it was.

And then the only thing I heard was the crack as her head hit the floor.

I will always hear the crack as her head hit the floor.

"Didn't you learn anything this semester?" Professor Link, the Lady of the Lake, asked, standing over me as I picked myself up. "Arthur dies at the end."

I remembered what I was. I spoke a word that flung her backward, then stood, shielding Sabra with my body, and said a binding spell to keep Link away from us. Bent over, barked out the words for healing. No response from Sabra.

"Morgan?" Liam said.

"Can you help me get Sabra to the lake?" I grabbed her bag, glad that the hilt of Excalibur showed through the top.

His eyes skipped from me to Sabra to Excalibur to the empty space in the room where Professor Link had been. "You're sure not the hospital?"

"Yes."

A breath.

"Okay." He brushed Sabra's hair away from her face, then picked her up, so carefully.

"Let me know if she gets heavy," I said. "I can help."

"Not to imply that you didn't just do actual magic in there, but maybe modern medicine?" Nirali asked.

"You read the old stories when you were doing your Green Knight research, right? I have the cauldron from the 'Preiddeu Annwn' in my bag."

She stopped. "Seriously?"

"What is that?" Liam asked.

"It's one of the treasures of Britain. Arthur went into the afterworld and brought them back. There's a theory that this is the thing that got turned into the Holy Grail when Christianity got ahold of the story. It supposedly resurrects the dead," Nirali said. "But you need blood. From a willing sacrifice."

"There's an island in the middle of Lake Severn. King Arthur is on it. In the exact condition as Sabra. I'm going to wake him up. And save her life." I prayed that saying the words would make them true.

"This is officially the weirdest semester of my life," Liam said.

"No shit," Nirali said. "But I'm coming with you guys."

No crew shell this time—a low black barge waited against

the shore, Cabal already there. Liam set Sabra in it. He took my hand, held on hard as I stepped in.

"Do you want us to wait for you?" Nirali asked.

"Yes." The sky was growing dark, the temperature dropping. "But be careful. I think there's about to be a storm."

Once

I CAN FEEL WHEN THIS STORY'S ARTHUR FALLS. IT is, as it always is, as a sword piercing my heart. There is no change in my brother, but he is still here, and so am I, and so the story is not yet finished.

The story will not end here. It never does. This is the place for after the ending.

There is always an after.

I can feel a storm coming. I brush the hair away from my brother's face and follow my flock to Viviane in her tower.

— 10 —

And so here we are, on the section of the map that has monsters. Arthur is here, but he's still not awake. I've brought Sabra, and I lay her carefully on the bier next to him, and this is . . .

This is . . .

This is all that's left. The sword, the cauldron, and the sleeping king, and I'm the one who needs to turn them into a living Sabra.

Over the water, the chiming of the bells. The carillon, not ringing an hour, just ringing, over and over. Calling the souls of the dead home.

I cut Excalibur across my palm and, using blood for ink, say the words of the scrying spell. Once more, looking for Arthur, even though I am standing next to him. I'm looking for the truth at the heart of the sleeping king, looking for the missing piece that made him, that will wake him up, bring him back.

What I am looking for isn't the part of the him that's here, but the part that has paused, all this time, beyond the end of the story. I am calling it home.

I finish speaking and watch as my blood sinks into his skin. As his breath catches, hitching his chest. As his eyes open.

As he sits up.

Once

VIVIANE DISAPPEARS. APPEARS AGAIN. BY MAGIC, but not by her own. She looks as confused as I am. There is no sound in the room, no color. And then, light, sound again. The story is telling itself around us, trying to decide how we fit.

"She's done it," Viviane says. "Your namesake. She's woken him. I wonder if soon enough?"

I can hear the bells ringing, carrying the souls of the dead in their sound.

I could have been with him, said hello, or perhaps goodbye, had I not come here, but I can feel the ending tightening around me, and I have no choices left, not this time.

I hope he knows I love him. In every story, I love my brother. In every story, I did what I did for love.

Viviane's hand, that has been Elaine's, and Nyneve's, and Nimue's, takes mine. "Let's wait for the end together," she says.

THE END

There is no change in Sabra. Her breathing is still shallow, her pulse still thready. I pick up the sword and cut myself again, ignoring Arthur's gasped shock. Hold the blood in my hand as I say the magic, then fling it into the air. It pauses, holds, beading up like rain on thin lines between Arthur and Sabra, marking the pattern that binds them together.

"What is that?" he asks.

"Your story. Morgan's magic. Our story. Some combination of all of them. Whatever it is, you're still linked."

"Do you know how to unlink us?"

"Yes," I say. I look straight at him as I say it, hoping there is a part of him that has been awake through all these stories, that knows what the end is supposed to be. That there is a part of him that remembers that once he wanted to be better than he was, and that will spare me from having to speak the words out loud.

"The story needs a death," he says. "I would rather it be mine."

I show him the cauldron. "If you agree, this will keep her safe."

A smile of recognition flashes across his face. "Do you know how to make sure I truly die this time?"

"Excalibur." The beginning of the story, the weapon that never missed.

He nods.

"Are you ready?" I ask.

His hand tightens on Cabal's fur. "I am afraid I must ask for your help. I do not think I can manage it on my own."

I swallow hard. "I wish I could tell you to take whatever time you need, but I don't think we have a lot of it." The trees are falling now, not just the apples but the trees themselves, and the lake sounds like the roar of an ocean. The ending has been written, and it is coming for us fast.

"I have already taken more time than I had any right to," Arthur says. He picks up Excalibur and hands it to me. "It is a good blade. Do not hesitate, and it will strike true."

"I am ready." His eyes are clear, and steady on mine.

"We still tell your story," I say, and I strike him through the heart.

He smiles as he falls.

The cauldron cracks in two.

There is no slow motion, no time to process. Only, one second I think that I have a solution, a way to be sure that Sabra comes back from wherever she is, and the next . . .

Arthur is dead.

There's just me.

And I can feel magic ending.

The trees are falling and the island is sinking, and somehow Cabal is still here, and that's good because I don't think I could take watching that dog wink out of existence with Arthur's blood still on my hands, and Sabra . . . not awake.

The lines of story connecting her to Arthur are gone.

That's good, I think. I rack my brains for some magic, something from the grimoire that will wake her. Something fast, because I can feel the magic leaving my body like a fever burning. I don't think I'm going to be Morgan the sorceress much longer.

The beginning.

I hold Sabra's hands in mine and whisper, *"Fiat lux."*

There is a gasp, and I don't know if it is Sabra or the story, but her hand clenches, and she wakes up.

Magic is falling around us like snow as we stumble through the ending apple trees. The barge is still waiting on the shore, and it takes us halfway across the lake before the magic is completely gone, before it falls away into the dark waters of the Severn. The three of us, Sabra, Cabal, and I, swim the rest of the way. Everything hurts, and the cuts on my hands reopen and bleed. Sabra so tired that Cabal and I half drag her, her arms slung around both of us.

Dawn cracks across the sky. A shout and a splash and Liam is there. He swims Sabra to shore. Nirali takes my hand and pulls me from the water, while telling Cabal that he's a good boy, the best. Somehow there are dry towels and Niv is there and she's crying and she kisses me on the forehead and says, "Thank you." And there is Nora, and she hands me a flask: "Nice job, wizard."

And it's over, and we're safe.

The tower that used to hold Professor Link's office is gone.

And so I set down the story, the true story of what happened that semester. To be a candle, to be a light in the darkness. So that none of it is forgotten.

Translatio Corporis

The city began building itself when Lena was nine. It was a labor of love.

Construction started with a fountain, ornate and elaborate, full of leaping fish, out of whose mouths smaller fountains splashed, a tridented Poseidon proud at its apex. Lena liked how the bright sun turned the splashing water sharp and clear like diamonds, how the wind brought the spray to tingle, cool against her skin.

She closed her eyes, lifting her face to the warmth of the sky, and an afterimage of the fountain burned on the inside of her eyelids. She heard the wild laughter of her best friend, Catherine, the two girls so inseparable they appeared like twinned shadows, as a sudden gust dampened the front of her sundress. Lena smiled and wished she could keep the place forever.

"Girls, let's go! Come away from those steps before you

fall. We're going to be late." Her mother's voice, impatient.

Lena opened her eyes, and the sky blinked. She climbed down from the steps she had been sitting on—the grey, worn pedestal of an ancient memorial, so old it was crumbling into dust at the touch of the breeze.

Near the bottom, her foot caught. She fell, bloodying her knees.

"What did I tell you?" her mother asked, brushing grit and gravel from the scrapes. "Are you all right?"

Lena nodded, half looking back over her shoulder, as if she might see what had tripped her. But the only thing behind her was an expanse of space—a cracked courtyard where idle pigeons strutted through.

"Catherine, how did your dress get wet? What have you girls gotten into?" Lena's mother twitched Catherine's dress straight and shook her head.

"There was water? Before?" Catherine, hesitant. Unremembering.

"Well, I don't know where. Come on, girls."

"There was water. Right?" Catherine whispered to Lena.

Lena nodded. She knew there had been. Splashing through the sun like diamonds. But she couldn't call to mind what it had been or where it had gone.

Somewhere, an other where, the splash of a fountain with the faintest trace of red in its waters echoed through an empty square.

. . .

There are metaphors that can be made on cities as bodies.

One can discuss the life of a city, the way it grows, the way it develops, as if one were discussing the life of a person. One might consider arteries for traffic and whether they might be clogged, or ponder whether there is breathing space between places as they are built. We speak of the faded glory of a building with the same words we speak of a formerly beautiful woman, the cracks that show in the facade.

We can think about foundations as skeletons—Does the place have good bones? the architect considers, when looking at a building. We talk about a body, with its architecture of muscle, of skin, hung on the bones beneath, like we might talk about a building.

Lena's city, embryonic as it is, does not consider metaphor.

As yet, the city considers almost nothing. All it knows is it is hers, and it loves her.

As she dreams, Lena almost remembers the fountain. It is there, locked behind a door in herself. She can feel it.

And though she doesn't think of it as missing, there is a piece of her that has gone too. The red scabs on her knees. The blood that was left behind on the ground, that might splash through a fountain like water. The tiniest missing piece of a self, wounds that she covers over with her hands.

Every city needs its foundation.

. . .

The fountain was the only occupant of Lena's city for quite some time, long enough for its copper splendor to oxidize to a blue-green patina. Long enough to feel like it had been alone forever. But it knew it was a city, and knew that name meant becoming more than a singular place. The air around it was made of time and memory, and so it waited, almost patiently, for the next inhabitant.

Then, later, the cathedral arrived.

"Did you know they used to grind the bones of saints into the mortar?" Catherine asked. "Something about making the space holy, sanctified. Some of the really old churches have whole bodies of saints buried in the cornerstones. Sometimes they weren't even dead before they were immured."

"You sound a little too excited about buildings with people built into them," Lena said.

Catherine grinned.

"Besides, you have to be dead before you can be a saint," Lena said. "Otherwise the miracles don't count."

"They don't happen?" Catherine asked.

"They happen. They're just not miracles. Not officially."

"I'm going to guess that distinction doesn't mean much to the poor suckers who get walled up in buildings because someone thought they were holy," Catherine said.

"Probably not." Lena shuddered.

The setting sun made the shadows of the gargoyles' wings

bend and flex, as if their stone shapes might spring into the air, unmoored from the foundation made sacred by the presence of the bodies of the dead. They were so beautiful. The whole building was.

Lena closed her eyes in happiness; opened them.

A blink, a scraping of stone, and the two young women stood before a rattling chain-link fence, posted with signs warning caution, red-letter danger. Nothing behind it but a vacant lot. Catherine pinched the screen of her phone, swiped out. "I need to download the update. The map says the cathedral should be right here."

Lena winced, pressing her palm against a sudden ache in her side. "You are the only person I know who can get lost with a GPS in your hand."

Some other where, strange air ran over a gargoyle's wings, and a cathedral settled into place, a new sacred relic contained within it.

Lena's illness began with feelings of exhaustion. The kind of tired even ten hours' sleep and coffee doesn't cure, the kind of tired that made Lena's bones ache, made her skin seem ill-fitting.

There were doctors, then, and blood work and the thousands of small indignities and embarrassments that come with a body that is not quite doing what it should, that feels like it is missing some essential piece.

Which, it turned out, it was.

"An entire rib?" Lena asked.

The doctor shook her head. "Have you ever been x-rayed before? I'd feel better if I had results to compare these to."

"No," Lena said. "I was a healthy kid. No broken bones. I never even had stitches."

Dr. Rhys flipped through Lena's file again, her eyes sharp. "The thing is, the edges of the removal are smooth. Beyond surgical."

"Are you saying I maybe never had that rib at all?"

"That's certainly possible." Dr. Rhys did not sound as if she particularly believed that option.

Lena pressed her hand against her side, against the absence she knew was recent. She said nothing.

Lena's city went through a spate of rapid growth. Gathering place after place that she loved, collecting them all for her. A park, lush green grass and riotous flowers, trees old enough to give looping, shaded canopies. A library, small. The kind that was inside an old house, where you had to make an appointment to look at the collection, but you did, because it was filled with books of magic, descriptions of illusions that were hundreds of years old, with titles like *Upon the Disappearance and Return of Objects* and *The Illusions of Other Spaces*.

In the places the buildings had left behind on their way

to this new, other city: scars. Shadows. Ruins. Blank spots on maps that hadn't yet realized they were inaccurate.

Pleased with its efforts, Lena's city stretched its bones, flexed its muscles, and waited. For her to notice it, the beauty it had made for her, and for another thing too. As it had grown, the city had learned. It had realized that it was missing a heart that didn't yet beat, to know that while places in it had age, it did not yet have history. It needed something else for that.

Something or someone. The city wasn't sure yet.

Lena began to feel depopulated, unpeopled. As if her body had gone traveling and her soul had yet to catch up. Too many tests, she told herself. Too many sterile rooms and needles sucking out bits of her. Too much inconclusive. Too many hushed voices, and maybes, and consultants.

"Of course you feel weird. No one could feel normal in a place like this," Catherine said. "Let's go. Let's get you out of here."

"You're right," Lena said, pulling electrodes from her skin, leaving behind sticky, raw patches and wailing machines. They weren't telling anyone anything useful anyway. "Let's go. Anywhere but here."

They went. Away from hospitals and maybes and uncertainties. From shadows on screens that were not shadows of things that shouldn't be resident in Lena's body, but shadows of things that should, that had somehow gone missing.

Not just a rib, now. Other bones. The iron in her blood. Some strange missing space that made Dr. Rhys turn pale and quiet, made her unable to quite meet Lena's eyes.

From far away, from an other where, Lena's city had found a way to connect to its foundation, to weave arteries to its heart. It could feel itself breathing. It was almost.

"Look," Lena said, leaning over the edge of a bridge. "It's like there's an entire city under there." She could see it, shining under the water. Not drowned, just beneath. Familiar somehow, like she had known it, once.

Catherine looked down at the surface of the water. She looked sideways at Lena. Her face was not the face of someone witnessing the appearance of the miracle of an underwater city. It had a different expression altogether. One of recognition, like Lena could walk those underwater streets from memory. "Maybe we should go inside," Catherine said. "Get out of the sun."

Lena looked back, searching, as they walked away.

That was the first place Lena saw her city. After, she saw it elsewhere, other where too. Behind her mirror, reflected in a window, always just on the other side. She thought maybe it was waiting; it seemed crouched, expectant.

She did not tell the doctors about this reflected, half-seen city shadowing her. It was not something she wanted to be cured of.

. . .

There were no clouds in the sky of Lena's city, nor were there footprints in its streets. It was a city unghosted, newly forming. Still, it knew what it wanted, whom it longed for, whom it loved.

It was not enough for traces of blood to flow through its waters, for bone to seal its foundations. A city was a living thing, needing blood and a heartbeat. Needing the person it had built itself for.

The city had doors. It would open them.

More inconclusive, more tests. "Inconclusive," Lena learned, was what you were told when the truth was too strange to fit in a scientist's mouth. "You are disappearing, from the inside out" was the kind of thing impossible to say, and so it wasn't.

Lena was stripped of iron, like someone in a fairy tale, and passed through vibrating tubes, where series after series of ever more elaborate images were taken of her. Blueprints, she thought, when she saw the cross sections of herself cast up on screens. The pictures looked like blueprints.

Inside those beige tubes, fire burning through her veins to make them visible, Lena imagined that she was in her city, the one she saw in mirrors and in water. The one she dreamt. She imagined the grass of its park beneath her head, spray from the fountain cool against her skin, the sacred shadows of the cathedral offering her refuge.

When she closed her eyes, she could almost remember these places. When she closed her eyes, she could visit them again.

She took herself to her city while her body was in the hospital, while hands that weren't hers rearranged her limbs, while tiny pieces of her were collected in glass tubes. She felt like she had come home.

The city trembled at her appearance. Lena glitched in and out of it like the rattle of broken celluloid, like a retro film negative, silvery and inverse.

Her feet bent no blade of grass, yet the city arched itself beneath them like a cat. Soon, it thought. She would see how beautiful it had made itself, full of places she loved, places that were part of her. It had made itself almost perfect enough.

Soon.

"Are you sure you want me to keep reading this?" Catherine asked. "It seems like it might be kind of creepy, given the context."

An overnight stay this time. For observation. As if things might change when seen in the dark. As if Lena's missing pieces might crawl out of the shadows and return.

She shifted on stale, rough sheets. The floor was cracked linoleum, once white, now dinge. The walls a similar shade.

The air reeked of various flavors of fear, acid and sweat and salt from weeping. Monitors beeped constantly.

"That's exactly why I want to hear it," Lena said. "Besides, it's interesting."

Catherine was reading from a book on medieval holy women. About their miraculous bodies—women who wept sacred tears, and virgin saints who lactated spontaneously and fed their villages from their breasts, or whose corpses exuded holy oil. About their relics, the bits and pieces of their bones, and vials of their blood, and locks of their hair, parceled out after their death, collected by those who thought that proximity to the holy would cause miracles to spontaneously generate around them.

"If you're sure," Catherine said. She continued reading the life of Christina the Astonishing, who—among other things—had astounded her neighbors by grinding her own body in the village mill, without apparent damage.

"Do you think they missed them? The women, I mean. Do you think they missed their relics, the bones and things that were stolen from them?"

You had to be dead to be a saint. Maybe you didn't notice the missing pieces, then.

Catherine closed the book. "Do you miss yours?"

Lena turned her head toward the window. The night shone through, and she looked into darkness, into the half-reflected shapes that appeared in the glass.

"Not really," she said. "I feel like I should, when I think about it, but I don't. It's more like I feel out of place. Homeless, almost. Like part of me has gone on ahead, and I don't belong here anymore.

"And I worry," she said quietly, "about what will happen when too much of me is gone."

Catherine reached out and held Lena's hand, hard, hard, as if by doing so she could keep Lena anchored, keep her pieces from disappearing.

The city had opened all of its doors in welcome. In anticipation. In desire. She had not walked through. She was there, and she was not there.

More not.

The city reached into itself. It slid through its streets and reached its vaulted roof to the sky. Its waters coursed through the fountain, her first presence. Her oldest.

It reached for all the pieces of her that it held, and then it knew.

There was one more door to open.

It was almost possible for Lena to ignore the disappearances, even though they were pieces of herself gone missing. They did not register when they occurred. The aches, the emptiness that was left behind, they felt like echoes.

But this. This shaking, this tearing, this sloughing of the

inside of herself, this was unignorable. It was as if someone had reached inside her chest and was tearing out her heart.

Every piece of her that had gone elsewhere hurt. She knew now that the saints had felt the pain of, had missed, every scattered relic.

Reflected in a monitor—its alarm screaming now—was a city. A place she had almost been.

She could see the ghosts in its windows, in its streets, in the cathedral. Ghosts that she had been. Pieces of her that used to be.

A door opened.

She walked through.

Every monitor in the room shrieked. Catherine sprang up as Dr. Rhys burst through the door, then froze.

"Where is she?" Dr. Rhys asked, staring at the empty bed.

"I don't know," Catherine said. But she thought of cities, reflected and lost, of bodies taken to make places holy, and wondered if, perhaps, she did.

"Come back," she whispered. "Come home."

The pain disappeared as she entered the city. Lena felt her heart thud hard against her breastbone and then fall back into its regular pattern of unnoticeable beats.

She had never set foot on these streets before, and still, she knew them. All the places—the buildings, the green of the park, the splash of the fountain—were hers. Lena felt them in her blood and in her bones. She felt them pull at the empty places inside her, offering comfort, welcome, a sort of home.

She walked toward the soaring lines of the cathedral. Up the steps and through the doors, carved with angels. Into the beeswax and incense-scented quiet. She walked through shadows and cold stone, past stern-faced saints bathed in stained-glass light.

The door to the tabernacle was open. It had been years since she had gone to Mass regularly, but Lena knew that was wrong. It should be closed, a border between the sacred and the profane.

The thing she found in it was wrong too. Not the Eucharist. A rib bone. Smooth-edged and curved. Human.

Hers.

Lena pressed her hand to her side, to the empty space.

The shadows in the cathedral trembled; the foundation of the city shook.

Lena picked up the bone and pressed it against her side.

The cathedral shook hard enough to shatter, stained glass crashing around Lena in a broken kaleidoscope.

The bone disappeared. The relic, translated.

The ache in Lena's side was gone, and beneath her hand, a rib.

She ran from the building as it collapsed in her wake.

Stopped at the foot of what had been the cathedral steps, gathering her breath as the walls fell down.

The ground trembled beneath her feet, and the shaking increased as she walked to the next building, and the next, regathering pieces of herself, leaving a city of ruins behind her.

The city wept. It could not understand, and it could not tell her. It could only watch as she took herself back from it, could only mourn as she ripped out its heart.

It had given her everything she loved.

It had opened all its doors and she was slamming them shut.

The city lay crumbled at her feet. The ground no longer trembling beneath them, but heaving, weakly. Gasps for breath.

Lena stopped in front of the fountain.

There were scars, still, on her knees.

She felt the city's sorrow like an ache. She knew what it was to be taken apart, piece by piece.

They were only scars.

Lena walked back through the empty streets of her city, the echo of a fountain splashing behind her.

She stepped across what had, this where, other where, been the threshold of a cathedral and went home.

Dreaming Like a Ghost

I f I tell you to think about a ghost story, you will probably imagine that it takes place in the dark. Perhaps your
mind will conjure up the darkness of a campfire, the
scent of woodsmoke and burnt sugar from making s'mores,
the crackle of the wind in the trees. The feel of your friend's
arm pressed to yours as you all sit tight, tight together, shoulders and hips rubbing in darkness that is companionate, but
still eerie enough to prickle the hair on the back of your neck
pleasantly as you listen.

Perhaps you imagine the darkness of the place the ghost
haunts. The shadows of an abandoned house, the black smear
left on the air by violent death. The pale figure that rises out
of midnight, the inverse of a shadow. You know the shape of
the thing, the form. You know what to expect from a ghost
in the dark.

This is not that kind of ghost story.

. . .

The first time I saw the ghost, it was in the light. That pale-gold slant of afternoon, the kind of light that wraps around you like linen drapes.

She smelled like spring rain. Not just the wet mineral scent that rises from the earth, but that particular way the near-black bark of a tree and the almost-green of buds smell, thick heavy mud burying the remains of winter underneath. Life beneath death, not the other way around.

In a nod to convention, a tribute to the power of story to arrange things, the first time I saw the ghost, she was in a graveyard.

She smiled at me.

"I saw a ghost today," I said as we were washing the dishes.

"Really?" Josh asked, and passed me a plate. Water dripped from it, spattering the tails of Josh's shirt and the thighs of my jeans. "What was it doing?"

"She. Not 'it.' She was in the graveyard." I had stood at the window, when I saw her, watching. She looked like she was about my age. Her face even seemed familiar to me, though I was sure I didn't know her.

She smiled, and her hands curved, like claws. Then she was gone.

"Well, isn't a graveyard sort of the logical place for a ghost to be? I mean, better there than in our bedroom, or the pantry." He stacked the silverware in the drying rack.

"You seem fairly unconcerned about all of this." I hadn't expected Josh to freak out—Josh didn't freak out about anything—but I had been expecting a reaction stronger than mild relief that at least our canned goods weren't being haunted.

"I don't believe in ghosts, Tamsin. Dead is dead, and when you're buried, you stay where you were put. I'm sure you saw something. Just not something I need to be concerned about."

I looked through the window, out into the night, at the gravestones standing sentinel, silent and waiting. My left hand curled into a claw.

We moved here for a job. A good opportunity—for one of us. Josh promised it would be my turn next time. It was a nice community, he was sure I could find something.

I'd had a good life where we were before: a job, friends— the things that ground you. I'd given them up.

Now I had him, and a house to unpack.

I kept finding bits and pieces left over from the people who had lived here before us. Not just forgotten trash: an armoire, with a drawer full of men's T-shirts, still folded; a woman's silk robe, embroidered with a pattern of ivy leaves, hanging in the closet; one high-heeled shoe, spangled with silver glitter; a battered paperback—poetry—with a picture of a smiling couple tucked inside the front cover.

There was a tear in the photograph, splitting them almost in two, but they looked happy.

I wondered if they'd moved in a hurry, if they hadn't been able to supervise the packing. I had been gathering up the things I found, so I could ask the Realtor to send them on.

It seemed like a lot to forget.

The night after I first saw the ghost, I didn't sleep well. I didn't sleep at all, really. My skin itched and felt too small, too tight. I tossed, tangling the sheets, throwing the pillows to the floor. After the first hour, Josh went to sleep elsewhere. Finally, I gave up too and stood at the window, watching. Through the open window I breathed in the scent of a storm, but the sky was cloudless.

As far as I could tell, the graveyard was empty, but that's the thing about ghosts, isn't it? They might be there—anytime—filling the spaces where we are. We just don't see them.

The graveyard was small and oddly haphazard. The markers weren't arranged in the precise, sterile rows of modern cemeteries, but scattered here and there like they had grown from the ground where they stood. The stones were weather-faded and overgrown with weeds. An enormous wild rosebush curled its thorns over at least two plots, like something out of a fairy tale before the curse was lifted.

One of the graves was recent—the date on the headstone was from this year. The earth still hadn't quite settled, and the grass spidery threads over uneven ground.

The earliest grave dated to the mid-seventeenth century. The house dated from around then too—the one growing up with the other. Old for America, but the kind of old that made my friends in England half laugh when I described it that way. Still, the graveyard felt ancient when I walked in it, as if holding the dead pushed a place backward in time, so that a grave with a stone that marked it as being there for one hundred years was actually half a millennium old.

I liked the graveyard. The real estate agent who had shown us the house clearly hadn't—her smile was plastic as she assured us that at least the neighbors wouldn't be noisy; then she refused to meet my eye after I said that graveyards were among my favorite places. I found them fascinating— the names, the dates, the lives marked by single lines of poetry. When I visited new cities, I would go to the cemeteries. I would walk through the rows and make up lives for the people, speaking them aloud to the quiet air. When I died, I wanted someone to walk past and trace my letters, say my name, make sure I didn't disappear.

It was late summer and the air smelled of grass that had been baked by the sun; of fat, pollen-drunk bumblebees; and of the bitter milkweed of monarch butterflies. But the head-stones still smelled cool, slate and stone.

Walking among the stones, trying to imagine which of the residents had walked out of her grave, I noticed something I hadn't before: all the people buried there were women.

All of them were women who had died young—between fifteen and twenty-five. Each of the stones had the same phrase beneath the name and date: BELOVED SISTER. Any of them could have been the ghost's grave. I traced my fingers over their names: Rosalind and Stephanie and Helen and Liza. Nora and Alanna and Sarah and Maude. I whispered each name to the air.

But I told no stories. Not then. What kind of story do you tell about a garden of dead girls?

Another drawer of forgotten objects, this time in the kitchen. Maps, flyers for local cleaning services, food-stained delivery menus. Pens with the names of banks and hotels on them. Smashed at the back of the drawer, a snake's length of foil-wrapped condoms.

It felt like finding a dirty secret, like I had opened the door and seen the former residents of the house fucking. I washed my hands after I threw them away.

As I dried my hands, I heard a woman weeping. I looked all through the house, and the yard, and walked through the graves again, but I didn't find her.

. . .

Josh brought takeaway home for dinner. Thai—which I liked spicy enough that tears would roll down my cheeks as I ate, and he liked not spicy at all; so I was unpacking the containers onto very separate plates before bringing them to the table.

It was clearly a peace offering, a way of saying "I know this sucks for you," without saying "I'm sorry," but he was trying, and so I let him.

"Did you see any ghosts today?" he asked.

I looked at him before I answered, trying to gauge his tone. Was it simple curiosity—no more nor less than asking if I'd had a chance to go to the grocery store—or was there some other note beneath the words?

I couldn't guess, so I just answered. "No, but I went looking to see which grave might be hers."

"Did you figure it out?" He sat at the table, unbuttoning his cuffs and rolling them up.

"If you don't believe in ghosts, why are you asking me questions as if you do?"

"This supposed ghost seems to matter to you. I'm trying to understand why it does."

And then: a peace offering. I almost told him what I'd found. Not just a cemetery, but a cemetery full of girls— beloved sisters. But I closed my mouth over the words. It wasn't like it was even a secret—he could go to the graveyard and see the same thing for himself—it just wasn't something I wanted to share. It was mine.

"Or maybe you've decided to take up a career in fiction, and I'm the one you're trying out your stories on. Have you decided being J. K. Rowling is easier than unpacking?" The line came out smooth, practiced, the kind of thing he'd tried out in the car first to see how it sounded.

The woman's voice again. Not weeping this time, but laughter, mocking. Josh didn't react.

"No," I said, and passed him a plate of spring rolls.

The scent of a spring storm came through the bedroom window, thickening the air, waking me from a tangle of dreams— the weight of dirt on my body, blood drying on my skin and wet in my mouth. The pressure of other bodies near me, voices crying out words that didn't linger past waking. My fingers, still dreaming, clenched like claws and remembered rending. My muscles ached as if I had spent the night running. Through the mattress, I could feel bones beneath me.

There was mud, streaked, at the bottom of the sheets.

Here is another way you can be woken up: rolling over onto something small, something that stabs you in your soft places. An earring. Not yours. You gasp, and you inhale—on your sheets—someone else's perfume. Jasmine. It's an old story, older even than ghosts.

And so when he asks you to move, to make a new start, you say yes.

You say yes, but you hate yourself a little, because what comes out of your mouth is "yes," not "fuck you" or "I know" or "in our *bed*." But you're not ready to say those things, those endings. Not yet.

You say yes, but you think maybe. Maybe if he sees you and not her, things can go back to how they were. Maybe then you won't feel like the ghost haunting your own life.

Clouds rose like bruises against the sky, and thunder rumbled in the distance. The air was heavy and thick, clinging to my skin, but no rain fell.

I peeled back lids of boxes, unwrapped the packed-away pieces of a life. Candlesticks and pairs of shoes and picture frames with photos of a smiling couple I still recognized but wasn't sure I believed in anymore.

A set of small crystal stars, which I hung on the bedroom windows to catch the light. The wind tossed them about, rattling them against the glass.

Outside, the ghost stood in the graveyard again, her hair still in the rush of wind.

She smiled.

I knew that smile. One half of a couple, in a photo nearly torn apart but preserved inside a book. The ghost was the woman who had lived in the house before me.

I ran from the house, from the piles of half-unpacked boxes, to her. The dry grass sliced at my calves, the bottoms of my feet, a thousand small knives, and so I ran faster, as if that would be enough to let me escape.

She was gone when I got there, but I flung myself backward onto the ground where she had been standing, pressing my bones into the earth above where hers lay. I dug my fingers into the dirt and held on tight, tighter. Voices rose up through the ground.

The voices of the dead, full of decay, of worms, choked with rot. I felt their words in my bones. Sister, they called me. Same.

They spoke of a storm, and wind and rain washed over me, soaking my skin. They spoke of betrayal, the death of love, and my mouth ran red with blood, thick and salt.

They whispered of vengeance, and my legs ached from the chase, and the howls of the hunted echoed in my ears.

They told me of falling beneath the ground and dreaming the graves that covered them. Beloved sisters.

I opened my eyes to dry grass and the setting sun.

"Were you out there playing dead?" Josh asked. There was a smudge, just below his ear. Lipstick. A color not mine. I didn't look at it. Sometimes you don't need to turn the page to know how the story ends.

"I don't know what you're talking about," I said, slicing tomatoes for the salad.

"Lying out in the graveyard. I don't know, sunbathing? Tamsin, you still have grass in your hair."

I set down the knife. The wind carried a woman's laugh through the room. "Were you spying on me?"

"Was I . . ." He pinched the bridge of his nose. "Just put mine in the fridge. I'm going for a walk."

I curled my hands into claws, and when I inhaled, I tasted blood.

Lightning strobed across the sky, shocking the night into something sharp-edged. Josh, I supposed, was still out walking in it. He could, if he wanted, find his way back.

I walked too, pacing the house, through the hallways and up and down the stairs, my breath coming quick, my pulse beating against the inside of my skin.

I drank a glass of wine, gulping it, my lips stained red, wine falling from my mouth in my haste, my thirst.

Lightning struck, and thunder shook the house so hard the windows rattled. The electricity snapped, sparked, and went dead.

I scrabbled for candles, the matches flaring high in my shaking hands, then opened the closet where the fuse box was. Hanging there, a man's shirt. White, button-down. Torn, bloodied. On the collar, a different shade of red. Lipstick.

Laughter, laughter, laughter.

I dropped the candle, and it guttered as it fell.

The sky opened, rain sheeting down in heavy drops, and I ran into it, my teeth bared. The wind whipped through the grass. The air smelled burnt, and the ghost girls rose from the ground. Not just one. All of them, a spectral sorority. They stepped up and out of their graves, and I felt something inside me tug loose.

The ghosts' stories rose in the air around me, and I breathed them into my lungs. I held the ghosts' hands—solid now, or mine had grown unso—and knew their loves, their losses.

I knew the dreams of the ghosts, of a world where they could hurt those who had hurt them, where they might make themselves ghosts to do so. Sisters.

The wind whipped my hair to snakes, and the long grass clung to my feet and legs. The storm was the dream of ghosts, time and desire stripped raw. Rain flattened the grass, and wind tore branches from trees. Hail left bruises on my skin.

The ghost girls and I gloried in the storm, throwing ourselves through the night, through the air, between the stones, out of our graves.

Then they stopped, stilled.

Turned.

The back door opened, and Josh stepped out onto the porch.

There are stories, of course, about the transformative power of love. Almost as many of these as there are ghost stories. About how if you hold on as your lover turns into a swan, and then a snake, and then a burning-hot brand, you will save him. With belief, you can steal your lover back from the very gates of hell. With belief, you can save your lover from whatever dire fate the story dangles over his head.

The stories, the ones that tell you this, they all make the same mistake: they assume that every story is a love story.

I don't know if he saw the ghosts. I know he saw me.

He tried to run.

I tore, my fingers like knives, like claws. Rent and howled with my sisters, with the storm. Felt bones break and tissue give. Tasted blood, thicker and richer than wine.

I heard him, over the storm. Telling me to stop. Telling me he was sorry. Telling me things would be different. After a while, begging. Then, just noise.

We took him to pieces.

After, I lay on the cool, wet ground, my bones falling through it to rest, to sleep, the gravestone even now rising above my head.

The dream of a ghost, wrapped in the earth.

Murdered Sleep

K ora had heard the rumors. They were everywhere
that fall, blown on the wind along with the golden
fans of fallen ginkgo leaves. Everyone claimed to
know someone who had been invited, though Kora spoke to
no one who had attended. People told stories of masks and
decadence, of a play that might have been a bacchanalia, of
something that wasn't a play at all, but rather an enfleshed
dream masquerading as a drama. Of impossibility made concrete and stone in the condemned hallways of an abandoned
building.

The invitation arrived with the rest of Tuesday's post,
unstamped and unmarked. Heavy black stock, printed in silver gilt, and sealed with bordeaux wax. Impressed upon the
surface of the wax was a pomegranate, split, seeds spilling
like blood.

Kora's hand trembled only slightly as she broke the seal.

There were three lines written on the inside of the card. An address. There was no need to print a time: midnight was ever the hour of the impossible.

Sleep is dying, and has been for a long time now, through uncounted ticks of clocks and the flickers of thousands of too-brief candles. Sleep is dying, a slow exsanguination of dreams, a storm-tossed suffocation of nightmares. Sleep is dying, and she is not alone in her throes.

The building looked like nothing from the outside. Or rather, it looked like the kind of place where the latest victim in some murder-of-the-week show would be found, the building's state of destroyed decay a metaphor for her own. Kora picked her way over trails of broken glass, amber-brown and snake-green, and climbed stairs that canted out from the rusting iron doors at an Escheresque angle.

The doors groaned open as she reached their threshold. Kora glanced around, looking for CCTV units, and decided that whoever had installed the system had done an excellent job hiding them.

The designer also had a fondness for Cocteau, Kora thought as she stepped into the entryway. It was mostly dark, lit only by torches in fixtures made to resemble white-gloved hands. The doors echoed shut behind her.

As one, the torches shifted, lighting Kora into a hallway.

She followed them, nerves making her blood fizz and her steps come fast and short. At the end of the hallway was an outstretched pair of white-gloved hands. The one on the right curled and beckoned, then opened flat.

Kora stood, puzzled. The hand repeated the gesture. Kora removed the invitation from her beaded purse and placed it on the hand. The hand snapped shut, then flung open, empty. On the previously empty palm of the left hand was a deck of cards. They looked like plain Bicycle playing cards, but when Kora picked the top card from the deck, it was the Lovers, reversed. The card was from the Marseille deck, the young man pinned by the gazes of the two women he was to choose between as much as by Love's arrow in his chest.

The left hand snapped shut, disappearing the deck. Kora tucked the tarot card into her purse, a replacement weight for the surrendered invitation.

The right hand offered itself to her, and when she took it, it became the handle of a door that opened before her. The room she stepped into was full of masks.

They hung on the walls in beautiful chaos, in every imaginable variety. There were plain strips of fabric, glittery half masks balanced on thin rods, and layers of leather curled and pressed into shapes from the sublime to the grotesque.

Kora selected a Venetian mask of tarnished silver, filigree wings at the temples. It tied with ribbon the violet-red of the seeds at the heart of a pomegranate, and settled onto her skin as if it had been made for her alone.

Mask in place, Kora walked back through the door she had entered by, and into a new part of the building. Her heels were sharp against the warped wood of the floor, purposeful cracks swept up by the dragging hem of her skirt.

There were doors along the hallway. Some shut, some cracked open, some gaping like mouths. Kora heard fragmented conversations, and the tingling jauntiness of a circus organ. Ice-blue light burned beneath one door, and her fingers ached from cold when she placed them on the handle.

A laughing woman ran out of one room, and she threw a smile over her shoulder as she ran. Three figures in masks and capes ran after her, racketing down the stairs. Kora followed at a more sedate pace, letting the character of the building sink into her skin.

As she walked, Kora caught a hint of some wonderful fragrance, burnt caramel perhaps, or the dark clouds at the heart of a storm. It curled through the air, invitation and seduction both. She followed the scent instead of the people, passing down a second flight of stairs, and then a third.

Kora stepped through dust and cobweb, and past heavy velvet curtains, and into the extraordinary.

Dancers spun by, no darkling throng, but color and light and texture glittering in kaleidoscope. Flames flickered in the air, without even candles beneath them. The air was scent and sound, and Kora barely had time to breathe it in before she was pulled into it.

She stepped, stepped, stepped, her feet skipping in a mad waltz. Her partner's mask was horned like a stag, and it seemed for a moment that Kora heard the baying of distant hounds somewhere beneath the music as they danced.

And then there was only the dance.

As she became accustomed to the hectic pace, Kora was able to see the wonders she had fallen into.

One of the walls was a celestial map, and the stars and planets moved across it in stately progression. In the center of the room was a fountain, bubbling with a liquid the pale green of perfect porcelain. When Kora came closer to it, she could smell the sunburned darkness of butterflies.

At the head of the room was a banquet table. Upon it, a pastry burst into flame, and from the flame arose a phoenix, which circled the room, dropping rubies in its wake.

"It's like the inside of a dream," said Kora.

"It is made of dreams," said the man she was dancing with. "Sleep's abandoned children, all gathered home and called to their revels."

Kora and her partner continued to dance. Other dancers were unpartnered, or gathered into ecstatic knots, but no one walked, and none remained unmoving. It seemed, as they crossed over a mosaic floor, past a woman with owl's wings whose mask was made of flowers, that the room had grown larger.

Vines crawled over a wall, and they were thorned about with roses, the air near them thick with the scent of raspberry jam. Kora thought she saw a snake coil its way through them, poison-green and hissing, and she shuddered.

"How long have you been here?" Kora asked.

"Have you seen clocks or shadows in this place? Or any other devices used to capture time, and parcel it out in captive bits? Time is only breath and heartbeat, only now, only tomorrow and tomorrow and tomorrow."

Kora wondered then how long it was that she had been there, masked and dancing, but then snails, delicate and jeweled, fell from the ceiling like rain, and she decided it did not matter.

And so she danced from partner to partner, from mask to mask. She gazed upon the Medusa and did not turn to unfeeling stone. She spun in the arms of a woman whose mask was a living butterfly, its acid-green and black wings gently opening and closing on her face. She watched as the liquid in the fountain turned to poetry, and calligraphed sonnets and cinquains unfurled from it.

She had dreamt something similar once, ink running like water from a fountain, drying in splashes of iambic fragments.

The music stopped, and with it the call to dance. Kora

reached behind her head, to check the ties on her mask. They were gone, though filigree wings still curled up past her temples.

Kora looked around the room and could no longer see the door through which she had entered.

She had followed all the rules. She had neither eaten nor drunk. She had spoken no promises, no insults, no prophecies.

"To stay is not a trap, but a choice. Will you choose to remain?" The horned man. Kora could see now that his was not a mask. That the horns climbed from his head without artifice.

"I am supposed to say no." Her hand traced the wings of her mask. "To lie, and cast aside my wings. To weep for lost mundanity, mourn my ordinariness, and beg you to send me home, back to broken glass and shit-smeared streets.

"To walk from here, into the harsh light of the ordinary, and never once look back.

"Are there any who actually do?"

"Most. The comforts of known life are powerful."

"I have never found them so," Kora said. She took the tarot card, the lover pierced by the arrow of choice, from the beaded bag still dangling from her wrist and handed it to him. "I choose to remain."

At the height of dreams, a clock rang out.

· · ·

Sleep is dying. This is no longer secret. Nights full of twitches and wakefulness fall like curses upon unslept beds. Night's hours stretch into fire-eyed forever. Somnambulists pace, and pace, and pace.

Kora danced again in the arms of the horned man. In the air above them hung an unseen orchestra. Passion sobbed from the strings of violin and cello, and drums counted the time between steps, between heartbeats, but no musicians could be seen.

So close to her partner, Kora could smell the deep green fragrance of forests, the pleasant rot of leaf mold and loam, and the vague musk of some great furred beast. Again, in counterpoint or descant, she heard the baying of hounds.

Then the music fouled, shattered, stopped.

A man lay on the floor. A tidy figure, in neat black velvet, dark hair a disarray of curls. His mask, sly and vulpine, had cracked down the center. A snake curled, green and jewel-like, in the empty socket of his eye.

Kora felt the floor beneath her sway, as if the building stood on fault lines shifting sideways from each other. The other dancers in the room were turning away, deliberately cutting the fallen figure from their line of vision. A scream tore the air, and the phoenix burst, once more, into flame.

Beneath the burning feathers, the body on the floor did so as well.

. . .

After the flames died, only the mask was left. The face of a fox, cracked in half, the ribbons that had held it on the dead man's head still knotted.

"Will you help me?" the horned man asked.

"How?"

"I need to take the mask outside, into the air, so that it might speak. But if I touch it, I cannot be certain of its answers—I am too close to require truth."

Kora's hand reached out, fluttered, paused. "Will I need to wear it?"

"No." He sounded sickened by the idea. "No. Such a thing would be abomination, like dressing yourself in someone's skin without asking them first.

"No, it will serve for you to carry it."

"Then I will help." Kora knelt down and gathered up the pieces of the mask.

They passed through the door and into the night sky. A night sky stranger and more star-filled than Kora had ever seen, in her city full of buildings and lights. The waxing moon seemed close enough to touch, if one were brave enough to risk the silver pinpricks of the stars that thorned around it.

Some other time, when she did not carry such a burden in her hands, Kora would have liked to stop. To look at what other wonders might be in the small pool where a ghost-white octopus roiled, to revel in the sharp scent of rosemary and lemon thyme that rose from beneath her feet as she walked, to stroke the leonine flanks of the sleeping gryphon. Those things would wait for some other when.

She had not known the man who had chosen for himself the face of a fox, but she owed him, she thought, the respect of her attention. In the midst of such overwhelming presence, she would mark his absence, and she would not look away.

The mask in her hands shuddered and strained, and the rent edges slipped over and under each other, until the mask was again whole. The strings unknotted, and coiled tight, tight, tight around her wrists. Kora's hands grew heavy and numb, but not before she felt blood drip through the lines of her palms to fall on the ground.

Carnelian starfish bloomed where the drops landed.

"I think, if you were to ask your questions now, it would answer," Kora said.

The man in the horned mask looked at Kora, and held silence long enough that five more starfish grew at her feet. His shadow behind him, a darker spot on the nap of the velvet sky, was first a stag, and then a cauldron, but never the shape of a man.

Something greener than envy hissed and slithered in the darkness.

When the questions were asked, they were not the ones Kora had been expecting.

"Did you choose the mask for yourself?"

The mask took on weight in her hands, and Kora felt her heart go four-legged and furred, felt the glory of a hunt through sun-dappled forest, tasted the salt-copper brightness of blood in her mouth.

"I did."

The dead man's voice was a pleasant tenor, with the trained elasticity of a singer or actor. And though it was not her speaking, his words ravaged Kora's throat, filling it with cinders and smoke.

"Were there any who sought to influence your choice?"

"I was swayed by nothing other than the memory of my lady, a fair vestal throned in the east, and the burning glory of her hair."

"Did you tell the cards for yourself, before entering?"

"The Ace of Cups, reversed. I read my own destruction, carried it in my hand."

As he finished speaking, the mask rent itself once more, and the two halves tumbled from Kora's hands. Its strings unwound from her wrists, and the pieces of the mask drifted to the ground, soft on the fragrant air, Goldengrove unleaving.

There was a crack at her feet. The octopus, bone-white, had devoured the last of the carnelian starfish.

Kora knelt and watched as the flesh of the octopus, lachrymal-sheened and opalescent, turned blush, then rose, then heart's-blood red. It crawled, suction cups like cold kisses on her skin, over her hand and braceleted itself around her wrist, color flooding and drowning from its surface in syncopation with her pulse.

Once again, the air trembled as the cry of a clock rang through it.

Even eternal places change.

"Drink this. It will help the pain." The horned man handed Kora a cup, full of a pale-gold liquid. It smelled of apricots and summer meadows, and when she drank, it was thick like honey, cool and fresh like the first snow of winter. When the last drops—three, two, one—fell upon her tongue, the ashes and smoke disappeared from her mouth, and her own voice returned.

"He is dead because he chose a card and a mask." Her thoughts trembled around her own card and mask, chosen not for remembrance, but for the sake of choice, for the desire for wings.

"No, he is dead because he was murdered, cracked open so that his dreams might spill out and populate the air.

"I asked for his card and his mask because they were the reason he came, and who he was when he was here. His dreams of himself deserved to be remembered, to be spoken, to be known to all the ghosts of this place."

The belling of the hounds was louder this time, a wild howling that raised the hairs on Kora's arms and coursed adrenaline through her muscles. The wind, which caught her hair in greedy fingers and tied it into one thousand and one lover's knots, was full of souls.

Sleep is dying, and does not want to be. So sleep steals here and there, from wreck and ruin, from blood and dream. Small pieces, never missed.

Until they are.

Every paradise has a serpent.

The octopus, again ghost-white, had taken up residence in Kora's hair, wrapping the strands around itself like sea wrack. It seemed content to perch there as Kora danced her way through the strange party that had become her life, never-ending and sleepless.

The woman that she danced with wore the mask of a white hound, with ears red and wet with blood. As they danced, the woman's eyes shaded from a warm brown to a bright poison-green.

Serpent green.

The woman's mask trembled, and her feet faltered in the dance.

Kora reached up and held the woman's head in her

hands, fingers pressed against the mask. Fur prickled beneath them, and the urge to chase, to hunt, quivered against Kora's skin.

The phoenix rose, burning, and Kora heard, as if from some great distance, the belling of the hounds.

The hiss of a serpent.

The strings of the woman's mask untied from her head and wound themselves around Kora's hands, and still she held the mask to the woman's face. She could smell the forest, fecund and dark, and could hear the inexorable chime of a clock. A small green snake, whip-quick, slithered over her foot. Poison-green, like the snake coiled in a dead man's eye. Kora stepped, once, twice, and crushed its skull.

The woman sank to the ground. There was no body where she fell. Instead, a white hound with ears of blood red, the incarnation of the mask that dangled from Kora's hands. Not dead, but translated.

And then the room was full of the howling of the hounds of hell, the red-eared Gabriel Ratchets, full too of the souls they carried. One more joined their number as they harried the steps of the masked dancers. In the center of the room, the horned man, the phoenix mantled on his shoulder, the hunt wild around him. He met Kora's eyes and bowed.

Even eternal places change.

· · ·

Kora wrote in ink that matched the pale luminescence of the octopus braceleting her wrist. Three lines. An address. She slipped the card into an envelope sealed with bordeaux wax, the phoenix in flame impressed upon it.

Dreamers were everywhere that fall.

The Speaking Bone

The island itself was made from bones.

There was a church, in another land, similarly constructed. The decayed flesh of the saints slipped from its underlying architecture, the white bones, sacred and incorruptible, incarnating the holy place. But the Sedlec Ossuary had been built. Hands that would become bones themselves set the pieces in place. Divinely inspired, but a mortal work.

The island had made itself.

It began, as these things do, with a woman, and a man. An unanswered question, and a death by water.

It began with the shipwrecked and the lost. Their bones were whited of excess flesh by the small and skittering denizens of the sea. The shapes were purified, rendered down to their essence, and then coral-encrusted, decorated with the care a medieval artisan would have lavished on a reliquary.

The first bone to break the surface was the iliac crest of a suicide. As the surf foamed over it, a tempest broke from the heavens.

The island grew quickly then.

From the time of its birth, there were always three women who dwelt upon the island.

Thin and wraithlike, barely enough flesh to cover their own bones, very nearly ghosts. All had long, tangled hair, woven with sea wrack, and though they were never old, their hair was white, white as bone.

If you were to ask one of these votaresses of the bones how she came to the island, she would not speak. If you were fortunate, she might smile and place a scaphoid or a hamate in your palm. Worn smooth by wind, polished by the sea, the bone would be the only answer your question required.

There were those who asked. There were always those who asked.

Most who did were satisfied by the small weight of some-one else's death pressed into their hand. The island held its secrets close. This was known and had always been.

But there were those who arrived in search of secrets of their own, who came to the island to divine runes, to read entrails, to throw the bones.

They arrived by casting themselves upon the shore, with the other flotsam and jetsam carried on the tide. They made pilgrimage from the edge of the salt-tear sea. Over bones whiter than cloud, whiter than page, whiter than death, they walked. Past bones lachrymal and parietal they quested.

Then, of a sudden, they would begin to collect: phalanges, proximal and distal. Scapula, calcaneus, and hyoid. The pilgrims would gather bones until they could articulate a complete skeleton of disparate parts.

The bone-priestesses would not hinder the gathering, but neither would they assist. They stood witness. They anticipated the miracle.

The pilgrims would take care not to choose bones that had known one another in life. Even malleus, incus, and stapes must never have heard the same sound. Otherwise, it risked the oracle speaking in a singular voice, and who consults an oracle in the hope of hearing sense?

The pilgrims could not eat while making their collections, for nothing living could grow in a field of bones, and as their flesh evaporated, they became like skeletons themselves, animate only by blood and questions.

When all the bones had been found, the quest completed, the pilgrim would speak a question to the wind. In many cases, this was even the question she had come to the island to have answered. When the last echoes had vanished to the air, the pilgrim would lie down on top of the collected skeleton, with grace and care, so as not to disturb the bones so carefully assembled.

There, she would wait.

In most cases, the skeleton never spoke. The pilgrim would lie in the calcified embrace of the lover she had labored to create, and thin, until a second set of bones fell to intermingle with the first.

Sometimes, so rarely it seemed as if this were a thing more impossible than the island itself, the bones chose to answer.

When the bones spoke, it was with the voice of the island. The very place convulsed as the answer was given.

The bones spoke only at dawn, when the newly born sun streaked the sky and water with its red-gold palette, mingling blood with ambrosia on the canvas. The voices of the three women who lived on the island at its beginning, now, and ever after, would rise in a song of transformation and mourning. Thus was the miracle marked and encouraged into being.

The song would continue until the pilgrim screamed. Once: the keening of a storm-tossed gull. Answers, true answers, like miracles, come at a cost.

The three women, the sisters of the bone, too sharp to be graces and surely too kind to be fates, would bend to lift the pilgrim off her skeletal lover.

One bone would be removed from the pile. It would be covered over in writing: ink dark as blood, dark as night, dark as truth. The words there written would spell out the answer to the question that had been whispered on the wind.

This bone, it should be noted, was not from the collected skeleton. It was from the pilgrim.

The bones were exchanged, one for the other, question for answer. The body of the pilgrim reshaped around the speaking bone, much the same as her life would reshape itself around the answer inscribed upon its twin.

The three sisters would guide the pilgrim to an ossuary at the center of the island, where she would remain for three days—yes, ever and always, three has been the proper length of time for resurrections—while she meditated upon her miracle. While her blood bathed the bone—lunate, perhaps, or sacrum—that had translated itself beneath her skin.

At sunset on the third day, the pilgrim would place the bone that had been hers, the one now scrimshawed over with knowledge, into the walls of the ossuary. She would be met at the door by one of the bone sisters. "Return," the bone woman would tell her, and kiss her once on each eyelid, so the path might be seen.

The next of the three would meet her at the place where the pilgrim had lain in communion with her bones. "Return," she would say, and kiss the pilgrim once on the breast, so the heart might remember. The last of the three would meet the pilgrim where the sea wept upon the shore. "Return," she would say, and kiss her once upon the mouth, so that nothing that had passed there might be spoken of.

Then the pilgrim would cast herself upon the waves, to

be borne back to the land less strange, where she had formerly lived.

In time, in days, or months, or decades, the bones of the pilgrim would return to the island. They would be reverently collected, examined, spread beneath the wind and sky. The mirror bone to the one that had been placed into the ossuary would be removed and reunited with its twin. Question with answer, speech resolved into silence.

The remainder of the skeleton—no longer pilgrim now, but saint—would be scattered across the island, the architecture of future miracles, to whisper answers to those brave enough to ask.

Those Are Pearls

E laine broke her curse like a mirror, heedless of the shards that scattered across the floor. The guests at the party laughed, applauded, whooped with delight at her reckless abandon. She offered them an exaggerated curtsy, holding the pose as she held their eyes, reveling in their gaze, in the simple pleasure of being seen.

The broken pieces of the curse slid into liquid, shimmering like mercury before fogging into smoke and disappearing. A minor curse, to be gotten rid of so easily. Nothing that had grown thorns and teeth. Nothing that had developed a craving for breath or blood.

Color high in her cheeks, Elaine plucked a glass of champagne from a passing server and drank. Her laughter was as bright and sharp as the bubbles, as sparkling as the crowd that surrounded her, all of them here to celebrate her freedom.

Her guests traded stories as they drank and danced, reminiscing about their own curses—"Ah, yes, sleeping does tend to run in families; certainly it is painful for words to turn to diamonds in your mouth, but when it was over, I had them made into this tiara"—and the breaking of them. They marked their relief at being past such things with every clink of glass upon glass.

They would drink until their memories were replaced with a shining haze. Until their own curses were nothing more than half-remembered shadows, until they could look at their tiaras without remembering the taste of blood and saliva as the diamonds fell from their lips.

Glass in hand, I left the too-bright room, the aggressive celebration. Happy as I was for my sister, that room wasn't mine.

Curses can be lingering things.

My own curse had been silence. It's common enough, particularly for girls. We're so often encouraged not to speak, and that practiced quiet makes it easy for a curse to steal our voices.

Because silence was one of the traditional curses, there was already a plethora of known ways to break it: I could weave or sew a certain number of shirts out of some material rough enough to cut my hands and stain the fabric with my blood, all without weeping. I could endure a loveless relationship for a year and a day. I could perform some tremendously useless task: find one mis-sorted seed in a barrel of its near-identical cousins and nurse the plant to flowering, my voice to return with its blooming.

There were traditions. Established guidelines. The curse fell, you purchased the way of breaking it, you moved on. That was what was done. Expected. Traditional.

Safe.

And in that safety, the seeds of the second curse. To have a voice only when it is given, only after asking nicely, following the rules. So I had decided to break my curse myself.

It wasn't the done thing, but it wasn't impossible. I could afford to be eccentric, and people don't mind a curiosity, so long as she's quiet about it.

"I don't know why you were worried that something would go wrong." Elaine stood in front of her mirror and rubbed at her eyes, smudging the memories of the party into her faded eyeliner.

"Curses aren't always easy to see in their true form. They lie and twist things around, and if you don't break them fully, you might not notice what's left until it's too late."

"You worry too much, Rose." She brushed her lips against my cheek, then yawned so hugely I heard her jaw crack. "Good night."

• • •

I worried just the right amount.

You'll see them sometimes, people with pieces of their curses still clinging to them. Half-transformed into birds—taloned feet, and feathers instead of hair—or with snakes slithering through their teeth along with their words. And then it gets worse, until there is nothing left but a sad-eyed bird that doesn't quite understand wings, a knot of serpents, a pool of silence in the shape of a girl.

Curses, if not properly broken, put roots into your blood and bones until you are nothing but a garden of misfortunes.

Elaine acted as if she'd never been cursed. That's tradition too. When it's over, there's no need to look back.

But in the days after the party, mirrors began to appear. Logical places at first—windows silvered over and offered reflection rather than transparency. Puddles became glass underfoot.

"There's something different, though," Elaine said, looking from our images in the shop window to the passing street behind us. "Look."

I stopped and stood next to her. Sister dark and sister fair. She was right. The reflected colors of her clothing were wrong, faded somehow. She wore an eye-catching blaze of red, but it looked barely pink, and she was nearly transparent.

"So strange," she said. "I'm almost gone, but you look the

212

same. Maybe it's just the angle." Elaine smiled at her reflection and kept walking.

I looked at the mirror slantwise, my gaze unfocused, searching for the haze of a curse. Nothing. But as I turned away, the glass seemed to alter, to shimmer like liquid, like mercury. I froze, then shook my head. Only a window again.

Most people only ever notice the manifestation of the curse. You know that your sister has fallen into an unwakeable sleep, that your brother speaks only truth, no matter how brutal, and those things are enough.

But each curse has a shape.

This is what a curse looks like: a necklace of thorns, bright against a throat, sharp enough to open a vein.

To break it, you see that the curse is water, and you drink it deep.

Or a curse may look like a vine of ivy, lush and green, roots almost unseen but hooked like claws beneath the skin.

You make yourself salt and ashes, inhospitable ground.

A curse may bind you, like a gag of shadows.

And your words are knives, cutting through.

All at once the mirrors, like curses, were broken. They did not return to what they had been before, windows and water and other, more usual things, just sat cracked in their stolen frames.

"It's creepy, seeing yourself in pieces like that," Elaine

said, gaze averted from her shattered reflection. "Someone should clean this up."

I reached a hand out, wanting one of the fractioned pieces of glass, then yanked it back, hissing. "It's sharp. Like teeth." Drops of blood welled on my finger. "Maybe that's why no one has cleaned them up."

"Ugh." Elaine shuddered. "I like them even less now."

The sensation of the mirror's teeth reaching for me lingered. I didn't like them at all.

When a curse is broken, nothing of it remains. It's swept away with the faded party decorations, poured out with the flat champagne.

The parties where we celebrated their breaking were the only places we spoke about the curses, after. Safe, light phrases. It was tradition not to speak seriously about them, no matter what the curse was. To ask someone what it was like to be shifted out of their shape every full moon, to be winged and feathered, to be unseen.

To tell anyone what it felt like to be strangled by your own words. To drown on unspoken poetry filling your lungs. To taste every silenced hello and goodbye like grit on your tongue.

All gone. Except for the memory.

Most people will not see you if you cannot speak. When I was cursed, I was ignored, shoved aside, treated as if I didn't exist.

Elaine made a point of carrying paper, so I could still talk to her, after a fashion. She asked me questions, as if expecting an answer. She said hello when she saw me. She said "I love you."

My curse breaking was the sound of locks flinging open. It was shadows falling away and ropes unraveling.

I wrote down all the things I would have said. Every word, every shout, every hesitation. I unsilenced myself, writing each unspoken thing over and over until the pages were covered in my unheard voice.

I lit the pages on fire, giving my words air the only way I could.

And I spoke.

My voice was a rusted hinge, so quiet I thought for a moment that I had done something wrong, that instead of breaking the curse, I had bound myself in it forever. My heart clenched around the thought that I could have been safe, that I should have asked nicely. There were reasons for the traditions, and I was no better than anyone who had followed them. I should have known.

Then I realized the weeping, howling animal sounds I heard were my own.

"I think something went wrong," Elaine said.

"Wrong how?"

"With my curse."

Elaine's curse had been invisibility. Again, a common

one, with well-established traditions. Quests were the usual thing in this circumstance—finding someone to fall in love with her, or to speak to her achievements rather than her physical beauty. Instead, she captured her reflection in a mirror and then shattered it.

She held the sliver of glass out to me. "When I broke it, it didn't all disappear."

"This is the original curse?" I asked. "From weeks ago?"

She nodded.

I took the glass from her. It was cool, like water in my hand, a blur across its surface as if some part of Elaine's reflection still colored it. "Why didn't you say anything before?"

"I didn't want to give it up. Being invisible. Not all the way. I wanted there to be times when I could just walk around, just exist, and not have to be looked at. I thought if I kept part of it, if I just let a little of it stay, it wouldn't be a curse anymore, and that could happen." She closed her eyes. "Stupid, I know."

"Why show me now? If you've had that piece of it the whole time, why decide now that something is wrong?"

"Look at yourself in the glass."

"Elaine, I am not using a curse to check my reflection."

"Pick another mirror, then. Any of them."

I stood before the mirror in the corner of my room. I could see everything in it. Except for my sister, and myself.

. . .

There are rituals. Traditions. A curse, once broken, breaks easier a second time. Death becomes one hundred years of sleep, becomes one thousand and one nights telling stories. We know what our curses are when we see them, and we know their undoing.

But there is a catch. We may know how to break curses, but they knew how to bind us in the first place.

It wasn't just our mirrors that were affected, but all of them, everywhere. No matter who gazed into them, no reflection showed. It was as if everyone had turned invisible.

"I hate it," Elaine said. "I look in the mirror and it's as if I'm a ghost in my own house. And the worst part of it is, everyone looks at me now. They know the mirrors are my fault because they know what my curse looked like, and so they stare. They don't even pretend not to. I can't be seen when I want to be, and still, no one will stop looking.

"I wish they knew what it felt like, to always be stared at."

After I learned how to see my own curse, I discovered that I could see other people's too. It wasn't difficult—once you know that something is there, know the way you need to look to make it visible, it's more effort to ignore it. Seeing the curses, understanding them, had the same sort of pleasure as fitting pieces into a puzzle. I liked the small click.

And what I could see, I could break.

It didn't take long after I broke my own curse for word to get out, for people to come to me for ways of undoing when their own curses fell. My methods were of interest at parties, and besides, it was easier to listen to me explain how to slip off shoes of red-hot iron than to walk until they were worn through.

I had seen Elaine's curse too. Tiny mirrors, strung together like bracelets and a necklace, a matching set, reflecting only her face. I would have unstrung them carefully, one by one, rather than smashing them to pieces—bad luck to break a mirror.

But she wanted to break the curse herself, and who was I to judge her for that? I loved my sister, so I did not tell her to be safe and to hope for good luck.

The piece of her curse was missing from my room. I went looking for Elaine to see if she had taken it back, to try to undo that final tiny bit herself.

She was looking out her window, a window that was transparent, as expected. Across the wall, the edge of her— shoulder and elbow and thick curls of hair—reflected in her mirror.

"Elaine?"

She turned to me, and I saw myself, perfectly reflected in the mirrors of her eyes.

. . .

This is what it means to break your own curse. It means knowing what the curse is. Not how it manifests, not why it fell upon you and not upon some other, not what people say it means, that such a curse has chosen you. It means seeing it truly, recognizing the truth at its red and bloody heart.

And so it means knowing your own red and bloody heart as well.

I repeated her name and closed my eyes. Seeing myself looking back instead of Elaine looking out was an ache.

"You worry too much, Rose," she said. "I'm fine."

"How?"

"It's not a curse. Look."

It took an effort to open my eyes to meet the mirrors of hers, to confront myself, reflected back. I stepped closer, looked sideways, walked around my sister while she stood perfectly calm.

No hook, no thorns, no sharp edges or claws. No trace of the curse that the transformation had come from.

"They can look all they want now. All they'll see is themselves."

She looked, I thought, happy. I closed my eyes again so hers wouldn't reflect my tears.

We don't talk about how the curses happen. We grow up knowing that certain curses run in families, that boys get cursed into monstrosity and girls into sleep, and we leave it at that. It is easier to imagine that our curses simply fall on us like shadows, inevitable at certain times, rather than to acknowledge the unseen truth: someone, somewhere, sets them in motion.

If you know the heart of a curse, you can break it. If you know the heart of a person, you can give them a curse that thinks it's a blessing.

We don't talk about the memories, and we imagine that silence is the final act in the curse's disappearance. In our hearts, we know that's not true. There is always something left.

I hugged my sister hard. In my finger, tiny slivers of a mirror, like small biting teeth, pressed against the inside of my skin.

All of Our Past Places

Aoife always told me that you could go anywhere, as long as you had the right map. So when it happened, my first thought, when I let myself into her apartment after not hearing from her for three days, was this weird feeling of pride. She'd done it. She was gone.

Then the fullness of what had happened hit me: she was gone.

I checked, and checked again.

Her apartment was nearly empty. The refrigerator had a couple of cartons of takeaway, whose contents ranged from edible to Dear God, and cream for her coffee. The usual.

And then there were her maps, covering almost every flat surface in the place. The ones she had collected, the ones she was sure were the way there.

All the maps that had St. Patrick's Purgatory marked on them had been unrolled, tacked flat, arranged one on top of the other. I was sure there was a reason for their order and that I would have understood it if I were Aoife. Whatever the reason was, though, without her I couldn't parse it. What I could see was that, on each of the maps, St. Patrick's Purgatory was gone. In its place, a small hole with burnt edges.

With the maps arranged as they were, the burned-out places were all exactly the same, as if a fire had caught, right there, and then been immediately extinguished.

I yanked my hands away, stepped back from the table, and reminded myself that I was being ridiculous. People didn't go to purgatory, or if they did, it was after they were dead. If they went to St. Patrick's Purgatory, that blip on the map of Lough Derg, in Ireland, it was by taking a ferry to Station Island. They didn't go by disappearing into a map, like some faux-charming "This is how our story begins" cold open from a crappy animated movie.

Except. Aoife was gone. And there was a hole in each map in the place where St. Patrick's Purgatory had been.

The thing, of course, that's supposed to happen in a situation like this is that you follow the other person to the underworld. You bring them back. I mean, I'd been around Aoife long enough to be familiar with the stories. I knew the rules. Someone went to the underworld, someone else came to get them, and then things didn't work out. The end.

Still, as far as underworlds and afterlives went, purgatory was a little different. The writers who'd claimed they'd been had also usually claimed that God had sent them back to tell the story.

Let's be honest. I had no idea what sort of framework I was operating in here, but waiting around and relying on God to zap Aoife back home so she could write about her purgatorial experiences in verse as if she were Dante wasn't a plan I could get behind.

If there was going to be a way out of this mess, the maps would be the key. That was how things worked: if you wanted to get somewhere, you needed a map. The only problem with that was, whatever Aoife had done had erased St. Patrick's Purgatory from them.

Places disappear from maps all the time. Maps from today will not include Czechoslovakia, East Germany, or the free, independent Republic of West Florida. There are reasons for these disappearances: places choose new names, wars are fought, peace is won. It sounds simple, but it isn't. We say the borders of countries are just lines on a map, but places run deeper in us than that.

When Aoife and I were in high school, the boundaries of Prussia had been an ongoing joke in our AP European History class. Constantly altered by reasons of conflict and history, they seemed to have been redrawn on a whim, traced one way and then the next with the specific intent of frustrating us, all those years later.

We never gave any thought to the people in those redrawn boundaries. We never asked ourselves what happened when a country was literally erased from the map.

We met because of a map, Aoife and I. When we were kids, Aoife would make what she called atlases. It's as good a word as any for them, I guess. She would take maps, any kind she could get her hands on—the kind you buy on impossible-to-fold paper at the gas station, or the blue-edged chunks of appendixes at the backs of social studies books, or, once, the surface of a globe, peeled and laid flat—and she would cut them into pieces and tape them back together.

They were impossible to use if you were actually trying to get somewhere. The last time I checked, Mordor had no contiguous boundaries with Bismarck, North Dakota.

She'd walk around the neighborhood with them, a cartographer examining her work. One day, she was standing at the bottom of my driveway, pencil in hand, making notes.

"What are you doing?" I asked.

"Checking locations," she said, looking from the plum tree in the yard back to her map and nodding.

"Why?"

"So the map will be right. So I can go."

"Go where?"

"Wherever I want. Somewhere else."

"Can I come with you?"

She looked at me, very seriously. I fidgeted under her scrutiny, raising one foot up to scratch at a mosquito bite behind the other knee.

"Okay," she said finally. "I'm Aoife."

"I'm Miren."

After that, we went everywhere together. Until she went to purgatory.

So I would need a map. A map to go to purgatory, to get Aoife back. I left her pile of maps untouched, afraid that if I moved them, it might close whatever door it was she had opened.

I went back to the beginning, to the maps Aoife had made when we were kids. Her atlases. They were carefully folded and stored inside a cedar chest that had seventeenth-century shipping routes carved on its lid.

She had never let me help make them, those summers of fourth and fifth and sixth grade. I could go on the adventures, but she always picked the places, always was the one to craft our way there.

I never fought with her about that. Even then, I knew she was the one of us who needed to get away.

I opened the chest to find it packed full of maps, folded one on top of the other. Taped and stapled pages creating countries that never existed. I shook my head at myself, acknowledging the ridiculousness of what I was doing, and began unfolding them.

They smelled like youth and summer. Like dried grass and melted ice pops that turn your tongue neon blue. Like the coconut of sunscreen and the dull plastic scent of Band-Aids. Grains of sand fell from them to the floor, and I found a piece of a crayon wrapper—one of the darker blues—and the orange-and-black wing of a butterfly, still bright.

Mile markers of our summers, of going anywhere but here, of finding all the possible somewhere elses, of always feeling found, as I walked on those impossible quests of Aoife's, even though I never knew from day to day where we were going.

The one place I never walked her to was her house. "It's better if we go to yours, Miren. We need a fixed point, like true north."

I had seen the bruises on her arms, heard my parents talk about Aoife's dad when they thought I wasn't around, so I understood, a bit, why she needed a reason to center the maps somewhere other than her house.

"Plus, I live on Rose Avenue," I said. "Like a compass rose."

"Exactly," Aoife had said, and her smile had bloomed across her face.

I brushed my hand across my eyes so my tears wouldn't fall on the maps and obscure them.

We think about maps like they are a kind of great truth. Like, if you find the right one, then you'll know the one true way to where you're going, and you'll be able to get there safely, on the most direct path. The straight and narrow, that avoids both the woods and the wolves within them.

But as anyone who's ever gotten lost while reading a map, or stopped just short of the lake their GPS was trying to drive them into, knows, it's never quite that simple.

Maps are often made with small, deliberate errors, cartographers watermarking their work. Paper towns and cartographic graffiti. Sometimes the errors persist, and we navigate around someone's imaginary land. Sometimes you just keep going, astounded when you don't run out of road.

Even when she stopped making maps of her own, Aoife never lost interest in them. She was my best friend, so I adopted her obsessions as my own. It was what you did when you were eleven, twelve, and I never grew out of it. I studied cartography. I learned how to draw a compass rose, and the difference between a sidereal rose and the classic twelve-wind rose. I drew them in the pages of my notebooks, increasingly elaborate in their construction, full of symbols for the winds, whose names I wrote out in all the old languages of mapmaking.

I got comfortable with the idea that there were monsters in the margins, and when I turned eighteen, I had "HIC SVNT LEONES" tattooed on the inside of my left wrist: "Here are lions," the words that denoted unknown territories. Aoife went with me, and had "Ultima" written on her left ankle and "Thule" on her right. Another phrase from the edges of maps: "Past the borders of the known world."

Like wherever she was now.

It was the old maps, the ones with things like "HIC SVNT LEONES" on their outermost margins and sea monsters drawn in their oceans, that had started Aoife's obsession with purgatory. There was this map from 1492, by the cartographer Martin Behaim. It was meant to be a map of the entire world. The only thing marked on Ireland was St. Patrick's Purgatory.

Aoife cocked her head and traced her finger over the tiny, mostly unmarked Ireland. "Hmmm," she said. "Why does this place matter so much?"

That started a flurry of searching for other maps, looking for ones that had St. Patrick's Purgatory marked. I waited for this to be a thing like her earlier obsessions, for her to begin making maps that were palimpsests of instructions to the underworld, that sent Inanna walking side by side with Persephone.

"They call it the Forgotten County, you know," Aoife said, bent over a stack of books and papers. "County Donegal. Where St. Patrick's Purgatory is. Parts of it permanently depopulated during the Famine. Whole towns just disappeared from the map. Even today, it only has just over half the population it had when the Famine started."

Lost and disappeared. "Seems like the kind of place where you might find purgatory, then."

There were people who said they had. Old, old stories. Some medieval knight who actually slept in the cave on Station Island, the actual St. Patrick's Purgatory, back when you could still do that. When he woke up, he said he'd had visions of purgatory, before Dante was even born. So it's not like Aoife was the first person to think the place really was a gateway to purgatory.

But I am pretty sure she was the first person to think she could get there through a map.

She scoured the internet for them, bought any map she could that had St. Patrick's Purgatory marked, regardless of provenance or condition. Some were torn and stained, burnt. Some were barely more than fragments. She kept them all.

"How many do you need?" I asked her.

"Enough to have confidence in the boundaries."

"I'm just going to remind you again that for the money you've spent collecting these, you could have bought multiple trips to Ireland." I set a plate of pasta with butter and cheese next to her, hoping she would eat.

"I keep telling you: I'm not trying to get to Ireland. I'm trying to get to purgatory."

It was like walking backward through our childhood, looking through Aoife's maps. Not just in the sense of nostalgia, but in the sense that these maps were our compass rose, illuminating the cardinal directions of our past. I hadn't known, then, what she was making when she put together these atlases, hadn't realized that she was making maps of us.

There was a map made up of all the cities we had said we wanted to live in when we grew up, choosing them only by the sound of their names: Shanghai, Abu Dhabi, Kilkenny. There was another made of some of the countries we wanted to travel to, Prussia in the center because, as Aoife said, no place deserved to disappear forever. Our own city, sliced into pieces and collaged with maps of impossible places—Atlantis and Avalon.

I studied that one carefully, looking for a border in common with purgatory, but no. Only the river Lethe, cut from its banks and spiraled on top, connecting all of them like a thread.

Aoife was still gone.

I marked on the calendar all the days I thought she might come back—feast days and holy days, forty days and forty nights, and other dates from other pilgrimages to the lands of the dead.

"Dead," I said out loud, letting the weight of the word fall flatly against the air in this room full of maps. I said it again: "Dead."

Because of course, it was possible. Possible that she hadn't passed through the maps like a glowing spark, possible that she hadn't gone to purgatory at all, at least not as a living woman, but was somewhere else. A body, not Aoife. Possible that, even if she had gone to purgatory, there was some sort of expiration date on her visit, that when her visa expired, she wouldn't get deported, but instead made like all the other souls there.

I didn't say it a third time.

Cartography, the making of maps, is based on the idea that we can model reality. When it comes to a map, the reality being modeled is usually some kind of physical location.

I looked at the room I sat in, covered with Aoife's maps. Maps that modeled no reality, except the one she wanted them to have, the river Lethe as red thread connecting the pieces. Maps to places she imagined into being. Maps to the places we once were.

A pile of maps, purgatory burnt through, erased from existence. You could go anywhere, so long as you had the right map.

That was what I needed, if I was going to bring Aoife home again.

I left Aoife's for the first time in days, blinking wraithlike against the sun, walking a path of circles through all the places that had been our maps. I gathered take-out flyers from our favorite restaurant, with their delivery ranges hand-scribbled over the dessert list, and folded concert posters from the club we'd sneaked into with bad fake IDs to dance at, directions stamped in the bottom right corner, and an old history text-book from our high school, one that had a map of Prussia in it. Bits and pieces of our reality.

I took them back to Aoife's and got to work. First, I drew the compass rose, sidereal, because the stars were every-where. All thirty-two points—the rising and setting positions of the brightest stars in the Northern Hemisphere, with myself as Polaris in the north and Aoife as Sigma Octantis, the true southern pole star, which is almost impossible to see unaided. Then I cut pieces from all the things I had gathered that afternoon, and all the maps Aoife had made.

I cut the burned-out center from one of Aoife's maps that had shown St. Patrick's Purgatory, a reproduction of Behaim's, the map that had started all of this. A map should reflect reality, and I would use that piece as the blinking "You are here" icon that would help her find her way home.

I fit all the pieces together, taping them tightly, until the borders between one and the next were erased. When it was almost complete, I wrote the words "HIC SVNT LEONES," not at the traditional place on the margin, but over the one place on the map I was unsure of. The center. Purgatory. The last piece I fit in the map was the marker for St. Patrick's Purgatory. I had mended the burned-out spot, made sure that it was no longer missing from the map.

And nothing happened.

I thought it would be enough—finish the magic, bring back Aoife. But nothing.

I closed my eyes tight and clenched my fists until my hands hurt. She was gone. Really gone, and I didn't know how to find her.

Once I felt like I could breathe again, I got up. I folded all Aoife's maps, the atlases, and put them back in the chest. I set my map on top of all her maps of purgatory.

Maybe I would buy a ticket to Ireland, go to Station Island. To a purgatory, even if it wasn't the one where Aoife was, where I could atone for not knowing how to find my lost friend.

It was dark when I walked home, but I knew the way. My parents' home, which I had come back to for the summer between college years. Knew it well enough to walk it half-blinded by tears and exhaustion.

"So hey. Nice map. You ended it at your house, though, not mine. Still our true north, I guess." Her voice was rough—a glitch recording. She stood up from the front step, stumbled, then caught herself on the doorframe. "Thanks for bringing me home."

Aoife.

"How?" I asked.

"Just like the way there. Through the map," she said, hugging me.

Her hair smelled like stale earth, and I could feel the

knobs of her spine. Her hands dug into my arms. "I couldn't find a map. After I got there, after I realized I wanted to go home, I spent the whole time looking. But I couldn't find one. Not until you made it."

I didn't ask, not about anything. Not then. I just held her, held her here, a fixed point in a map of turning stars.

Saints' Tide

When the saint came to the baptism, the entire church went silent. Even the baby, who was only a second before screaming her indignity at the wet, cold process, hiccuped and hushed.

I don't even remember hearing the church door open. Only that sudden silence, and then looking up to see a miracle walking through the church.

The saints don't speak. It's said they can't, that their voices are one of the things the tide takes from them. Maybe they just don't need to speak. It is enough, I suppose, to *be* a miracle. And that, they certainly are. They used to be people, the saints. People we grew up with, who lived here with us. But once they become saints, they look like impossible, not like human. Bones the bleach white of driftwood visible beneath skin that is glass. Lightning-struck sand turned into a person, the translucent softness of sea glass in some places and perfectly clear in others. Salt water rather than blood in their veins. The light shines right through them, blinding. Pearls, which were once eyes. The Saints' Tide takes and the Saints' Tide transforms.

The saint continued their progression toward the baptismal font, toward the child. They walked slowly, taking the tide's own time, then stopped. There was a noise then—a gasp—from my sister, Rinna, the child's mother, as the saint took the baby from her arms and lowered her into the salt water of the baptismal font. Fully. Rinna's face was terrible—torn between her obvious desire to rescue her child, and the knowledge that what was happening was an unasked-for wonder. The baby didn't cry at all, not even when the water closed over her head, and not when she returned into the world of the air. She simply opened her eyes, the holy water beaded on her lashes like glass.

The saint handed her back, nodded once to Rinna, and left.

The Sister of the Tide who was performing the baptism reached for the baby, then dropped her hands back to her sides. "Truly, the ceremony was performed, and I can add nothing to what has been done. Do you have a name for the child?"

"Her name will be Maris," Rinna said, her voice almost steady, "for the sea."

· · ·

In the beginning was the sea. The saints came after.

Word of the saint's visit, of their participation in my niece's
baptism, traveled fast, and it seemed like everyone in town
tried to squeeze themselves into Rinna's small house that day.
It was a miracle, certainly, and one everyone wanted proximity to. A sign—though no real agreement as to what. Perhaps
that Maris would someday be a saint, though that was said in
whispers.

I wished they wouldn't say it. A sacred destiny is a hard
thing to wish upon a child.

But whatever it meant, the saint's participation in Maris'
baptism was a wonder, one large enough that contingents of
both the Sisters of the Tide and the Sisters of Glass stood in
knots on Rinna's front porch. Separate knots, of course—the
Sisters did enjoy their disagreements over the finer points of
doctrine.

No matter what you believe, the saints are inescapable.
They live among us, they walk our streets, they gather at the
edges of the beaches, but there is something in them that
changes when they become saints and not people. Their
past washes off of them—they return smooth-faced and
unrecognizable. After the sea, they don't interact—they
are observers, silent and lovely and strange, but they are
like statues, untouchable signs and symbols, not participants. The fact that this one had broken that distance was

something remarkable and something everyone was talking about.

I nodded and smiled and said hello to more people in the time I spent crossing my sister's living room than I had in the entire month. It was a relief to finally make it into the kitchen.

"How are you doing?" I asked Rinna as I took the sleeping Maris from her arms. She was a small bundle of warmth, her dark hair a silk fuzz. I pressed my cheek to the top of her head.

"I don't even know," she said. "I haven't had time in all this to breathe. A saint baptized my daughter, and all I can think is that Sean Locke ate at least three pieces of honey cake! Three! I'm running out of food because the entire town has come by, there are no clean dishes left in the house, and I still need to make the offering to the tide sometime today."

I laughed. "Sean knows you'd never bake him your honey cake, so he's trying to take advantage while he can. And I can make the offering for you."

"Are you sure you don't mind?" She brushed her hair back from her face and ran water into the dish-filled sink.

"Honestly, I'd rather be out there than in here with all these people."

"No, but I mean—I know that isn't really your sort of thing. It was enough that you came to the baptism."

"It's not the sea I have the problem with," I said. "I promise, I'd be happy to do it."

"Thank you," she said. "The stuff's by the door. I really appreciate it."

"No problem." I tucked Maris into her little baby seat, wrapped the ends of the blanket around her feet so they wouldn't get cold, and kissed her head. Then I grabbed the basket of things Rinna had assembled, and went out to the beach.

The quiet was a relief after the press of people and voices in Rinna's house. It was growing late, the approaching winter bringing on the darkness sooner and sooner each day. The sky was a cauldron of clouds, slate splotches pushed about by the wind. There were streaks on the sand, patterns left by the wind. The air felt thick and heavy, like a storm coming in. My favorite sort of weather.

After I'd walked far enough that the waves broke over the tops of my feet, I stopped. I set the basket on the sand and waited, breathing in and out with the tide until I felt quiet and peace in the rhythm of the waves. Then I made the offering.

"I offer these gifts in thanks for the gift of Maris, and in hope that she may one day be safely returned to the sea," I said. I poured out the jar of seawater Rinna had collected on the day she learned she was pregnant, the source of life held as a promise for the life to come. I scattered salt on the waves, to take bitterness from Maris's days. Finally, I dropped a tiny, clear piece of glass, that the saints might bless her. The waves grabbed it, tumbled it across the sand, and then pulled it under.

A good sign. Rinna would be happy. She'd been religious enough when we were younger that I wouldn't have been surprised if she had chosen to cast herself on the tide, to aspire to sainthood. I was glad she hadn't—I liked my sister here, and speaking. I'd never really understood the holiness in silence. To me, holiness should be a living thing—not a glass example, but something that breathes and feels with you. The sea, not the saints.

Even though the offering was finished, I stood, lingering in the quiet, in the setting sun. The waves swept back and forth over my feet, the tides pulling at the sand beneath them, sending me just enough off-balance to remind me that the sea was not my place. Something smooth bumped against my left ankle. I looked down.

A glass heart.

A saint's heart.

I'm not the sort of person who's used to dealing with miracles.

I didn't take the heart into my sister's house. I knew how she would react—it would terrify her. She'd see all the day's previously good signs as twisted, as bad omens, as things of terror gathered around Maris. The saints go back to the sea one last time when they are ready to end. After that second, final death, they break apart, and their relics occasionally wash up. This heart was a piece of one the sea hadn't kept— nothing soothing in it. I left it on the edge of the sand, then went inside, slipping in the back door so I could avoid any remaining crowd.

"It's all taken care of," I said.

"And the glass?" she asked.

"The waves took it."

Relief softened the lines of her face. "Thank you for doing that. I just want everything to be right for her."

"Of course you do," I said. "So do I."

"The house has cleared out some—most everyone's gone home. Do you want to sit down and have a drink? I think there might even still be some food somewhere."

"No—it felt like a storm was coming in. I want to get home. But before I go—how are you?" She looked drawn. And it had been a day, and probably more of an exhausting one than she had planned for, but she looked thin around the edges.

"I'm fine," she said, and pressed the heel of her hand to her heart. "It's just—everyone kept talking about what this means for Maris. Her future. Her destiny. When she would become a saint herself. She's only little, you know? I want her to have a life first."

Rain hissed and spattered, the first part of the storm. "Anyway, you better go if you don't want to get drenched. Good night."

"Good night." We hugged, and I left. I took the saint's heart with me. I wanted Maris to have a life first too.

The storm roared through the night, the rain falling in sheets, the wind a constant howl. I wondered if Maris slept through it, or if she was keeping Rinna as tired and wakeful as I was.

I kept thinking of the heart. Occasionally fragments of the saints wash back up after their return to the sea. Partial hands and feet are the most common. But never a heart. Or at least I'd never heard of such a thing washing up before. The tide brought many blessings, but this—I wasn't sure what this was.

The storm tapered off just before dawn, but its remnants clung to the morning like sea wrack. I walked through gusts and drizzle, stepped over puddles and downed branches. I passed a clutch of people, stopped to let a saint make their slow way across a street, rain streaking iridescence on its glass skin. I looked as closely as I could but saw no heart beating beneath the shining glass.

Then I walked inside the Convent of the Sisters of Glass.

I hadn't been in the convent in years, but muscle memory is a powerful thing: without even thinking, I dipped my left hand into the basin of seawater just inside the door and traced the sign of the wave over my forehead and my heart. The convent was quiet—the silence held, purposeful.

There relics were displayed in the long hallway that was the public part of the convent. Hands, it seemed, tended to last—there were three, two of which were complete. One foot, the big toe missing. Part of a head. Nothing even remotely like the glass heart I had, wrapped in fabric and tucked into my bag.

Aside from being unlike any of the other pieces here, the heart was in immaculate condition—not a chip, not a scratch. It was as if the heart had been made separately, or perhaps never used, to still be so perfect.

I pressed my hand against my chest.

"Can I help you?" Unlike the Sisters of the Tide, who dress in sea colors—blues and greys and greens—the Sisters of Glass dress in white and silver. They each wear beads of sea glass strung into a circle and wrapped around her wrist. This one wore glass that was all clear, clear as the saint's heart. She was my age, which seemed young for a nun. Usually, women don't choose to care for the saints until after they've had lives of their own. But vocations come when they will, or so I've always been told. She smiled. "My name is Olivia. I'm sorry to disturb you if you wished to keep silence, but you looked a little lost."

"I found something," I said. "I think it might be from a saint."

"What is it you've found?" Her voice low and calm, her expression polite interest.

I looked around. The hallway, people passing through, an older woman praying in a corner, seemed like too public a place for what I had to show. "Here?"

"We stand amongst holy relics."

She had a point.

I pulled the glass heart from my bag and opened the wrappings. Olivia turned fish-belly white, stepped close, and silently re-covered the heart. Her hands still on the fabric, she said, "Perhaps someplace less public would be more appropriate. If you'll come with me?"

She walked in that way that eats the ground while still being graceful enough not to look like hurrying. I followed her down the long hall and into a small room. There were windows open—I could hear the waves crash.

She closed the door behind us. "Let me see the heart again."

I passed it to her.

Her hands shook as she unwrapped it. "Where did you find this?"

"In the sea, last night. It washed up right before the storm came in. I had just finished making the offering to the tide for my niece, and there it was."

"Your niece. There was a saint at her baptism, yes?" The question sounded like an afterthought. All her attention was on the heart in her hands.

"Yes. Do you think that could be related?"

"I wouldn't think so—the saint's appearance at the baptism is a blessing on the child. Did the offering to the tide go smoothly?"

I let pass the fact that the heart's appearance had not been described as a blessing on anyone. "It did—the waves took the glass. Then I stood in the water for . . . a while. I'm not sure how long. Then the heart washed up."

"I won't say they aren't connected—the tide does as it wills. But I believe the heart is a sign for you, not for your niece."

"I'm guessing since we're tucked away in here, it's not a good sign." The weight of it in my hands was as heavy as a secret.

"You are holding someone's preserved and unbroken heart in your hands. What kind of a sign do you think it is?"

It felt like the sort of question that was almost rhetorical, that had an expected call-and-response answer that I was supposed to give regardless of how I actually felt. "I'm holding a saint's glass heart, and whatever it means, I think it's a sign that should have gone to someone else."

"It's natural to feel unworthy of a gift of this nature," she said.

"It's not that I think I'm unworthy," I said. "It's that I don't want it."

I remember the first time I saw a Saints' Tide. They're not common, which is a mercy; it's not the sort of thing that you're likely to forget.

The years it happens, it happens in the late spring—Resurrection Season. That first year, I was ten. I remember the moon was full, and glass had washed ashore, pieces and pieces of it, coating the beach into shining, for three tides. The necessary signs were there: the next low tide would be the Saints' Tide. There was a crackle of excitement in the air, the same sort of electric feeling that comes in before a hurricane.

I went to the beach with Rinna. Playing saints had been her favorite game that year, even in the cold of the winter. She'd walk out into the water, then immerse herself, then come back—silent, solemn. Sometimes she'd drape herself in tiny pieces of seaweed, crown herself with driftwood and beach glass.

I'd thought it would be like that to watch. That it would be like a party almost—people walking out into the waves, then coming back all glass and shine and holiness.

It wasn't.

Most of them turn back, the people who think they are going to walk into the water and walk out saints. It's a glory to think of—the transformation, the sacredness. But it's also a death. You walk into the water and then you keep walking. You walk until your lungs fill with salt water. Until your heart stops. Until you die. There is no guarantee that you will return. Most people—even the ones who make it as far as letting the waters close over their head—thrash their way back to the surface, to dry land and a life no holier than any other.

Most of the people who do walk into the water and hold themselves there beneath its surface drown.

I didn't realize it that day—too young, too excited. They disappeared, yes, and it was strange, but so was everything else that happened. So I didn't count, didn't think about how many went in and how few came back out. But there is always a second, darker tide that returns.

Only one saint walked out of the waves that day.

I admit, it was like seeing a miracle. The shine that began below the surface, the way the waves parted and fell away, the person now glass and pearl and bone. The hush that followed it out of the sea, the only noise the breaking of the waves. The beauty was almost unbearable—I had to turn away.

We waited after that. Hoping for another saint. After a while, the afternoon shifted. The voices of the remaining watchers were less anticipation, more dread. The first body washed in as the sun set.

Rinna didn't play saints anymore after that.

All that day, the heart was a weight on me. Heavy, rewrapped and tucked in my bag as I walked home. Heavy in my thoughts as I tried to go about my day. It pulled at me like the tide. That night, I took the glass heart back to the beach. Not because I was considering tossing it back into the waves. Not seriously, anyway. That wouldn't solve the problem. But I needed to think about it, and that seemed the best place.

I had asked Olivia if I could leave it at the convent, to be placed with the other relics. I'd hoped she would say yes— that would make its appearance just a thing that had happened, not a puzzle to be solved. She'd said it was best that I keep it—it was an unanswered question, and even if I didn't want to hear the answer, she didn't think it would speak to anyone else.

I'd refrained from mentioning that the saints never spoke.

I sat just above the waves, took my shoes off, and let the water wash back and forth over my feet as I held the heart in my lap. The glass was cool to the touch, only just warmer than the seawater. It was an oddly pleasant shape in my hands. Comforting, almost. Almost.

I wondered if I had known the saint, before they were transformed. I wondered if I would have said they had a good heart.

No one really knows why the tide chooses some and not others to be saints. The Sisters of the Tide say it's holiness, that the sea knows the truth of the heart, but everyone has stories of someone whose sainthood was a surprise to everyone who knew them in their life before. The Sisters of Glass say it's a desire to be better than you were, the willingness to let the water wash everything from you, until you are clear like glass.

That version makes a little more sense to me, but I don't know. I've lived with them around me my entire life, and almost everything about the saints still seems strange.

The tide rose up higher, soaking the hems of my jeans. The damp fabric clung uncomfortably to my legs. I stood up and took my tossing thoughts and the glass heart home.

Olivia was standing in front of my door when I got home, her white robes stark against the night sky. She twisted her beads around and around her wrist. "I'm sorry for showing up unannounced, but I can't get the heart out of my thoughts."

"Look, I'm freezing. My clothes are soaking wet and uncomfortable. All I want to do right now is go inside and have the world's hottest shower, and then a whiskey. So unless this is some sort of an emergency, I'd appreciate it if we could have this discussion some other time." It was, perhaps, not my most pious moment.

"It's not an emergency. It's just—my husband left me for the tide," she said. "To become a saint. That's why I became a nun. Because I didn't know what else to do to make that okay."

"Come in," I said. "You can have some whiskey, but I'm still taking a shower."

"Thank you."

She was holding the heart when I came back down. "I wondered if I could tell if it was his. But it just feels like glass to me."

"Does that make it better or worse?" I asked.

"I don't know. Neither, I suppose. He's still unrecogniz-able, silent and glass, and I'm still the woman whose husband would rather be that than warm and in bed beside her." The sea's own bitterness in her voice.

"What do you"—I gestured at her robes—"say about people who choose to become saints?"

"Officially, of course, it's a sacrifice. A calling. A miracle. On my good days, I truly believe that." She finished the whis-key in her glass.

"And on your not-good days?"

"It feels like cowardice."

I nodded. I'd never really known anyone who became a saint, not beyond the casual sort of way you know every-one when you live in a small enough place. To me, going to the waves seemed a way to walk away from a life, and not a way to live it.

"How can you bear it, then?" I asked. "Living among the relics?"

"Because I hope that it will help me understand. That if I can sit in the quiet, with the glass, somewhere in that quiet, I will know why he felt called to go to the sea, and that some-where in that understanding, I'll find peace."

It's easier, I think, to be a saint than to be a human.

. . .

The next morning, Rinna came over to tell me that Maris was sick.

"The doctor says it's her heart," Rinna said, red-eyed and splotchy from weeping. "It's not fair. She's so small, just such a tiny thing."

Maris was sleeping in her carrier at Rinna's feet. She looked delicate, even more than would be expected of someone so small. Her skin more translucent than before, the colors of the veins showing through, instead of healthy pink.

"We're going to go to the Sisters of the Tide. I want them to pray for her."

"Of course," I said.

"Plus, you know how the saints like to walk the grounds there. I'm hoping we'll find one that I can beg for a blessing for her, the poor little love. . . ." Her voice trailed off.

"I'll go make an offering to the waves," I said.

"Thank you." Rinna's hand clutched mine, hard, hard. "I trust the doctors, of course I do. I know they'll help her. But the saints can too."

"Of course," I said.

The saints, of course, are miracles. It is impossible to see them and think of them as anything else. They are the numinous given form. We give thanks to the sea for their presence among us. We ask them for blessings, for benedictions.

They walk through our streets, all hours of the day and

night, sacred and silent. Every so often, they will stop, will lay hands on someone. It happens rarely enough to be seen as a blessing.

It's a dark thought, I know, but sometimes I think that we look at the wrong thing. The saints are walking miracles, yes, but I wonder if the miracle is that moment of transformation, of walking into the tide as one thing and out of it as another. I wonder if that moment of transformation is the only miracle that belongs to the saints. If everything else we've built around them is just our own hope.

If that occasional laying on of hands isn't an act of blessing, but one of regret—of reaching out for a humanity they no longer have. Of them wanting connection with warmth, and with life once more.

We pray to the saints, and I don't know if they hear us. They have certainly never spoken an answer.

It became clear, soon enough, that no offerings to the tide or prayers to the saints were helping.

"Glass?" I asked, the word falling dully from my mouth.

"Look," Rinna said. Her hand shook as she pushed Maris' shirt aside. A small spot of glass shone on her chest.

"A saint," I whispered.

"Maybe?" Rinna's voice cracked. "I don't know. I don't know what to do, how to help her."

I kissed the soft swirl of Maris' dark hair. Maybe I did.

. . .

It's always been the sea I've believed in—had faith in—more than the saints. I can feel the holiness in the turn of the tide; the crash of the waves is sacred music. It's the sea, after all, that transforms people into saints. The miracle isn't in us.

That afternoon, I took the glass heart to Rinna.

She stared at it, then at me. "You've had this how long? And it only now occurred to you that it might help?"

There was nothing I could say in the face of that—even my fear that it was a bad omen, well, she had a sick daughter, of course it was. But maybe if I had brought it earlier, it would have been a good omen, would have prevented Maris from getting sick. Everything that I hadn't done was the one thing that would have helped.

"Take it away," she said. "I don't want it here. I don't want it anywhere near Maris. And I don't want you near her either."

"Rinna?"

"I mean it. If saints themselves are giving warnings, maybe you're what's being warned against. Stay away." She turned her body, holding Maris as far away from me as she could, and clutched her tightly.

"I'll be praying for her," I said.

"Like that will help. You barely even believe."

"Rinna, I—"

"I don't want to hear it. Go. Take that thing and go."

I love my sister. I went.

The saints began to follow Maris.

"They've never done anything like this before," Olivia said.

I hadn't seen it yet. Rinna was still furious with me, and so I had been staying away from her, so as not to add to her stress. "Following?"

Olivia nodded. "Just one at a time at first. Trailing after her in the street, on the convent grounds. There are more now. I saw five this morning, standing outside your sister's house."

"Like a vigil," I said.

"Yes."

"What do you think they're waiting for?" I asked.

"I wish I knew."

So did I. A vigil ended with change or with death. And Maris was such a small thing.

Glass covered the beach with the next tide. A rough line of it, broken and shining, clear as tears, mixed among the more usual driftwood and detritus cast up by the waves.

"It'll be a Saints' Tide," Olivia said. She bent, lifted a handful of the glass, then let it rain back through her fingers. Other Sisters of the Glass walked the shore, their robes flapping like wings in the wind. Some bent and gathered the glass—they'd string it together for their holy beads.

"How can you tell?" I asked.

"There are signs. The heaviness in the air. The amount of glass that's washed up, and the way it reaches out from the waves. The saints are restless on the convent grounds, walking in circles. They can feel the pull in the tide."

"Will you watch?" I asked.

"No," she said. "I'm a Sister of Glass. My work will come after."

"After?" I thought of the bodies, that second, gruesome tide. There must be someone, I thought, who helped the families when they realized that the sea had taken from them and would not give back. But that wasn't what she meant.

"There are always saints who return to the sea then. We see them out, and we collect what returns."

What returns. Broken glass hands, reverently displayed in the convent. A glass heart, sitting on my kitchen table. "Can you tell which ones will go?"

"No," she said. "But some of them always do. It's as if there has to be a balance—a tide that goes out for every tide that comes in."

I picked up a handful of glass and let it fall back to the sand, and I thought of a heart of glass that had come in on the tide, a heart of glass that beat in my niece's chest.

Olivia stood next to me, her hand on my shoulder, as I wept.

. . .

The next morning, a second glass tide came in, thicker than the first, turning the beach into a hard, merciless glare. I stood, shivering in the late-spring wind, on Rinna's porch. There was a ring of saints, silent behind me, watching the house, the sea beyond it.

The door opened. "What?"

"How is Maris?" I asked.

"No worse," she said, beginning to close the door again.

"It'll be a Saints' Tide," I said.

"And why do you care?" she said.

"I just thought you'd want to know." The excuse wasn't quite true—I was sure she did know. I wanted to see her. To see Maris.

"Well, now that you've done what you came for, you can leave again."

"Rinna, please," I said.

"No." She closed the door.

The saints were still silent as I walked past them. I hadn't expected anything else.

Rinna was there on the beach with the next tide, the third glass tide. Her hands were fisted at her sides, and her eyes hard on the horizon. "I'm going out tomorrow. I'll offer myself to the tide."

My entire body went cold. "You're doing *what*?"

"For Maris. When I'm a saint, I can cure her." She didn't

256

look at me, just kept her face turned to the waves.

"She doesn't need a saint, she needs a mother."

"What would you know about either? You don't know what it's like, to sit there and watch her, and watch the doctors not be able to help her, and just have to do nothing. At least this way"—a sob cracked through her voice—"at least this way, I would be doing something. Something that might actually help. Something other than just watching."

"And then what is Maris supposed to do? Because it's not like you'll be able to come back. Even if you become a saint, you'll be glass. You'll be like that." I jerked my head back, to where a phalanx of saints stood. Silent.

"Are you saying you won't take care of her?" Rinna looked at me.

And there was nothing I could say to that. I've never wanted a child, but of course I would.

"I'm doing this," Rinna said. "This is how I can help."

"And what if you die?" I asked. "You know that's more likely—you go out into the water and you don't come back a saint, you come back a corpse. How does that possibly help Maris?"

"At least I will have tried. I'm her mother. My job is to do everything I possibly can to save her."

"No," I said. "Your job is to raise her."

"Don't you think I know that?" Tears poured like glass from her eyes. "Don't you think I'd rather hold her and laugh with her and watch her take her first steps? Don't you think

I'd die to hear her say 'Mama'? But my baby's heart is turning to glass, and she won't ever say anything if she doesn't live.

"My job is to do whatever it takes to help her. If I have to die for her, I will."

I don't pray, not to the saints, anyway. I know the gestures and the rituals, and I'm happy to follow the forms when asked. I don't begrudge anyone their beliefs, and I would never turn my back on a blessing when offered. But I can't bring myself to ask for one, not directly.

Not even for Maris. For me, asking the saints to help would be mouthing empty words, and why would they listen to that, from me, instead of Rinna, or Olivia, or any of the Sisters, the people who meant what they said?

But I believe in the power of the sea. My whole life, that's what I've looked to. So I took the glass heart, and I went to the beach, and I sat vigil for Maris, all night and into the dawn. I matched my breath to the waves, in and out, and I hoped that what I was doing was enough like prayer that the sea would hear me.

The Saints' Tide. The wind whipped the water white. I pulled the blanket tighter around Maris. She was so small in my arms, and I could feel the fluttering thump of her glass heart against my chest. "Rinna, please."

"You tell her that I loved her. More than anything. That she was why I did this." She shook as she spoke.

"You should stay here and tell her yourself. Please, Rinna." Salt stung my eyes.

"She's not getting better. I have to go."

I set Maris down in her carrier, the glass heart next to her, and embraced my sister. "I love you."

She reached her hand out, shaking, and brushed it against Maris' hair. "Goodbye."

Rinna walked toward the waves. She didn't falter, didn't look back. Not even when Maris cried, sobbing that seemed far too loud for her small body.

Then a voice cracked out like the breaking of ice. "Stop!"

A saint. A saint had spoken.

That one word, in that unheard voice, was enough to command. No one moved. Not even Rinna. We barely breathed. And so the crack, when it came, echoed even over the sound of the tide.

The saint was shattering. And still they walked forward, down the beach, toward the tide.

Toward Maris.

The saint held out their hands, and I put Maris in them. The saint shuddered, cracked further, but held Maris safely, carefully, as they walked with her to the waves. The cracks widened; glass fell to the sand.

The saint paused at the edge of the tide and lowered Maris into it.

Another shattering. The saint crumbling now to pieces and Maris falling into the water and Rinna pulling her out.

"She's fine!" Rinna gasped. "She's healed!"

At my feet, the glass heart cracked open.

I took the two halves of the broken heart to Olivia at the Convent of the Sisters of Glass. "I thought these might belong here."

"Are you sure?" she asked. "You seem hesitant."

"I think that they need to go back to the sea," I said. "But I don't really know how any of this works."

"None of us do," she said. "We just hope things become clear someday. If you think they should go back to the sea, then that's what you should do with them. The heart came to you in the first place."

And so that night, I took the heart back out to the waves. I stood, the salt water washing over my feet, one broken half in each hand. "Thank you," I said. To the sea. To the saints. To whatever might be listening.

I placed the glass heart into the water and watched as the tide carried it away.

Painted Birds and Shivered Bones

The white bird flew through the clarion of the cathedral bells, winging its way through the rich music of their tolling to perch in the shelter of the church's walls. The chiming continued, marking time into measured, holy hours.

Maeve had gone for a walk, to clear her head and give herself the perspective of something beyond the windows and walls of her apartment. She could feel the sensation at the back of her brain, that almost itch that meant a new painting was ready to be worked on. Wandering the city, immersing herself in its chaos and beauty, would help that back-of-the-head feeling turn into a realized concept.

But New York had been more chaos than beauty that morning. Too much of everything and all excess without pause. Maeve felt like she was coming apart at the seams.

In an effort to hold herself together, Maeve had gone

to the Cathedral of Saint John the Divine. There, she could think, could sit quietly, could stop and breathe without people asking what was wrong.

Midwinter had been cold enough to flush her cheeks as she walked to the cathedral, but Maeve couldn't bear being inside—large as the church was, she could feel the walls pressing on her skin. Instead, she perched on a bench across from the fallen tower and pulled her scarf higher around her neck.

Maeve sipped her latte and leaned back against the bench, then sat up. She closed her eyes, then opened them again.

There was a naked man crouched on the side of the cathedral.

She dug in her purse for her phone, wondering how it was possible that such a relatively small space always turned into a black hole when she needed to find anything. Phone finally in hand, she looked up.

The naked man was gone.

In his place was a bird. Beautiful white feathers trailing like half-remembered thoughts. Impressive, to be sure, especially when compared with the expected pigeons of the city. But bearing no resemblance to a man, naked or otherwise.

Maeve let her phone slip through her fingers, back into her bag, and stood, shaking her head at herself. "You need to cut down on your caffeine."

* * *

"You thought what?" Emilia laughed. "Oh, honey. The cure for thinking that you see a naked man at the cathedral isn't giving up caffeine, it's getting laid."

"Meeting men isn't really a priority for me." Maeve believed dating to be a circle of hell that Dante forgot.

"Maeve, you don't need to meet them. Just pick one." Emilia gestured at the bar.

Maeve looked around. "I don't even know them."

"That's exactly my point." Emilia laughed again. "Take one home, send him on his way in the morning, and I can guarantee your naked hallucinations will be gone."

"Fine." Maeve sipped her bourbon. "I'll take it under advisement."

Surprising precisely no one, least of all the woman who had been her best friend for a decade, Maeve went home alone, having not even attempted to take one of the men in the bar with her. She hung up her coat and got out her paints.

Dawn was pinking the sky when she set the brush down and rolled the tension from her neck and shoulders.

The canvas was covered in birds.

Madness is easier to bear with the wind in your feathers. Sweeney flung himself into the currents of the air, through bands of starlight that streaked the sky, and winged toward the cloud-coated moon.

Beneath Sweeney, the night fell on the acceptable madness of the city. Voices cried out to one another in greeting or curse. Tires squealed and horns blared. Canine throats raised the twilight bark, and it was made symphonic by feline yowls, skitterings of smaller creatures, and the songs of more-usual birds.

Not Sweeney's.

Silent Sweeney was borne on buffeting currents over the wild lights of the city. Over the scents of concrete and of rot, of grilling meat and decaying corners, of the blood and love and dreams and terrors of millions.

And of their madness as well.

Even in his bird form, Sweeney recognized New York as a city of the mad. Not that one needed to be crazy to be there, or that extended residency was a contributing factor to lunacy of some sort, but living there—thriving there—took a particular form of madness.

Or caused it. Sweeney had not yet decided which.

He had not chosen his immigration, but had been pulled over wind and salt and sea by the whim of a wizard. Exiled from his kingdom, in truth, though there were no kings in Ireland anymore.

On he flew, through a forest of buildings built to assault the sky. Over bridges, and trains that hurtled from the earth as if they were loosed dragons. Over love and anger and countless anonymous mysteries.

Sweeney tucked his wings and coasted to the ground at the Cathedral of Saint John the Divine. The ring of church bells set the madness on him, sprang the feathers from his skin, true. But madness obeyed rules of its own devising, and the quietness of the cathedral grounds soothed him. He roosted in the ruined tower and fed on seed scattered on the steps after weddings.

He had done so for years, making the place a refuge. There had been a woman, Madeleine, he thought her name was, who smelled of paper and stories. She had been kind to him, kind enough that he wondered sometimes if she could see the curse beneath the feathers. She scattered food, and cracked the window of the room she worked in so that he might perch just inside the frame and watch her work among the books.

Yes. Madeleine. He had worn his man shape to her memorial, there at the cathedral, found and read her books, with people as out of time as he was. She had been kind to him, and kindness was stronger even than madness was.

Maeve stood in front of the canvas and wiped the remnants of sleep from her eyes with paint-smeared fingers.

It was good work. She had gotten the wildness of the feathers, and the way a wing could obscure and reveal when stretched in flight. She could do a series, she thought.

"I mean, it's about time, right?" she asked Brian, her

agent, on the phone. "Be ambitious, move out of my comfort zone, all those things you keep telling me I need to do."

"Yes, but *birds*, Maeve?"

"Not still lifes, or landscapes, if that's what you're worried about."

"Well, not worried exactly.

"Look, send me pictures of what you're working on. I'll start looking for a good venue to show them. If it doesn't work, we'll call this your birdbrained period."

It wasn't the resounding endorsement of her creativity that Maeve had been hoping for, but that was fine. She would paint now, and enthusiasm could come later.

She could feel her paintings, the compulsion to create, just beneath the surface of her skin. She gathered her notebook and pencils and went out into the city to sketch.

Sweeney perched on a bench in Central Park, plucking feathers from his arms. He had felt the madness creeping back for days this time before the feathers began appearing. Sure, he knew it was the madness. His blood itched, and unless that was the cursed feathers being born beneath his skin, itchy blood meant madness.

Itchy blood had meant madness and feathers for close to forever now, hundreds of years since the curse had first been cast. Life was long, and so were curses.

Though when he thought about it, Sweeney suspected curses were longer.

Pigeons cooed and hopped about near the bench's legs, occasionally casting their glinting eyes up at him. Sweeney thumbed a nail beneath a quill, worried at it until he could get a good grip. The feather emerged slowly, blood brightening its edges. He sighed as it slid from his skin. Sweeney flicked the feather to the ground, and the pigeons scattered.

"Can't blame you. I don't like the fucking things either." Sweeney tugged at the next feather, one pushing through the skin at the bend of his elbow. Plucking his own feathers wouldn't stop the change, or even slow it, but it gave him something to do.

"The curse has come upon me," he said. Blood caked his nails and dried in the whorls and creases of his fingers.

And it would. The curse would come upon him, as it had time and time again, an ongoing atonement. He might be occasionally mad, and sometimes a bird with it, but Sweeney was never stupid. He knew the metamorphosis would happen. A bell would ring, and his skin would grow too tight around his bones, and he would bend and crack into bird shape.

Sooner, rather sooner indeed than later, if the low buzz at the back of his skull was any indication.

"But just because something is inevitable doesn't mean that we resign ourselves to it. No need to roll over and show our belly, now." Sweeney watched the pigeons as they scritched about in the dirt.

There were those who might say that Sweeney's

stubbornness had gone a long way to getting him into the fix he was currently in. Most days, Sweeney would agree with them, and on the days he wouldn't, well, those days he didn't need to, as his agreement was implied by the shape he wore.

You didn't get cursed into birdhood and madness because you were an even-tempered sort of guy.

"You guys all really birds, there beneath the feathers?" Sweeney asked the flock discipled at his feet.

The pigeons kept their own counsel.

Then the bells marked the hour, and in between ring and echo, Sweeney became a bird.

Dusk was painting the Manhattan skyline in gaudy reds and purples when Maeve looked up from her sketchbook. She had gotten some good studies, enough to start painting the series. She scrubbed her smudged hands against the cold-stiffened fabric of her jeans. She would get takeout—her favorite soup dumplings—and then go home and paint.

The bird winged its way across her sight line as she stood up. Almost iridescent in the dying light, a feathered sweep of beauty at close of day. Watching felt transcendent—

"Oh, fuck, not again." In the tree not a bird, but a man, trying his best to inhabit a bird-shaped space.

Maeve closed her eyes, took a deep breath, opened them again. Still: Man. Tree. Naked.

"Okay. It's been a long day. You forgot to eat. You have

birds on the brain. You're just going to go home now"—she tapped the camera button on her phone—"and when you get there, this picture of a naked man is going to be a picture of a bird."

It wasn't.

Sweeney watched the woman pick up her paintbrush, set it down. Pick up her phone, look at it, clutch her hair or shake her head, then set the phone down and walk back to her canvas. She had been repeating a variation of this pattern since he landed on the fire escape outside her window.

He had seen her take the picture, and wanted to know why. The people who saw him were usually quite good at ignoring his transformations, in that carefully-turned-head, averted-eyes, and faster-walking way of ignoring. Most people didn't even let themselves see him. This woman did. Easy enough to fly after her, once he was a bird again.

Sweeney wondered if perhaps she was mad too, this woman who held the mass of her hair back by sticking a paintbrush through it, and who talked to herself as she paced around her apartment.

She wasn't mad now, though, not that he could tell. She was painting. Sweeney stretched his wings and launched himself into the cold, soothing light of the stars.

. . .

In the center of the canvas was a man, and feathers were erupting from his skin.

"Oh, yes. Brian is going to love it when you tell him about this. 'That series of paintings you didn't want me to do? Well, I've decided that the thing it really needed was werebirds.'"

It was good, though, she thought. The shock of the transformation as a still point in the chaos of the city that surrounded him.

The transformation had been a shock. The kind of thing you had to see to believe, and even then, you doubted. Such a thing should have been impossible to see.

And maybe that was the thread for the series, Maeve thought. Fantasy birds, things that belonged in fairy tales and medieval bestiaries, feathered refugees from mythology and legend scattered throughout a modern city that refused to see them there.

She could paint that. It would be a series of paintings that would let her do something powerful if she got them right.

Maeve sat at her computer and began compiling image files of harpy and cockatrice, phoenix and firebird. There were, she thought, so many stories of dead and vengeful women returning as ghost birds, but nothing about men who did so. Not that she thought what she had seen was a ghost, or that she was trying some form of research-based bibliomancy to discern the story behind the bird (the man) she kept seeing, but she wouldn't have turned away an answer.

"And would it have made you feel better if you had found one? Because hallucinating a ghost bird in Manhattan is so much better than if you're just seeing a naked werebird? Honestly." She shook her head.

Though it wasn't a hallucination. Not with the picture on her phone. Why it was easier to think she was losing her mind than to accept that she had seen something genuinely impossible was something Maeve didn't understand.

She printed out reference photos for all the impossible birds she hadn't yet seen, and taped them over the walls.

In the beginning, when the curse's claws still bled him, and Sweeney had nothing to recall him to himself or his humanity, he would fly after Eorann, who had been his wife before he was a bird. She was the star to his wanderings.

Eorann had loved Sweeney, and so she had tried, at the beginning, to break the curse. Unspeaking, she wove garments from nettles and cast them over Sweeney like nets, in the hopes that pain and silence spun together might force a bird back into a man's shape. Had even one perfect wing lingered as a reminder of his past and his errors, it would have been change enough. More, it would have been stasis, a respite from the constant and unpredictable change that, Sweeney discovered, was the curse's true black heart.

When that did not work, she had shoes made from iron, and walked the length and breadth of Ireland in an attempt to wear them out. But she was already east of the sun and west of the moon, the true north of her compass set to once upon a time. Such places are not given to the wearing out of iron shoes.

Eorann spun straw into gold, then spun the gold into thread that flexed and could be woven into a dress more beautiful than the sun, the moon, and the stars. She uncurdled milk and raised from the dead a cow that gave it constantly, without needing food nor drink of its own. If there was a miracle, a marvel, or a minor wonder that Eorann could perform in the hopes of breaking Sweeney's curse, she did so.

Until the day she didn't.

"A wife's role may be many things, Sweeney. But it is not a wife's job to break a husband's curse, not when he is the one who has armored himself in it."

Those were the last words that Eorann had spoken to him. From the distance of time, Sweeney could admit now that she was right. Still, from the height of the unfeeling sky, he wished that she had been the saving of him.

"Well, they're different. That's certain," Brian said, walking between the canvases.

"If 'different' means 'crap,' just say so. I'm too tired to parse euphemisms."

Maeve had only one completed canvas—the man transforming into a bird. But she had complete studies of two others—a phoenix rising out of the flame of a burning sky-line, and a harpy hovering protectively over a woman.

"They're darker than your usual thing, but powerful." Brian stepped back, pacing in front of the canvases.

"They're good. I've a couple galleries in mind—I'll start making calls.

"You'll come to the opening, of course."

"No," Maeve said. "Absolutely not. Nonnegotiable."

"Look, the reclusive artist thing was fine when you were starting out, because you didn't matter enough for people to care about you. But we can charge real money for these. People who pay real money for their art aren't just buying a decoration for their wall, they're buying the story that goes with it."

Maeve was pretty sure no one wanted to buy the story of the artist who had a panic attack at her own opening. No, scratch that. She was absolutely sure someone would want to buy that story. She just didn't want to sell her paintings badly enough to give it to them.

"Well, then how about the story is I am a recluse. A crazy bird lady instead of a crazy cat lady. I live with the chickens. Whatever you need to say. But I don't interact with the people buying my work, and I don't go to openings."

"You're lucky I'm good at my job, Maeve."

"I'm good at mine, too."

Brian sighed. "Of course you are. I didn't mean to suggest

otherwise. But I don't understand why you don't just buy yourself a pretty dress and have fun letting rich people buy you drinks and tell you how wonderful you are.

"Let yourself celebrate a little. It's the fun part of the job, Maeve."

It wasn't, not for her. Of course, Brian wouldn't understand that. Maeve worked too hard to keep her panic attacks hidden. She had an entire portfolio of tricks to keep them manageable and out of view.

When she wasn't in the apartment, she was fine, as long as she didn't have to interact with too many people. Crowds were okay as long as she had someone she knew with her and she didn't have to interact with the people she didn't know. When she had to meet new people, she did so in familiar surroundings, either one-on-one or in a group of people she already knew and felt comfortable with. Even then, she usually needed a day at home, undisturbed, after, in order to rest and regain her equilibrium.

A party where everyone would be strangers who wanted to pay attention to her, who wanted her to interact with them, with no safety net of friends that she could fall onto, was impossible.

Even after Eorann had told Sweeney that she could not save him, it took him some time to realize that he would need to be the saving of himself. More time still, an infinity of church bells, of molting feathers, to understand that saving himself did not necessarily include lifting the curse.

In search of himself, of answers, of peace, long and long ago, Sweeney had undertaken a quest.

A quest is a cruel migration. This is the essence of a quest, no matter who undertakes it. But Sweeney had not known what to look for, save for the longing to see something other than what he was.

The Sangreal had been found once already, and though lost again, it was the kind of thing where the first finding mattered. The dragons were all in hiding, and Sweeney had never particularly thought they needed to be slain.

Nor had he known the map with which to travel by, save for one that would take him to a place other than where he was. He took wing. Over sea and under stone and then over the sea to sky.

Maeve saw the bird at the Cathedral of Saint John the Divine again.

Cathedrals, churches, museums, libraries, they were useful sorts of places for her. When the walls of her apartment pressed too tightly, these were places she could go, and sit, and think, and not have to worry about people insisting that she interact with them in order to justify her presence.

"I came here for peace and quiet, you know. Not because I'm hoping to catch a glimpse of you naked."

The bird did not seem to have an opinion on that.

When she sat, Maeve specifically chose a bench that did not have a line of sight to the bird's current perch. Not like it couldn't fly, but it was the principle of the thing. And she really didn't want to see it become a naked man again.

Stories about artistic inspiration that came to life and then interacted with the artist were only interesting if they were stories. When they were your life, they were weird.

The bird landed next to her on the bench.

Maeve looked at her bird, at her sketchbook, and back at the bird.

"Fine. Fine. But do not turn into a man. Not in front of me. Just don't. If you think you're going to, leave. Please." She tore off a chunk of her croissant and set it on the bird's side of the bench. "Okay?"

Maeve was relieved when the bird did not answer.

There was a package from Brian waiting for her when she got home. The card read, "For the crazy bird lady."

Inside was a beautiful paper bird. A crane, but not the expected origami. Paper made sculpture, not folded. Feathers and wings and beak all shaped from individual pieces of brightly colored paper. It was a gorgeous fantasy of practicality and feathers.

Maeve tucked it on a shelf, where she could see it while she painted.

He hadn't answered her today, the red-haired painter.

Sweeney could speak in bird form—he was still a man, even when feather-clad—but he had learned, finally, the value of silence.

This had not always been so. It had been speaking that had first called his curse down upon him.

He had called out an insult to Ronan. Said something he should not have, kept speaking when he should have driven a nail through his tongue to hold his silence.

Ronan had spoken then too. Spoken a word that burned the sky and shifted the bones of the earth. A curse, raw and dire. That was the first time the madness fell upon Sweeney. The madness, and the breaking of himself into the too-light bones that made up a bird's wing.

When it came down to it, it was pride that had cursed Sweeney into his feathers, as sure as pride had melted Icarus out of his. Pride and a too-quick temper, faults that dwelt in any number of people without changing their lives and their shapes, without sending them on a path of constant migration centered on a reminder of error.

Curses didn't much care that there were other people they could have landed on just as comfortably. They fell where they would, then watched the aftermath unfold.

. . .

Some days were good days, days when Maeve could walk through her life and not be aware of any of the adjustments she performed to make it livable.

Tuesday was not one of those days.

She had taken the subway, something she did only rarely, preferring to walk. But a sudden hailstorm had driven her underground, and sent what seemed like half of the city after her.

Maeve got off at the second stop, not even sure what street it was. Her pulse had been racing so fast that her vision had gone grey and narrow. If she hadn't gotten out, away from all those people, she would have collapsed.

Her notebook, her most recent sketches for her paintings, was left behind on the uptown 2 train. It had to have been the train where it went missing. She was sure it had been in her bag when she left her apartment, and it was clearly not among the bag's upended contents now.

Forty-five minutes on the phone with MTA lost and found did no more than she had expected, and reassured her the odds of its return were small.

And though it had smelled fine—she had checked—the milk with which she had made the hot chocolate that was supposed to make her feel better had instead made her feel decidedly worse.

The floor of the bathroom was cool against her cheek.

Exhausted and sick, Maeve curled in on herself and fell into tear-streaked sleep.

The bird was in her dream, and that was far from the weirdest thing about it.

The sky shaded to lavender, the clouds like ink splotches thrown across it.

Then a head sailed across the waxing moon.

Sweeney cocked his own head and shifted on the branch.

Another head described an arc across the sky, a lazy rise and fall.

Sweeney looked around. He could not tell where the heads were launching from, nor could he hear any sounds of distress.

Three more heads, in rapid succession, and Sweeney was certain he was mad again. He wished he were in his human form, so that he might throw back his own head and howl.

Five heads popped up in front of Sweeney, corks bobbing to the surface of the sea.

Identical, each to each, the world's strangest set of brothers.

They looked, Sweeney thought, cheerful. Certainly more cheerful than he would be, were he suddenly disconnected from the neck down.

Each head had been neatly severed. Or no. Not severed. They looked as if they were heads that had never had bodies at all. Smiling, clean-shaven, bright-eyed. No dangling veins or spines, no ragged skin. No blood.

Sweeney supposed the fact that the heads were levitating was no more remarkable than the fact that they were not bleeding. Still, it was the latter that seemed truly strange.

"Hail."

"And."

"Well."

"Met."

"Sweeney," said the heads.

"Er, hello," said Sweeney.

"A."

"Fine."

"Night."

"Isn't."

"It?" Their faces were the picture of benevolence.

"Indeed it is," said Sweeney.

"We."

"Would."

"Speak."

"With."

"You."

As they seemed to be doing that already, Sweeney simply bobbed his head.

"Do."

"You."

"Not."

"Remember."

"Us?" The heads circled around Sweeney.

He tried to focus, to imagine them with bodies attached. Nothing about them seemed familiar. He could not see past their duplicated strangeness. "Please forgive me, gentlemen, but I don't."

"We."

"So."

"Often."

"Forget."

"Ourselves."

"Or."

"Perhaps."

"We."

"Haven't."

"Met." They slid into line in front of him again, the last one bumping its left-side neighbor and setting him gently wobbling.

"Can you read the future, then?" It seemed the most likely explanation, though nothing about this encounter was at all likely.

"Yes."

"And."

"No."

"Only."

"Sometimes."

Sweeney appreciated the honesty of the answer almost as much as he appreciated the thoroughness.

"Listen."

"Now."

"Sweeney."

"Listen."

"Well."

"No."

"One."

"Chooses."

"His."

"Quest."

"It."

"Is."

"Chosen."

"For."

"Him."

"All."

"Quests."

"End."

"In."

"Death."

"So does life," said Sweeney.

"Then."

"Choose."

"Yours."

"Well."

"Sweeney."

The heads cracked their jaws so wide Sweeney wondered if they would swallow themselves. Then they began to laugh, and while laughing, whirled themselves into a small cyclone. Faster and faster it spun, until the heads were nothing but a laughing blur, and then were gone.

Sweeney, contemplative, watched the empty sky until dawn.

Maeve sat up, her head and neck aching from sleeping on the tile, her mouth tasting as if she had licked the subway station she fled from earlier that day.

Legs still feeling more like overcooked noodles than functioning appendages, she staggered into the kitchen and poured the milk down the sink. It was a largely symbolic sort of gesture, performed only to make her head feel better—it certainly wouldn't undo the food poisoning or the resulting fucked up dream, but seeing the milk spiral down the drain was still a relief.

Talking heads flying around Central Park and conversing with a bird who was sometimes a man. It was like something out of a Jim Henson movie, except without the good soundtrack.

Becoming involved enough in her work to dream about it

was, on balance, a good thing. But there were limits. She was not putting disembodied heads into her paintings.

Maeve painted a tower, set into the Manhattan skyline. A wizard's tower, dire and ancient, full of spirals and spires, held together with spells and impossibility.

She hung the surrounding sky with firebirds, contrails of flame streaking the clouds.

Dawn came, but it was neither rebirth nor respite. Sweeney was still befeathered. He turned to the glow of the rising sun, and the tower that appeared there, as if painted on the sky.

Every wizard had a tower, even in twenty-first-century New York. It was the expected, required thing, and magic had rules and bindings more powerful than aught else. It had to, made as it was out of words and will and belief. Certain things had to be true, or the magic crumbled to dust and nothingness.

Sweeney cracked open his beak and tore at the promise-crammed air.

A wizard's tower is protected by many things, but the most puissant are the wizard's own words of power. Even after they have cast their spells and done their work, the words of a wizard retain tracings of magic. Their echoes continue to cast and recast the spells, for as long as sound travels.

The words do not hang idle in the air. Power recognizes power, and old spells linger together like former lovers. Though the connections are no longer as bright as the crackle and spark of that first magic, they can never be entirely erased. They gather, each to each, and in their greetings, new magics are made.

Ronan had been a wizard for centuries now, perhaps millennia. A few very important years longer than Sweeney had been a bird.

Ronan had fled Ireland in the coffin ships, with the rest of the decimated, starving population. His magic, the curse's binding, had pulled Sweeney along in his wake.

In the years since his arrival, magic had wrapped itself around Ronan's tower like fairy tale thorns, a threat, a protection, and a guarantee of solitude. A locus of power that sang, siren-like, to Sweeney, though he knew it was never what he sought.

Sweeney flew around the tower three times, then three, then three again, in the direction of unraveling. The curse, as it always had, remained.

"How many paintings do you have finished?"

"Five."

"How long will it take you to do, say, five or maybe seven more?"

"Why?"

"Drowned Meadow will give you gallery space, but I think these new pieces are strong enough you'd be better served if you had enough finished work to fill the gallery, rather than being part of a group showing."

"When would I need them finished by?"

Brian's answer made her wince, and mourn once again the loss of the sketchbook, and the studies it contained. Still.

"It's a good space. I'll get the pieces done."

"Excellent. I'll email you the contracts."

"Wait, that's what the naked bird guy looks like?" Emilia stood in front of the first painting in the series, the man transforming into a bird. "No wonder you keep seeing him around the city. He's hot."

"He's usually a bird."

"Still, yum. And is that drawn to scale?"

Maeve snorted. "Fine. The next time I see him, if he's being a person, I'll give him your number."

Emilia laughed, but she looked sideways at Maeve while she did. "So, are you seeing all of the things from your paintings?"

Emilia had moved to the newest painting in the series, a cockatrice among the tents at Bryant Park's Fashion Week, models turned to statues under its gaze.

"Do you think I would be here with you, discussing the attractiveness of a werebird, after having consumed far too much Ethiopian food, if I had really encountered a bird that can turn people to stone just by looking at them?"

Maeve looked at Emilia again. "Or no. It's not actually that you think that. You're just doing the sanity check."

"I don't think you're crazy. But you know you don't always take care of yourself before a show. And this one did start with you thinking that you saw a bird turn into a naked guy."

"Which, I admit, sounds odd. But you don't need to worry that I've started the New York chapter of the Phoenix-Watching Club."

"That sounds very Harry Potter. You haven't seen any wizards wandering around the city, have you? I mean, other than the guys who like to get out their wands on the subway." Emilia twisted her face into an expression of repulsed boredom.

"And you wonder why I don't like to leave the house."

"No wizards?"

"No wizards."

There were wizards in New York City, nearly everywhere. War mages who changed history over games of speed chess. Chronomancers who stole seconds from the subway trains. And the city built on dreams was rife with oneiro-mancers channeling desires between sleep and waking.

Even the wizard who had set the curse on Sweeney looked out over the speed and traffic of the city as he spoke his spells, shiftings and transformations, covering one thing in some other's borrowed skin, whether they would or no.

But though Ronan was here, and had been, he was not the direction to which Sweeney looked to break his curse. Wizards did not, under any but the most extreme circumstances, undo their own magic. Magic, magic that is practiced and cast, is at odds with entropy. Not only does it reshape order out if chaos, but it wrenches the rules for order sideways. It rewrites the laws, so that a man might be shifted to a bird, and back again, no matter how physics wails.

To make such a thing happen, though it might seem the work of an incantation and an arcane gesture, is the marriage of effort and will. And will, once wielded in such fashion, is not lightly undone.

But just because the wizard would not lift his curse did not mean that the spell might never be broken.

It just meant it would require a magic stronger than wizardry to break it.

Maeve's apartment was full of birds. Photographs papered the walls, layered over one another in collage; Escheresque spirals of wings that had never flown together fell in cascading recursive loops of impossible birds.

The statue from Brian was a carnival fantasy among articulated skeletons in shadow boxes, shivered bones set at precise angles of flight.

Her own bones ached as if wings mantled beneath the surface of her skin and longed to burst forth from her back.

The canvas before her was enormous, six feet in height and half again as wide, the largest she had ever painted. On it, a murmuration of starlings arced and turned across a storm-tossed sky.

Among the starlings were other birds. Birds of vengeance, storm-called, and storm-conjuring. The Erinyes.

The Kindly Ones.

More terrible than lightning, they harried the New York skyline.

Cramps spasmed Maeve's hands around her brushes, and her eyes burned, but still she layered color onto the canvas.

It was a kind of madness, she thought, the way it felt to finish a painting. The muscle-memory knowledge of exactly where the brushstrokes went, even though this was nothing she had painted before. The fizzing feeling at the top of her head that told her what she was painting was right, was true. The adrenaline that flooded her until she couldn't sit, or sleep, or eat, until it was finished.

Madness, surely. But a madness of wings, and of glory.

The skies of New York had grown stranger. Sweeney was used to the occasional airborne mystery. It wasn't as if he had ever thought himself the only sometimes bird on the wing.

But a flock of firebirds had taken up residence in

CATHEDRAL OF MYTH AND BONE

Central Park, and an exaltation of larks had begun exalting in Mandarin in the bell tower of St. Patrick's Cathedral.

He thought he had seen the phoenix, but perhaps it had only been a particularly gaudy sunset.

Magic all unasked for, and stuck about with feathers.

Though perhaps not magic unconjured.

Sweeney paged through a notebook, not lost on a train but slid from a messenger bag. He had wanted, he supposed, to see how she saw him.

Of course, he was in none of the sketches.

But its pages crawled with magic. It was rife in the shadows and shadings and lines of the sketches. Sweeney didn't know if it was wizardry or not, what he was looking at, but there was power in her drawings.

Perhaps enough power to unmake a curse.

"You're sure I can't convince you to come to the opening?" Brian asked. "Because I think people are really going to want to talk to you about these paintings, and Maeve, do not say, 'My art speaks for itself.'"

"You have to admit, you pretty much asked me to."

"Maeve."

"They'll sell better if I'm not there."

"What would make you think that?"

Because if I'm there, I'll spend the entire evening locked in the bathroom, occasionally vomiting from panic, she

PAINTED BIRDS AND SHIVERED BONES

thought. "Because if I'm not there, you can spin me as mysterious. Or better yet, perfect. Tell them what they want to hear without the risk that I'll show up with paint still in my hair."

"I have never once seen you with paint in your hair. And even if I had, artists are supposed to be absentminded and eccentric. It's part of your charm."

"You told me I wasn't allowed to be absentminded and eccentric anymore, remember? Not in this gallery. Not at these prices."

"I suppose I did. Still, this is your night, Maeve. If you want to be here, even if there is paint in your hair, you should come."

"I can assure you, Brian, I won't want to."

Sweeney could, if he concentrated enough, prevent the shift in form from man to bird from happening. Usually, he didn't bother—the change came when it would, and after all these years, he had made peace with his spontaneous wings.

But he wanted to see the paintings. To see, captured in pigment and brushstroke, the birds that Maeve had made a space for in New York's skies.

He wanted to see her, just once, in the guise and costume of a normal man.

More, he wanted to see if the magic that crackled across the pages of her notebook was in the paintings as well, to see if she could paint him free. A request that might allow him to once again be a normal man, instead of what he was: a creature cursed into loneliness and the wrong skin, whose only consolation was the further loneliness of flight.

Sweeney's difficulty was that while he could, by force of will, hold himself in human form, it let the madness push further into his consciousness. The longer he fought the transformation, the more he struggled to be shaped like a man, the less he thought like one.

Sweeney slid on his jacket. He checked to make sure his buttons matched, his fly was up, and his shoes were from the same pair. He hailed a cab and hoped for the best.

On the night of the opening, Maeve was not at the gallery. She had been there earlier in the day to double-check the way the paintings had been hung, to see to all the last-minute details, and to tell Brian, one more time, that she was absolutely not coming to the opening.

"Fine. Then at least put on a nice dress at home and have some champagne with a friend so I don't get depressed thinking about you."

"If that's what will make you happy, of course I will," she lied, offering a big smile and accepting Brian's hug.

As the show opened, Maeve was wearing a T-shirt with holes in it and eating soup dumplings. Which she toasted with a glass of the very fine champagne that Brian had sent over. Emilia texted from the gallery that the "paintings are your best thing ever. So proud of you!" Comfort and celebration and a friend, even if far from what Brian imagined.

Strange to think that this show, which Brian thought could be big enough to change her career, had begun with seeing a bird turn into a naked man. Which was certainly the one story she could never tell when asked what inspired her work.

She hadn't seen the bird for a while now. Or, thankfully, the naked man. Some parts of the strangeness of the city were better left unexplained.

Too many answers killed the magic, and Maeve wanted the magic. Its possibilities were what made up for the discomfort and worry of everyday life.

The lights were too bright and there were too many people. Sweeney bit the insides of his cheeks and walked through the gallery as if its floor were shattering glass.

The paintings. He thought they were beautiful, probably, or that they would be if he could ever stand still long enough to really look at them, to see them as more than blurs as he circled the gallery. He felt too hot, his skin ill-fitting, his heart racing like a bird's.

Sweeney clenched his fists, digging his nails into his palms, and forced his breath in and out until it steadied.

There.

Almost comfortably human.

Sweeney walked the room slowly this time, giving himself space to step back and look at the canvases.

Feathers itched and crawled beneath his skin.

And there he was.

The still point at the center of the painting, and feathers were bursting from his skin there, too, but there, it didn't look like madness, it looked like transcendence.

Sweeney heaved in a breath.

"It does have that effect on people."

Sweeney glanced at the man standing next to him, the man who hadn't seemed to realize it was Sweeney in the painting hanging before them.

"Are you familiar with Maeve's work? Maeve Collins, the artist, I mean," Brian said.

"Ah. A bit. Only recently. Is she here tonight?"

"Not yet, though I hope she'll make an appearance later. But if you're interested in the piece, I'd be happy to assist you with it."

"If I buy it, can I meet her?"

"I can understand why you'd make the request, but that's not the usual way art sales work."

And now the man standing next to him did step back and look at Sweeney. "Wait. Wait. You're the model for the painting. Oh, this is fantastic."

Feathers. Feathers unfurling in his blood.

"But of course you'd know Maeve already, then."

"I don't." Sweeney braceleted his wrist, his left wrist, downed with white feathers, with his right hand. "But I think I need to."

He unwrapped his fingers and extended his feathered hand to the man in the gallery, beneath the painting that was and wasn't him.

Brian looked down at the feathers. "I'll call her."

"I don't care how good the party is, Brian, I'm not coming."

"Your model is here, and he would like to meet you."

"How many vodka tonics have you had? That doesn't even make sense. I didn't use any models in this series."

"Not even the guy with feathers coming out of his skin? Because he's standing right in front of the painting, and it certainly looks like him, not to mention this thing where I'm watching him grow feathers on his arms, and what the fuck is going on here, Maeve?"

"What did you say?" The flesh on her arms rose up in goose bumps.

"You heard me. You need to get here.

"Now."

Maeve took a cab and went in through the service entrance, where she had loaded the paintings earlier that week.

"Brian, what is—you!"

"Yes," Sweeney said, and in an explosion of feathers and collapsing clothes, he turned into a bird.

Maeve sat with the bird while the celebration trickled out of the gallery. She had gathered up the clothes he had been wearing, and folded them into precise piles, stuffing his socks into the toes of the shoes, spinning the belt into a coil.

At one point, Brian had brought back a mostly empty bottle of vodka, filched from the bar. Maeve took a swig, and thought of taking another before deciding that some degree of sobriety was in order to counterbalance the oddity of the night.

The bird didn't seem interested in drinking either.

Maeve dropped her head into her hands and scraped her hair back into a knot. When she sat up again, Sweeney was pulling on his pants.

"I am sorry about before. Stress makes me less capable of interacting with people."

Maeve laughed under her breath. "I can relate."

Brian walked back. "Oh, good. You're, uh, dressed again. Have you two figured out what's going on?"

"I am under a curse," Sweeney said. "And I think Maeve can paint me free of it. There is some kind of power in her work, something that I would call magic. I'd like to commission a painting from her to see if this is possible."

"That's . . ." Maeve bit down hard on the next word.

"Mad? Impossible?" Sweeney met her eyes. "So am I."

"I'm not magic," Maeve said.

"That may be. After all this time and change, I am not a bird, though I sometimes have the shape of one. Magic reshapes truth."

Maeve could see the bird in the lines of the man, in the way he held his weight, in the shape of the almost-wings the air made space for.

She could see the impossibility, too, of what was asked.

"Please," said Sweeney. "Try."

"I'll need you," Maeve said, "to pose for me."

"This has got to be the weirdest contract I have ever negotiated."

"Brian. You negotiated with a guy who had been a bird for a significant part of the evening. Even if it had been straight-up 'sign here' boilerplate, it still would have been the weirdest contract you ever negotiated."

"True."

"I'm surprised he didn't ask for a deadline." Maeve picked up one of the white feathers from the floor, ran it through her fingers. "Some way of marking whether this will work or not, rather than just waiting to find out."

"You say 'whether' like you genuinely believe it's a possibility, Maeve.

"And yes, this has been a night of strangeness, but magic

is not what happens at the end. The way this ends is that you're going to wind up painting a very nice picture for a guy who is, I don't know how, sometimes a bird, and he is still going to be sometimes a bird after it is signed and framed, and once it is, we will never speak of this again because it is just too weird.

"You're good, Maeve. But you're not a magician. So stop worrying about whether there's magic in your painting, because there isn't."

"You said people don't buy paintings just because of what's on the canvas, they buy the story they think the painting tells," Maeve said.

Brian nodded.

"Sweeney bought a story where magic might be what happens at the end. He's bought that hope.

"And that much, I can paint."

Maeve took a sketchbook and went back to the Cathedral of Saint John the Divine. It seemed like the right place to start, even if she didn't put the church itself into her painting. Full circle, somehow, to try to end the transformation in the same place she had first witnessed it.

Spring had come early, the buds on the trees beginning to limn the branches with a haze of green. The crocuses unfurled their purples in among the feet of the trees, and an occasional bold daffodil waved yellow.

And this was transformation too, Maeve thought. More regular, less astonishing than a man suddenly enfeathered, but change all the same.

Maeve sat beneath a branch of birdsong and cleared her mind of the magic she had been asked to make. If the bird—if Sweeney—was correct, it would be there anyway.

She opened her sketchbook and began to draw.

Sweeney walked the streets of his city. It wasn't often that he wandered on foot, preferring to save his peregrinations for when he wore wings. But tonight, he did not want to be above the grease and char scents of food cooking on sidewalk carts, of the crunch of shattered glass beneath his shoes.

He wanted the pulse and the press of people he had never quite felt home among. They would be his home if Maeve succeeded. Perhaps then he would feel as if he belonged.

He should have, perhaps, spent his night on the wing, the flight a fragment to shore against the ruin of his days once he could no longer fly. He would miss, every day of his life he would miss, the sensation of the air as his feathers cut through it. But he would have a life.

Sweeney bought truly execrable coffee in an I LOVE NY cup, because at that moment, with every fiber of his being, Sweeney did.

. . .

"Can I ask . . ." Maeve hesitated.

"How this happened," Sweeney said.

She looked up from her sketchbook. "Well, yes. I don't want to be rude, or ask you to talk about something that's hurtful, but maybe I'll know better how to paint you out of being a bird if I know how you became one in the first place."

"It was a curse."

"I thought that was the kind of thing that only happened in fairy tales."

Sweeney shrugged, then apologized.

"That's fine. I don't need you to hold the pose."

"And I'll stop interrupting." Maeve bent back to her sketchbook.

"It is like something from a fairy tale. I was angry. I spoke and acted without thought, and, in the way of these things, it was a wizard I insulted. He cursed me for what I had done.

"For over a thousand years since, this has been my life."

"I'm sorry. Even if it was your fault, over a thousand years of vengeance seems cruel."

Tension rippled over Sweeney's skin. He shrank in on himself, fingers curling to claws.

"What is it?"

Sweeney extended his arm. Feathers downed its underside. "I had hoped this wouldn't happen."

"Does it hurt?"

"Only in my pride. Which was the point of the thing, after all." He schooled his breathing, and Maeve watched him relax, muscle by muscle. Except for a patch near his wrist, the feathers fell from Sweeney's skin.

"May I?" Maeve asked.

Sweeney nodded.

Maeve stroked her hand over his wrist, feeling the feathers' softness, and the heat of Sweeney's skin beneath. Heart racing like a bird's, she stepped closer and kissed him.

A beat passed, and then another.

Sweeney's hand fisted in her hair, and he shuddered a breath into her mouth. She struggled out of her clothes, not wanting to break the kiss, or the contact.

Feathers alternated with skin under Maeve's hands, and Sweeney traced the outlines of her shoulder blades as if she, too, had wings.

As they moved together, Sweeney was neither feathered nor mad. Maeve did not feel the panic of a body too close, only the joy of a body exactly close enough.

White feathers blanketed the floor beneath them.

Maeve looked at Sweeney. "I don't think the painting is going to work."

"Why?" He tucked her hair behind her ear.

"I mean, I think it will be a good painting. But I don't think it will be magic."

"I'm no worse than I am now if it isn't. All I ask for is a good painting, Maeve. Anything beyond that would be"—he smiled—"magic."

The parcel arrived in Wednesday's post. Inside, the sketchbook Maeve had lost. In the front cover, a scrawled note: "Forgive me my temporary theft. It's long past time that I returned this. —S." There was also a white feather.

She flipped through the pages and wondered what Sweeney had seen that convinced him her art was magic, the kind of magic that could help him. Whatever that thing had been, she couldn't see it.

Maeve kept the feather, but she slid the notebook into a fresh envelope to return it to Sweeney. Even if she couldn't give him freedom, she could give him this.

That done, Maeve took down all the reference photos of mystical, fantastic birds that she had printed out and hung on her walls while painting the show for the gallery. She closed the covers of the bestiaries and slid feathers into glassine envelopes, making bright kaleidoscopes of fallen flight.

She packed away the shadow boxes, the skeletons, the figurines, reshelved the fairy tales.

The return of the sketchbook had reminded her of one thing. If there was any magic she could claim, it was hers, pencil on a page, pigment on canvas. It came from her, not from anywhere else.

The only birds Maeve left in sight were a white feather, a photo she had downloaded from her phone of a naked man perched in a tree, and the sketches she had made of Sweeney. Finally, she hung the recent sketches from the cathedral. She would have to go back there, she thought, before this was finished, but not yet. Not until the end.

At first, Sweeney thought it was the madness come upon him again. His skin itched as if there were feathers beneath it, but they were feathers he could neither see nor coax out of his crawling skin.

His bones ground against one another, too light, the wrong shape, shivering, untrustworthy. Not quite a man, not wholly a bird, and uncertain what he was supposed to be.

The soar of flight tipped over the edge into vertigo, and he landed with an abrading slap of his hands against sidewalk.

And then he knew.

Maeve was painting. Painting his own, and perhaps ultimate, transformation.

Dizzy, he ran to where he had first seen her, the Cathedral of Saint John the Divine.

Maeve hated painting in public. Hated it. People stood too close, asked grating questions, offered opinions that were neither solicited nor useful, and offered them in voices that were altogether too loud.

The quiet space in her head that painting normally gave her became the pressure of voices, the pinprick texture of other people's eyes on her skin.

She hated it, but this was the place she had to paint, to finish Sweeney's commission here at the cathedral. The end was the beginning.

On the canvas: the shadow of Sweeney rising to meet him, a man-shape greyed and subtle behind a bird. Sweeney, feathers raining around him as he burst from bird to man. A white bird, spiraling in flight, haunting the broken tower of the cathedral, a quiet and stormy ruin.

The skies behind Maeve filled with all manner of impossible birds. On the cathedral lawn, women played chess, and when one put the other in check, a man in a faraway place stood up from a nearly negotiated peace.

Behind Maeve, Sweeney gasped, stumbled, fell. And still she painted.

This time, it felt like magic.

The pain was immense. Sweeney could not speak, could not think, could barely breathe as he was unmade. Maeve was not breaking his curse, she was painting a reality apart from it.

Feathers exploded from beneath his skin, roiling over his body in waves and disappearing again.

He looked up at the canvas, watched Maeve paint, watched the trails of magic in her brushstrokes. In the trees were three birds with the faces and torsos of women, sirens to sing a man to his fate.

The church bells rang out, a sacred clarion, a calling of time, and Sweeney knew how this would end.

It was not what he had anticipated, but magic so rarely was.

Maeve set her brush down and shook the circulation back into her hands. A white bird streaked low across her vision and perched in front of one of the clerestory windows.

"Maeve."

She turned, and Sweeney the man lay on the ground behind her. "Oh, no. This isn't what I wanted."

She sat next to him, took his hand. "What can I do?"

"Just sit with me, please."

"Did you know this would happen, when you commissioned the painting?"

"I considered the possibility. I had to. Without the magic binding me into one spell or the next, the truth is I have lived a very long time, and I knew that death might well be my next migration."

Sweeney's following words were quieter, as if he was remembering them. "No one chooses his quest. It is chosen for him."

Sweeney closed his eyes. "This is just another kind of flight."

Maeve hung the finished painting on her wall. Outside, just beyond the open window, perched a white bird.

Returned

The shadows press on your skin, prickled velvet that shouldn't have weight, shouldn't have texture, shouldn't feel like you are wearing sandpaper and poison, but they do.

You are almost used to it, this new way that things that shouldn't happen do, but you do not like it.

Here is one of the things that shouldn't have happened: you are awake, and you do not want to be.

No.

No, that's not quite it, and you are going to be honest. You are going to put aside the polite fucking fictions that are in place to make everyone else feel better around you because you are done, done, done caring what they feel. Since you have returned, no one has given any indication that they care about what you feel.

So. To say the thing true: you are alive, and you do not want to be.

Well, you are not exactly sure about that one word.

Alive.

You died. Not the sort of dead on the operating table, light at the end of the tunnel, go back to those who love you, near-death kinds of dead. But dead dead. All the way gone.

A death certificate was signed. Your body was cremated. You were made into a thing of ash and air and some fragments of bone. All that was left to go wherever you were was a soul, and that had gone on long before the burning of your body.

Not that it had been your idea to die. You weren't a suicide. It had been

(a snake bite)

(a poisoned apple)

(a hand around your throat)

Anyway, you don't exactly remember, or rather you do. The problem is you exactly remember all those things, all those possible deaths, and you cannot say which one was yours.

Maybe that is why everyone looks at you, well, like that.

Maybe not. You've heard them talk.

You remember being dead. You remember passing over the white bone of the corpse road, feeling vertebrae, ribs, phalanges, crunch beneath your feet. You remember the air shivering as you passed beneath the lych-gate. The scale that weighed your heart. You didn't need coins to pay your passage, because . . . No. That part you don't remember.

(maybe)

(no)

The queen whose eyes were as cold as marble, who welcomed you with frostbite's kiss. You remember her very well. She smelled of winter and tasted like pomegranates.

You were neither particularly happy nor particularly sad about being dead. There were things you hadn't done—you had never learned French or how to make a soufflé. You never started the novel you had always meant to write, and you still couldn't run for more than a mile without stopping.

You regretted not doing those things, but in a dull, quiet sort of way. It seemed to you just as likely you would never have done them, only kept them on a list for someday, even if you hadn't been

(stung by a bee)

(hit by a car)

(drowned in your bath)

You got used to being dead. The way the sky was shades of red, purple, grey—always striated with black, and never any stars. The way voices carried in the land of the dead, sounding more hollow, less real than other sounds, as if they were coming from farther away than the mouths that spoke. The way drinking from the wrong river could make you forget what it had been like to be alive.

(You had known that, about the river, before you arrived

on its shore. But it was only a little that you drank, and you had been thirsty, or at least you had thought you should be after your travel there, and besides, you didn't want to remember how you'd died.)

(You wish there were a river like that here.)

Then he showed up.

The hollow voices of the dead sounded almost solid in their excitement over his presence as they told you he was here, he was speaking. If he spoke well, he would take you back. Back to life.

Excitement was not what you felt about him being there.

You didn't listen to him speak. You stayed away, until you couldn't.

He was, you guessed, the person you would call your boyfriend. Or lover. Which you mostly thought was a stupid word, but what else do you call the guy who walks into the afterlife and drags you back into your beforelife with him?

Bringing you back was, all things considered, easy for him. He had rules and he had tasks and he had warnings, and if he did all the things exactly as he was supposed to, you would have to go with him. He did, and you did.

No one ever asked you what you wanted.

The cold-eyed queen's goodbye kiss burned like ice on your lips from the moment they touched hers until the moment you stepped again into the sun. You think you remember seeing a tear on her cheek as she embraced you and bid you safe journey, but perhaps you only want to remember that.

Now that he has brought you back, he is bright-eyed and golden and so very pleased with his success, so very proud of himself. He is handsome on television, and in the photographs for websites and weekly magazines that write stories about what he's done, stories that say bringing you back was a miracle of love. He writes a "Top Ten List of Romantic Gestures Sure to Win Her Heart," and no one comments on the fact that, for number one to work, she has to be dead first. No one says that things are more romantic when the girl is alive.

You are a shadow in photographs, cold-eyed and frost-bitten, and everyone says they cannot tell what he sees in you. This makes them like him all the more. He must be a really great guy, to love someone like you. To stay by your side, even now, now that you are like this.

You cringe from the sun, too bright in a sky that is shades of blue, day and night, and full of the stark white light of stars. You step back when he tries to touch you.

He had sex with you once. The first night you were back. He had brought you back because he loved you, and now he was going to show you how much. He pushed himself inside you and withered almost immediately. You were too cold, he said. Like a dead thing.

He hasn't tried again.

Small mercies.

You'd walk away, leave, if you could, but whatever tether pulled you with him out of death, whatever magic reconstituted the pieces of your immolated body around your peregrine soul, still hasn't snapped. If you get too far away from him, well, you can't. You are dissolved, reconstituted, turned inside out. Returned to him, to his side, to this curse he has brought you to.

You wish he had looked back.

But he didn't, and you are here. Returned. And at the center of an attention that is just one more thing that you don't want. You hate how they look at you, with pity and puzzlement. You hate how they look at him, lust and belief.

No one cares about the truth of you. At first, they expected you to be happy. Not being dead was clearly superior to being dead. And how romantic, what he had done. He must love you very much.

No one asked you the opposite question—whether you loved him, whether you had wanted to return with him. The old magics are not without their flaws.

The people around him watch you as you turn from him, as you flinch from his hand, as you stay behind him, as far as you can without being snapped back to his side, as if you are ungrateful, as if you are some half-wild, feral thing, and you suppose you are.

The reason why is another thing they do not know, that you would tell them if they asked. Your body was not the only thing that came back when you were yanked between death and life.

Your memories did too, the ones you drank away with the river. Bits and pieces, here and there, more like a dream than like events you lived through (died in), but maybe that's how things are now. Even your dreams feel more real than this thing that happens when you're awake, this thing you used to call life.

But you are awake, and you do remember.

You remember that you weren't in love with him, not anymore. You were going to leave, you had told him.

You remember he reached past you, and closed the door, and said:

"No."

You remember the look in his eyes as he told you he would never let you leave his side.

You remember the weight of his hand as it crushed your throat.

You remember that, even though you were dead, you ran from him, under the red-black sky of the land of the dead, on the white, white bones of the corpse road. Ran much farther than a mile without stopping. Ran into eternity, fleeing into death, away from the pursuing voice that called out how much he had loved you, loved you so much, why couldn't you see it, he would make you see.

You crossed the river's shore and you washed your hands

in it, washed your hands of him, and drank its waters to forget.

But now you remember.

And the shadows fall painful on your skin, and the sky is too bright, and you cannot turn your back and walk away from him.

So you try to die. It's the only way you can think of to get away from him, and it wasn't bad, being dead. (The cold kiss of the colder queen.) You were just starting to get used to it. You miss the soothing darkness of the starless sky.

You open your wrists because the knife is close and you have never been afraid of blood, but the liquid that runs in the wake of the blade is darker than blood and your skin heals almost before the cut is finished.

You take pills, so many pills, and you do not even fall asleep.

You sink yourself beneath the waves and discover that you can breathe underwater.

He cries when you come back, dripping salt water behind you, and asks why you want to leave him again, when he loves you so much. He says that it is the power of his love that keeps you here. You should be grateful that he rescued you, that he has made it so you can always be together.

You think about that word: "always." It is stuffed to the letter with time; it is an alternate shape for an infinity symbol.

It is unbearable.

"I'll tell them," you say. "I'll tell them that you killed me."

He doesn't even bother to laugh. It's too ridiculous. You're clearly not dead. He has fixed things, taken it back.

Fixed. Things.

Rage is acid in your veins. Even the air on your skin is needles. Your lips peel back from your teeth and you hiss like a snake, like a Medusa, like a basilisk.

And perhaps your gaze is poison, because it fixes him like a stone.

You don't think of what happens next as murder. His death is only a side effect. But if you are going to be tethered to him for always, for that infinity-shaped word, you are going to choose where.

Your fingers are claws and you tear his fragile heart from behind the opened cage of his ribs, and when it ceases to beat in your hand, you feel the rubber-band snap of a loosed tether. This is not what you expected. This is better.

Free. You are free.

You drop the ruined thing from your stained hand. It is full of blood, and not love, after all, no matter what he said. You begin to walk away. You can feel the bones of the corpse road again, and you know that if you just keep walking, you will find it under your feet, that it will return you to where you belong.

Then you turn. You look back. There is one thing you need to bring with you. A talisman against future events.

This time when you leave, you don't look back. You carry

his head by the hair, and when the white bone of his spine, unstrung like a broken lyre, clatters against the white bone of the road, you stop and you fix it there. You place it very carefully. You make sure that his sightless eyes are always looking into the land of the dead, always looking in the wrong direction to walk out himself, or to drag you back with him.

This time, you do not drink from the river of forgetfulness. You do not even wash your hands in it. You return, covered in the price of your passage, to the cold queen on her colder throne, and she presses her cold lips to yours. Your hands smear her red, like the crushed seeds of a pomegranate, and she tells you how glad she is that you have returned.

The Calendar of Saints

14 February—Feast of Saint Valentine

Saint Valentine is often depicted surrounded by roses and birds. Popular poses include his officiating at a marriage or extending his hands in benediction over a couple. He is claimed as patron by affianced couples, those crossed in love, and beekeepers.

The first time I used a blade to defend a point of honor, both the blade and the honor were mine. I was perhaps eight, and Rosamaria Sandro had accused me of copying her mathematics exam. The next time we were in the salle, I told her I would prove her a liar with my blade. She stopped laughing at the idea when I hit her for the third time with the blunted end of my sword and made her tell our mathematics instructor the truth. The pomp and ceremony of today's events have nothing in common with that juvenile scuffle but the blade.

The blade, of course, is what matters. It is as sharp, as edged, as fatal as truth.

The subject of this Arbitration stands to the left of the dueling grounds, tiny white teeth sunk so deep into her lip that it, too, whitens. Her fiancé hovers close by, as if to shield her from the events or perhaps from their consequences. I wonder if he will put her aside if I am defeated. I want to think that he will stay with her, that his protective posture is a sign of genuine attachment rather than a signal of possession. Laurelle is beautiful and wealthy. The things that have been whispered about her would never have been said so viciously if it were otherwise. So it is possible he stands at her back because of reasons other than love, but I do not wish to believe in them.

Lost in my thoughts, I stumble in my warm-up, bruising the arch of my left foot against a stone I should have cleared from the ground. This is why I hate knowing the stakes when I take up my blade—they are a distraction. What I think should happen, what I would wish for the outcome to be, means nothing. If wishes mattered, there would be no need of swords.

My distracted thoughts focus as the Arbiter takes his place at the precise midpoint of the square, and I remind myself that Laurelle du Lyon's honor—or possible lack thereof—has not been placed in my keeping but has been entrusted to my blade, and my blade has long been dedicated to the will of

God. Not that I wish to believe in God any more than I wish to believe Laurelle's fiancé cares only for the social and financial benefits of his upcoming marriage. The only thing I have faith in is my blade. Still, the formalities must be observed, and there is something to be said for a system of order in the face of chaos. The Church is gifted at the maintenance of order.

The Arbiter reminds those watching that by the grace of God and Her holy saints, my victory will confirm the truth of Laurelle's claim to chastity. Should my opponent prevail, his victory will give divine imprimatur to the bragging of Count Gregorio. When directed to do so, I kneel, holding my sword before me like a cross, as the Arbiter invokes God's justice and mercy and asks that the light of truth shine down in judgment.

The count's claim is represented by the blade of Leviticus Cole. Thus, I do not need to hear the Arbiter announce that the duel ends with First Blood. Cole is known for neither subtlety nor endurance, but rather for brute force with a blade. He doesn't have the skill to fence beyond First Blood. Cole knows this and so has only taken preliminary vows. I have never understood why, if he is unwilling to risk his death, he took any vows at all. Truth feeds on sacrifice as much as it feeds on belief.

But I am not here to judge him, nor to judge anyone.

God's judgment is rendered on the third pass, when I supinate my wrist to bring my blade a hair above Cole's and lay open his cheek to the bone.

My role finished, I clean my blade as the Arbiter places his blessing upon Laurelle and her fiancé. They hold hands as they kneel before him.

30 May—Feast of Saint Joan of Arc

Saint Joan is often depicted as a young woman dressed in armor. Although she is usually shown carrying a sword, artists generally portray her gazing off into the distance, as if listening to her holy voices. She is claimed as patron by those in prison, victims of judicial abuses, and women in military service.

There were not many options available, here in the City of Seven Hills, for a girl who was a whore's bastard. Certainly, becoming a Sacred Blade was not one of the few options my mother offered me. There was no money for schooling. Everything extra was necessary for my mother to maintain the illusions of her profession.

But I was born on the feast day of Saint Michael, lord of hosts and patron saint of fencers, and my mother named me Jeanne, after another martial saint. When he found me defending his ridiculous lapdog from a rabid stray, holding a stick like I was wielding a rapier, one of my mother's clients decided it would be a good joke to pay for my education as a swordswoman. My training began as a joke, but the sword became my vocation.

It became my life.

I graduated undefeated. The next day, I took vows as a Sacred Blade.

17 September—Feast of Saint Robert Bellarmine

Saint Robert Bellarmine is often depicted in the red robes of his cardinalate. To his right are the scales of justice, symbolizing his work in founding the Lex Canonica, *and to his left hangs an orrery, symbolizing his advocacy of Saint Galileo. Saint Robert Bellarmine is credited with the first serious steps toward harmonization of the disciplines of theology and science. He is claimed as patron by lawyers, astronomers, and students.*

There are no fresh-faced lovers at the dueling grounds today. Instead, pinch-faced clerks with threadbare cuffs and ink-smirched fingers shadow their elegant patrons. The patrons offer precisely gauged deference to the Arbiter. It is an uneasy crowd, more used to the bloodless weight of precedent than the sharp cut of a blade.

I shake my hands as I stretch, limbering my muscles and loosening my fingers in the cool morning air. My feet slide through patterns of attack and retreat.

Although it hasn't always been, it is now rare for the Justiciar to send disputes to the dueling grounds to be arbitrated. The *Lex Canonica* is fussy and labyrinthine, but it is also widely considered just. It is possible this dispute is over a matter of faith or that one of the parties is a member of the cardinalate, although if that is the case, it is odd that the dispute has gone through the Justiciary at all. Perhaps the case is here because one of the parties understands that words obscure truth, while swords lay it bare, clean and to the bone.

I continue to shake my hands as I warm up, willing the stiffness and ache out of my fingers. The Arbiter arrives, red robes brilliant through the resinous haze of incense. I walk back to my end of the courtyard and wrap the black sash of the challenger around my waist, tucking the ends in tightly, then slide my misericorde through the sash at my left hip. The Arbiter's acolytes cover the dueling grounds in a thick layer of scented smoke. I listen for the tolling of the Bell, but it does not sound. Third Blood, then.

The stakes are not read. Perhaps I am in the minority, but I prefer it when the Challenges begin in silence. Arbitrations are cleaner when the only thing at stake is the skill of the two blades.

Magdalena Nero is representing the challenged party. I know her by reputation only—she trained at Maria, Stella Maris. Their students are known for stealth and cunning.

Since there is time to strategize, I let her score First Blood, a thin red line across my left bicep. I wince, as if it hurts, and let that side drag. Smiling, Magdalena comes in high and fast. Fire blossoms along my collarbone. I continue past her guard and flick my blade through the flesh of her sword arm and then across her back.

Second Blood to both.

Breathing rapidly, I retreat, then continue backward, pulling distance at the peak of her attacks to make her lunge, then pressing her recovery, hoping to annoy her into forgetting stealth, into forsaking cunning for an honest attack. Finally, when she has backed me into a corner, she redoubles her lunge.

I spin toward her outthrust blade, switch my own into my left hand, and continue the motion, driving my weapon into the soft flesh above her right hip bone. Third Blood.

Magdalena blasphemes loudly, cursing her blade. The focus of the clerks and their patrons snaps back to the dueling grounds. This place is sacred. There are consequences for blasphemy here.

Magdalena has already dropped her blade and fallen to her knees, begging for mercy. The Bell tolls, low and clear, and the Arbiter meets my eyes, then nods once.

I draw the misericorde from the sash at my waist, then step forward and slip the knife into her heart. It is a clean kill—she bleeds hardly at all.

The Arbiter steps onto the cold stone of the dueling grounds and I prostrate myself, cruciform, for absolution. He speaks the words by rote and turns away before I regain my feet. After a novena has passed, I will present myself and my sword at the Cathedral for reconsecration, my sin officially forgiven.

17 September—Feast of Saint Hildegard von Bingen

Author of the oldest extant scientific writings by a woman, Saint Hildegard is often depicted with pen and ink in hand. Paintings of her are often bordered by musical notation from one of her compositions, and a flask of boiling water usually sits in the background. Saint Hildegard is claimed as patron by women in the biological sciences, linguists, and migraine sufferers.

The man in black sets another whiskey in front of me and places enough money on the bar to cover the two that I've already drunk.

I push the money back. "I was paid well enough for this morning's work to cover my own drinks, thank you."

"One might think if you had truly been paid well enough, you would not now be drinking until you can no longer hold a sword."

"I'm not drinking over what I was paid to do."

"Over your opponent's death, then."

"She wasn't my opponent when I executed her." I accept mortal commissions; I've killed before. Those deaths were honest. Magdalena's was a waste, and my hands are filthy with it. With a casual nod, from a cleric who knew nothing about the sword edge of truth, I have been made to feel like a heretic. "Being wielded in that fashion perverts what a Blade is supposed to be."

He sips his drink once, twice. "And what is it that a Blade is supposed to be?"

I drain my own glass, feeling the flame of the alcohol lick its path down my throat and numb the raw edges of my thoughts. "Truth."

"Agreed. Which is why we'd like to place you on retainer."

"Forgive me, but who is 'we'?"

"The Ignatians." The man in black pushes back his hood to reveal the silk lining of ebon-shot burgundy, indicative of membership in that Order. "We would offer you a commission."

He pauses, then turns to face me directly. "And the holy sword of Saint Ignatius Loyola."

A large enough shock, it seems, actually can smack a person sober. Ignatius Loyola, a former soldier, founded the Sacred Blades when Arbitration became the legal method of answering the unanswerable. He never lost. Popular legendry holds his sword to be miraculous.

"Father, I appreciate the honor you do me, but I do not possess the faith I believe your Order would require in the wielder of that blade."

The Ignatian places his hands, sheathed in skintight

gloves of black leather that were bonded to his flesh at the wrists, on the scarred surface of the bar. "My name is Michael Gonzaga. Since the death of Saint Ignatius, my family has served as custodians of his sword, passing it from hand to hand. God Herself has shown me in a vision that the next hand to touch the sword is meant to be yours."

"God Herself has a strange sense of humor, in that case."

"Perhaps She does."

24 October—Feast of Saint Tycho Brahe

Saint Tycho is commonly depicted in full court robes, standing before a telescope. In the background can be seen a star in supernova and a comet. In his left hand, he holds a model of a human nose, cast in gold. Saint Tycho is claimed as patron by poets, makers of prosthetic devices, and designers of astronomical instruments.

I became the Sacred Blade of the Ignatians. Although they are an all-male Order, their rule makes provision for vowed female Blades. I kept my vigil in front of the crypt of Saint Ignatius, his sword gleaming coldly before me as I knelt on the marble of the Cathedral. The saint did not speak to me that night, but then, I did not expect him to. When dawn finally broke, kaleidoscoping through the stained glass of the rose window, I heaved myself up from my aching knees, bowed low before the altar, and picked up his sword for the first time.

My hand trembled only a little.

THE CALENDAR OF SAINTS

The hilt of the sword bumps against my hip as I walk to the library to meet with Michael Gonzaga to learn the commission I have been hired to defend.

He sits underneath an India-ink rendering of the Hazelnut Cosmos of Saint Julian of Norwich. His hands rest on his lap, and I can see the red line of skin where his gloves are bonded to his flesh. For as long as I live, mine will be the only hand to touch the sword of Saint Ignatius. When I die, it will return to the custody of Fr. Gonzaga or, in the unlikely event that he predeceases me, his successor.

The very unlikely event. Death is only one of the truths of the blade, but it is beatitude and commandment both.

Fr. Gonzaga begins speaking as soon as the backs of my calves brush the rungs of my chair. "Our Order has retained you because there have been a series of Challenges made to the teachings of the saints. None have been heard as yet, but we believe that it is only a matter of time before one will be."

"Which saints?"

"The scientists."

"Science has never been a matter for the Arbiter's jurisdiction." Not that there are never disagreements over the scientists' theories, but those play out in the Laboratories of the University.

"Not previously, no. But we hear rumor that a Challenge is being prepared that will claim that the Laws of Science contradict the Laws of God."

"That's heresy." During the time of Saints Robert

Bellarmine and Galileo Galilei, scientific law was infallibly declared divine truth.

"Yes. And heresy must be judged on the dueling grounds of the Arbiter."

"This is ridiculous. The Church believes in the saints of science."

"Not all of the Church. Some hold that complex science is simply miracles our pride has blinded us from recognizing as such."

"Your Order does not believe that. No sensible part of the Church believes that."

"Honoring our vows requires us to defend the Church."

Honoring my vows requires that I do so as well. Honor, which is as sharp as penance, as sharp as truth. As sharp as a blade.

22 June—Feast of Saint Thomas More

Saint Thomas More is depicted in his robes and chain of office as lord chancellor. An ax, the instrument of his martyrdom, crosses the field of the painting, left to right. On the desk in front of the saint are copies of two of his works, Moriae enco-mium *and* Utopia. *Saint Thomas More is claimed as patron by politicians, diplomats, and writers of fantastic impossibilities.*

Gonzaga hands me the curling sheet of paper. The scarlet ribbons signifying it has come from the Arbiter are affixed to the bottom of the page by a wax seal showing two crossed swords. "The Challenge is to Saint Rudolf Clausius's work on thermodynamics. They chose well."

He is right. The Challenge, which states that a universe in which chaos is increasing is incompatible with an ordered universe designed by God, is a smart one. "I don't see a resolution to this anywhere outside the Arbiter's jurisdiction."

I don't either, and even contemplating the Challenge repulses me. Heresy is judged on the dueling grounds, yet this Challenge, for all it follows the legal forms, is also a form of heresy.

I put my hand on the hilt of the sword I carry everywhere and worry my fingers across its curves. As the Branch Militant of the Church, the Ignatians are sworn to defend the *Lex Canonica*, and I am the sworn Blade of the Ignatians. "Will the Order command me to lose?"

Fr. Gonzaga looks appalled. "Jeanne, no. The Challenge is mortal. And even if it weren't, such an action would be a grave sin against the blade you wear.

"Our Order believes in the *Lex Scientia*, holds it equal to the *Lex Canonica*—Saint Bellarmine was an Ignatian, after all—but we recognize that we may not know the truth entire. Perhaps this Challenge is a way of showing us a new facet of the truth. For us to see that, you must fence as you always do, Jeanne. To win."

Good. This perverse Challenge may require my life, but at least I will be allowed to keep my honor.

"Jeanne, if you don't believe in the Church's doctrines,

why do you care about the outcome of the Challenge? Why does it matter to you whether the Church calls something divine miracle or human discovery?"

"Because, Father Gonzaga, it isn't that I don't believe. It matters because I do. I believe absolutely in the law of the blade. This Challenge is a perversion of that law. It is blasphemy.

"I believe in this," I say, and I draw the sword at my side. "I believe it means something beyond the desire of the person wielding it, or the person wielding me." I drag my left hand across the blade, watch the blood weep from the wound.

"Truth is a blade, Father. It requires that we bleed."

8 January—Feast of Saint Galileo Galilei

It has recently become fashionable for artists to depict Saint Galileo sitting with his daughters, the nuns Maria Celeste and Arcangela. Orbiting their heads are the four Galilean moons. Saint Galileo is hailed as the father of modern science and is claimed as patron by physicists, insomniacs, and the blind.

In the grey light of early morning, I stand listening to the last echoes of the Bell's toll through myrrh-scented smoke.

A mortal Challenge. As expected. The morning reeks of endings.

I do not listen as the official Challenge is read. I know

THE CALENDAR OF SAINTS

why I am here, what I stand for. I look for Fr. Gonzaga in the crowd and see him, his lips moving, I assume in prayer. On the far side of the dueling grounds, my opponent, Josef Benedictus, shifts his weight back and forth.

We kneel, and the Arbiter absolves our sins. He begs the light of truth to shine upon us. We come en garde, and the signal to begin is given.

I fling the holy sword of St. Ignatius—my sword—to the heavens. Fr. Gonzaga cries out as it arcs through the air. Thinking that I have forfeited, Benedictus launches himself at me like an arrow shot from a bow.

A forfeit is not truth. A draw, however, is.

I step into his guard and slide the misericorde from his sash, then continue the motion, driving the knife into his heart. At the same time, I pierce my own.

9 January   Feast of Saint Jeanne of the Knife

Saint Jeanne is always depicted in the white garment of the Sacred Blades. The broken blade of Saint Ignatius Loyola lies at her feet, on top of a formal Challenge, rent in two. Her breast is pierced by a misericorde. Saint Jeanne is claimed as patron by scientists, bastard born, and unbelievers.

The Green Knight's Wife

The boys arrive with the changing of the weather, ushered in by winter's cold. Once a year, at the beginning of December, those silly boys who think coming here means they are brave. All of them so eager to test their worth on the edge of my husband's axe.

For years and forever and for always, through one story and into the next, they have been as regular as the snowfall, these boys. They come in their shining armor, their expensive suits, their television good looks—alien things among all this green wildness, this unchanging cathedral of my husband's making. He feels more comfortable in a place that is like him: forest, secret, overgrown.

No one ever asked me what my comforts were, whether I wanted to press myself to holly and thorn in my marriage bed.

He gives the boys a year and a day to arrive, my husband

does. "I like to make it fair for them." He laughs and oak leaves fall from his beard, holly berries roll red and fall to the floor like drops of blood.

I do not believe him. I am also an edge that those boys must test themselves against.

Here are the rules for the game my husband plays. It begins at the heart of winter, the ending of the year, at the great feasts of those brightly lit holidays, meant to call back the sun from the darkness. Someone calls for a wonder, and he goes.

My husband is a wonder, you see. He is vine and leaf, oak and holly, tree and forest and winter, wrapped around the shape of a man. The heart of him is a green and secret thing.

And, well, there is the small matter of his head.

He will pound on the doors until they open before his blows, and stand before the one who called. In the early days of the story, the summoner would be a king, overfed and drunk, in his Christmas court. Now it is just as likely a CEO and corporate party—more drink, less food. Some-times even the staged reality of a television show, and a room full of cameras and calculated angles. Once he has arrived before his audience, my husband will brandish his axe and ask: "Who is so bold in his blood and his brain that will dare strike one stroke for another?"

Oh, it sounds archaic now, and every so often, someone

asks him to change the wording—"Why can't you just say, 'You try to cut off my head and then I try to cut off yours'?"—but there is a formula to these things. The words matter. Besides, regardless of the phrasing, there is always someone willing to take the second part in this game, and brains have very little to do with it. They all think that they are special, they are chosen, they are as much a wonder as my husband is.

Then my husband will hand the axe over to the volunteer—a knight in armor, a lawyer in a suit, an actor in this month's designer T-shirt—and will make a big fuss about kneeling down, bending his head, baring his neck to the blow.

The poor, silly boy who has no real idea what he's gotten himself into, how old and how unpitying this story is, who thinks he is clever enough to get himself out of it, will pick up the axe, and smile, rooster-chested, at the queen, at the boss's wife, at the starlet of the week, and strike. The axe will bite true, and my husband's head will fall to the floor.

The boy—he will not think of himself as a boy, he will think of himself as a knight, as a *man*—will pose with the axe, will bow. Someone among those gathered will apologize to the queen for the mess, the blood.

And then my husband's body will stand up from the floor, and my husband's hand will reach into his hair, and he will pick up his fallen head, and his head will speak: "You must come to endure what you have dealt."

Someone usually faints at this point. It's never the person with the camera.

The rules are given, the chapel green, a year and a day, otherwise all honor lost. Honor. As if that was ever what this was about.

Head tucked under his arm, my husband turns, and comes home to me.

They show up early, the boys. Days, even weeks before the deadline, even now, in these days of planes and cars and GPS. So concerned with honor and reputation, with not looking like a coward, a pussy, they must pretend they are eager for the axe's kiss, for a blow they must understand will be fatal if struck. But they think they are special. They think there is a way out, at least for them. They are almost right.

This is when the second part of the game begins.

My husband disguises himself as someone whose beard is not made of oak leaves, whose arms are not wrapped around with trailing vines of ivy, and whose head, if struck off, would remain decorously detached and would definitely not start speaking.

He invites them to stay with us—we're close by, after all—and isn't it better to go to such an ordeal well-rested and fed? He pours them a drink, ice rattling against crystal, and smiles.

The boys look at the warm amber color of the scotch.

They think of the thread count of the sheets in this house, versus those of the cheap hotel just down the road. The boys look at me. They say yes.

My husband smiles.

He makes a deal with them—it's the deal he always makes. "Anything you're given while you're here, you give to me." He knows they'll say yes, these boys. They are here precisely because they're the kind of people who take dares, who say yes, who gamble. They are here to take a blow from an axe.

They think they can cheat and never be found out.

I am to be the thing that tests their honor: to offer sweet words, to offer kisses, to offer a casual fuck. The reality TV people, they love this. It's their favorite part, the thing that really kicks the ratings up. It's so drama, it's edgy, it's just potentially queer enough to titillate once the camera cuts away.

The cameras always cut away. At least when the kisses are traded back to my husband.

When this game began, I would play along. I would tempt the boys and laugh to see which of my offers they would accept. I would kiss them and smile, knowing my husband would taste me on their mouths. If he was going to give me away, I would take what pleasure I could get out of it.

If they tell him what they've been given, if they return to him those kisses and more, my husband tells them he understands, that what happened was my fault, no man could resist what it is I offer. When they kneel and bare their necks to him, he swings the axe and holds, the thin and almost bloodless line on their skin just deep enough to scar—a reminder, nothing more.

I cannot remember the last time this was how the game ended.

If the boys keep their secrets and mine, my husband cuts off their heads, and then he looks at me and smiles. This is, after all, my fault.

The first time this happened, so long and long ago, I felt the blow. A thud that landed in my chest, as if my husband's axe had hit me in the heart.

When it happens now, the cameras cut away.

It's so easy, if you're watching, to tell yourself it's special effects. The blood is added in post. That it could never happen. Not really.

It's so easy to ignore all the hard parts of a story when you don't have to live it.

The boys' heads don't reattach.

No matter how you bleach it, bone is never as white as snow.

And then one year, the boy doesn't show up. It is two days after the New Year and snow is falling outside, and the cameras are waiting, and my husband, green and wild, is pacing back and forth, axe in hand. Phone calls are made, texts sent, emails written, and no one can find him, this boy that is now late to his appointment with an axe. They can't believe it; I can't believe it has taken this long for someone to realize there is no game if you simply refuse to play.

But there is such panic. There won't be an episode, there will be no story without some silly knight and his honor, kneeling at my husband's feet. Everyone is desperate for the end.

"I'll do it."

The cameras turn to me. My husband laughs.

"All I need do is trade blows, yes? I return to you everything that I've been given while I've been here?" The cameras love this idea. My husband shrugs. It's not precisely the game he wants, but it's better than nothing.

So we crunch through the snow to the chapel green, to the heart of the forest. The berries are red on the holly and the air smells of pine.

I do not look at the skulls that line the eaves of the chapel.

My husband says the words of the challenge and hands me his axe. He kneels at my feet, stretching his head toward the altar. There is blood, old, rust-colored, sunk into the stones.

I swing the axe, and it cuts through his neck as if it is nothing. His head falls to the ground. But I am not finished. I swing the axe a second time, cutting through his chest, through the twisted vines that grow where his heart would be.

"Everything," I say, "that I have been given, I give back to you."

My husband's eyes close. His body does not stand. His head does not speak. I drop the axe next to his corpse.

I walk from the chapel. Blood falls from my hands, red as holly berries on the white snow.

Breaking the Frame

Escape

The photograph is of a woman at the center of a forest. She is as slim and tall and pale as the birches she stands among. The shadows turn her ribs and spine into branches, into knots in the wood. Around her arms, the peeling white bark of the birches, curved in bracelets. Between her thighs, the hair is dense and springy like moss.

She is turning into a tree.

All the stories tell us that this sort of transformation is the kind of thing that used to happen all the time, when maidens fled—good, virtuous girls—before the rampant desires of the gods. When they could run no more, they stopped, put down roots, raised up branches, and made themselves inviolate. Very nearly always a god will prefer warm, wet flesh to splinters.

To escape a god, a woman must lose her self.

The wood closes around her.

• • •

It was the first photograph he took of her.

"I need a model," he said. "For an ongoing series of work. Photographs."

Francesca sighed and sipped her coffee. "And I'm sure it's very legit, really, and any nudity will only be tasteful and artistic, and—what are you doing?"

He had set a laptop on the table next to her and was opening files. "Here's my portfolio. My agent's card, and the information of the last gallery where I showed. Call them. Google me. Talk to anyone. Then call me."

The photos on the screen were good. If he was a creep, at least he was a talented one.

"And who do I ask for, if I decide I'm saying yes?" Her voice was warm at the end of the question, an answer already implied in the asking.

"You mean when?" He smiled, and he was gorgeous. "Vaughan. Vaughan Matthews."

She said yes. Of course she said yes. There are no stories when people say no.

Six Seeds from a Pomegranate

At the center of the photograph is a pomegranate, torn open. Seeds are scattered everywhere. At the right edge of the

*image is a young woman, hair tangled and eyes soft, as if she
has just woken from a lover's bed. Her hands are stained red.
Between her lips is a pomegranate seed.*

That was the first time they slept together. Francesca's hands
were still sticky from the pomegranate's juice, and she left
red smears across the white cotton of Vaughan's sheets.
When they kissed, their mouths tasted of the wine-dark fruit,
simultaneously sweet and tart, of desire so great that a person
might consign herself to the underworld in order to satiate it.

After, she sat up, the red-smeared sheets pooled around
her waist. "You realize the only way this would be more of a
fucking cliché would be if I asked you for a cigarette right now."

"What's wrong with being a cliché?" Vaughan asked.
"There's truth in them. They wouldn't last so long otherwise."

He tugged the sheet from her fingers, then laced his
hand with hers. Tenderness, not lust.

This, Francesca thought. *This* was going to be trouble.

Delilah

*The woman is shot from behind, thick, tangled hair stream-
ing down her back. She is barefoot, in a thin white dress.
Held lightly in her left hand is a pair of scissors, blades open.*

Transformation is a magic that becomes more natural with
repetition. It is difficult at first, to slide behind someone's

eyes, to pull their skin up and over yours. The seams show. The fit isn't quite.

The next time is easier, and then the next, until becoming a new person takes no more work than buttoning on a new shirt.

The thing about changing into someone else, inhabiting their life, even if only briefly, is that each time it takes a heartbeat longer to remember who you were. One more breath before your soul returns to yourself. You are never quite the person you were before.

Perhaps not pearl-eyed, but sea-changed. Something strange.

"I want to try the shot with you completely submerged."

"Vaughan. The water is cold. Not lukewarm. Not tepid. But freezing-my-tits-off cold."

"It's making the blue tone in your skin fantastic. I'll get some close-ups, too."

Francesca stared at him, then climbed back into the lake. The layers of skirts she was wearing clung to her legs, weighing her down, and the flowers that had been strewn across the surface of the water were bedraggled and worse for wear.

She supposed she was, too.

In and out of the water she climbed, Ophelia rescuing herself, only to drown again at her lover's request.

Vaughan showed her the digital shots as he worked, and he was right—of course he was—about what the cold water was doing to the color of her skin: bluing her lips and shadowing her eyes in ways that makeup never could.

Francesca looked haunted, broken, dead.

The photographs were gorgeous.

"One more, as the sun sets."

So numb she couldn't shiver anymore, Francesca slid back into the water. And she slid beneath the surface, and she slid into darkness.

Pray You Love, Remember

Taken as the sun sets, the living fire on the surface of the lake is a stark contrast to the drowned woman floating beneath it.

This photograph was exhibited only once, and Matthews has said he will never sell it. Speculation in the art world suggests this decision is due to the circumstances under which the shot was taken. The model, Francesca Ward, nearly died, and then fell ill from pneumonia.

Matthews did no new work during her illness.

Francesca fell in love with Vaughan when he brought a book of fairy tales to read to her while she was sick.

That's not quite true.

But she felt an ache inside her chest as Vaughan's voice broke over Beauty leaving her family and running back to the side of the ailing Beast, and the ache turned to warm honey as his hand fell from the page to hold hers.

It was safe then, his hand on hers, to say the word "love."

But really, the falling had been a foregone conclusion from the moment he showed her his photos and asked her to be in them.

Vaughan captured pieces of the world—never as it was, but as it could have been, as it *almost* was. As it might actually be, if we just looked around the edges and noticed the magic.

That was how he saw her, too, Francesca thought. As if she might be magic around the edges.

When someone sees you like that, falling in love is always only a question of when.

Beauty and—

In the foreground of the photograph is a rose on top of a cracked mirror. There are clocks everywhere, fallen, tilted, askew, and all with their hands fixed at three minutes to twelve. Given the shadows in the picture, one assumes the hour being chased is midnight.

At the left is a woman in a ruined ball gown. She holds the head of a beast.

There is a thing that happens to stories when you try to change them. Narrative is resistant to change. It clings to its themes, its arcs, its tropes.

If you find the fault lines along the story's center and apply pressure, you can expose the pulse of its bloody heart. You can draw your pen through its entrails and read the signs within.

But once you have, once you have gazed upon the heart of a story, your changes will be woven into its fabric, embraced as a variant text. The story will reshape itself around what you have written, will scar over the wounds that you have so carefully made.

You can change it, but the thing you loved in the story will always look different to you after.

Look Back in—
The woman is shot from the back, and there is a bright light before her, so we see her only in outline. She is climbing up a set of steps hewn into rock, climbing out of somewhere.

Or perhaps not.

A hand reaches through the light toward her. Instead of reaching for it, she looks over her shoulder, turning back.

"That wasn't the photograph I took. You saw the finished shot. You know."

"I was there, Vaughan. I know that's not the shot. I didn't turn my head, never looked back."

Why would she have? She knew the story of Orpheus and Eurydice. It was Orpheus who looked back, and Eurydice who disappeared, returned to death. She trusted him enough to follow him out of the darkness, but he had no faith in her silent footsteps.

"I didn't look back," she repeated.

"I know," said Vaughan.

"But I thought about it."

"What?"

"I thought about what it would be like, walking out of death, and back into life, and how my feet would ache from walking, and how the sun would hurt my eyes, and what if I didn't want to go with him?"

"What?"

"I mean, we assume Eurydice loved Orpheus because of the story, and how he goes down to Hades for her and everything, but no one ever asked her if she loved him. No one asked her if she wanted to go back."

"So you did."

Francesca laughed. "I guess I did. I'm sorry if I fucked up your picture."

"I'm not. And you didn't. It isn't what I thought I was getting, but it's good."

The problem with wonders is their duplication. When something happens once, it is a miracle. When the miracle recurs, it must be renamed.

Language is not meant to contain miracles. To manifest, they require somewhat else.

· · ·

Subtext

The photograph is a nude. The model's body is entirely covered by lines of text. The quotations are taken from fairy tale and myth, romance and fantasy, and they turn the model's body into a palimpsest from a commonplace book.

However, if the text on the body is read carefully, it becomes clear that certain of the stories have been altered from their known forms.

Which ones have been so rewritten is a matter for debate.

Shadows of words remained on Francesca's skin, ghost-tattoos of stories that almost were.

She had asked Vaughan not to tell her the lines he'd chosen, not to say which stories he was inscribing on her skin. She had kept her eyes closed, had not read what was written on her body.

And still.

"Some of them changed," he said. "Like this one: "'Find me,' she said, and stepped out of her shoes of glass.'"

"It makes the story better," Francesca said, "if it's told like that."

"How so?"

"Well, isn't it more fun to think of them in conspiracy together? Instead of the prince being some kind of foot fetishist and Cinderella just waiting around, happy to marry whoever shows up with her shoe?"

"When you put it like that, yes." Vaughan traced the words braceleting Francesca's wrist, words he had written there: "and only in the mirror to see the other." The phrase was unchanged on her skin, unchanged in the photograph. Others weren't and his skin prickled as he read them. "Francesca, I don't think it's my camera doing these things."

"No. I don't either."

Every Maze Has a Monster

This is a triptych of photographs, done in sepia. The first two are cross sections of a labyrinth, old, with crumbling rock walls. At the bottom, running through the twists of the maze, is a golden thread.

In the third photograph, there is the same labyrinth, the same thread, but now we are in its center. A woman stands there. She holds a spool of golden thread in one hand, and she is smiling.

It is impossible to tell if she is unwinding the thread or gathering it back up.

Stories change. They become unexpected and require a braver sort of belief. Not belief in what is, but belief in what could be.

Possibility.

Power.

. . .

"The picture didn't change," Francesca said.

"Did you expect it to?" asked Vaughan.

She thought of the cool air, the dry scent of dust, the strength of the cord she had wound through her fingers. "No. No, I didn't. The way you composed the shot, Ariadne was making her own choice."

"You're still not going to tell me what direction you were winding the thread, are you?"

"What direction do you think I was winding it?" Francesca smiled.

Half-Sick of Shadows

A boat rests beneath a willow tree.

Scattered near the boat are pieces of discarded armor. Among them, the white shield, three bends gules, of Sir Lancelot.

A white dress drapes the armor.

The lady is in the water, not drowned, but smiling.

The light on the water is brilliant, bright glints like scattered diamonds. Like the pieces of a shattered mirror.

"Have you ever," Vaughan asked, "thought about taking your own pictures?"

"Actually, yes. I know exactly the one I want to start with."

. . .

Freedom

Francesca Ward's photograph is composed in a manner that echoes Escape, *by Matthews. But while the two images are in dialogue,* Freedom *is no mere imitation.*

Rather, Ward's self-portrait is a reimagining. The strong lines of her body, the frank gaze with which she looks out from the photograph, make clear that this is the story of a woman, not of some thwarted god's prize.

The tree is split, and she is stepping out of it.

ACKNOWLEDGMENTS

Thank you to all of the editors who first published these short stories. I'm so grateful for your support and encouragement, and for the excellent homes you gave my writing. Thank you also to those kind friends who read these stories in draft, who gave me the tiny pieces of things that grew into ideas, who have been my support as a writer. In particular, thank you to Maria Dahvana Headley, Megan Kurashige, and Sarah McCarry.

Thank you to my agent, Brianne Johnson, who is a rock of support, and to my editor Joe Monti, who suggested that this book exist. Thank you also to everyone at Saga for all your hard work and support of my writing.

I could not have written "Once, Future" without reading Helen Macdonald's powerful book *H Is for Hawk*.

As always, my thanks and love to my family, and in particular to my parents.